10TH ANNIVERSARY

Special thanks to our well-wishers, who have contributed their congratulations and support.

"The best historicals, the best romances. Simply the best!"
—Dallas Schulze

"Bronwyn Williams was born and raised at Harlequin Historicals. We couldn't have asked for a better home or a more supportive family."
—Dixie Browning and Mary Williams,
w/a Bronwyn Williams

"I can't believe it's been ten years since *Private Treaty,* my first historical novel, helped launch the Harlequin Historicals line. What a thrill that was! And the beat goes on...with timeless stories about men and women in love."
—Kathleen Eagle

"Nothing satisfies me as much as writing or reading a Harlequin Historical novel. For me, Harlequin Historicals are the ultimate escape from the problems of everyday life."
—Ruth Ryan Langan

"As a writer and reader, I've always felt that Harlequin Historicals celebrate a perfect blend of history and romance, adventure and passion, humor and sheer magic."
—Theresa Michaels

"Thank you, Harlequin Historicals, for opening up a 'window into the past' for so many happy readers."

—Suzanne Barclay

"As a one-time 'slush pile' foundling at Harlequin Historicals, I'll be forever grateful for having been rescued and published as one of the first 'March Madness' authors. Harlequin Historicals has always been *the* place for special stories, ones that blend the magic of the past with the rare miracle of love for books that readers never forget."

—Miranda Jarrett

"A rainy evening. A cup of hot chocolate. A stack of Harlequin Historicals. Absolute bliss! Happy 10th Anniversary and continued success."

—Cheryl Reavis

"Happy birthday, Harlequin Historicals! I'm proud to have been a part of your ten years of exciting historical romance."

—Elaine Barbieri

"Harlequin Historical novels are charming or disarming with dashes and clashes. These past times are fast times, the gems of romances!"

—Karen Harper

Carolyn Davidson

THE WEDDING Promise

HARLEQUIN®

TORONTO • NEW YORK • LONDON
AMSTERDAM • PARIS • SYDNEY • HAMBURG
STOCKHOLM • ATHENS • TOKYO • MILAN • MADRID
PRAGUE • WARSAW • BUDAPEST • AUCKLAND

This book is dedicated to the memory
of Arnold "Jake" McDonnell,
brother-in-law and friend, a wounded warrior
who spent over 40 years in his wheelchair.
He was a hero to the end.
and
To Mr. Ed
Sweetheart, husband, lover and friend—
Father and grandfather extraordinaire—
A man who knows the meaning of romance

ISBN 0-373-29031-4

THE WEDDING PROMISE

Copyright © 1998 by Carolyn Davidson

All rights reserved. Except for use in any review, the reproduction or
utilization of this work in whole or in part in any form by any electronic,
mechanical or other means, now known or hereafter invented, including
xerography, photocopying and recording, or in any information storage
or retrieval system, is forbidden without the written permission of the
publisher, Harlequin Enterprises Limited, 225 Duncan Mill Road,
Don Mills, Ontario, Canada M3B 3K9.

All characters in this book have no existence outside the imagination of
the author and have no relation whatsoever to anyone bearing the same
name or names. They are not even distantly inspired by any individual
known or unknown to the author, and all incidents are pure invention.

This edition published by arrangement with Harlequin Books S.A.

® and TM are trademarks of the publisher. Trademarks indicated with
® are registered in the United States Patent and Trademark Office, the
Canadian Trade Marks Office and in other countries.

Printed in U.S.A.

"I didn't frighten you?"
His grin widened.

She met his gaze, her blue eyes shiny with the tears she had not shed. "I liked the kiss. I just didn't think it was proper, with me working for you, and all. I can't stay here if you intend to…"

"I won't take you to my bed, Rachel."

Her quick look was skeptical. "I don't know much about men, Cord McPherson, but my mother told me that when a man takes a kiss, he usually plans on… Well, anyway, she said I should be sure that a man has honorable intentions when I let him kiss me."

"Ah…there's the hitch, honey. You didn't let me. I just went ahead and stole the kiss without permission." His gaze was filled with the wonder of her, the glowing color she wore like the armor of a virgin bride.…

Prologue

"There's no way on God's green earth you young'uns can travel by yourselves." As if he pronounced the fate of the three people facing him, the weathered wagon master issued his ultimatum. "If your pa had listened when he should have, you'd have two good oxen pullin' your wagon instead of those horses. You'd have stood a chance, maybe."

The big man took off his hat and shaped it with a fist, his gaze avoiding the eyes of the young woman in front of him. "I asked around, Rachel. There's plenty of churchgoin' people in Green Rapids that'll be glad to give homes to all of you."

Rachel Sinclair's arms stretched like the wings of a mother hen to encompass the narrow shoulders of her small brothers. "I can tend to my family," she muttered stubbornly. "I don't need the charity of a bunch of church folk."

"You're nothin' but a child yourself, girl." With a rush of exasperation, Mr. Clemons denied her claim. His brow furrowed as he scanned the waiting wagons behind her. "You're a good girl, Rachel. You've held things together for your brothers real well, but the truth is, these men are in a hurry. They're haulin' freight, and besides that, I can't expect the rest of the people in the group to look out for you when things go sour. We're goin' to leave you here with the sheriff and that's that!''

Rachel's slender fingers tightened their grip, as if she must imbue her brothers with a trace of her determination. ''Go on then,'' she told the man in front of her. ''We'll be just fine.''

A look of sheer relief brought an easing of Tom Clemons's frown. ''Sheriff's on his way. Y'all just stay put here and he'll make some arrangements for you. I already talked to him.'' His gait was hurried as he made his way past the three young people, none of whom turned to watch his departure.

''Is he really leavin' us here, Rae?'' Barely a whisper, the voice reached her ear and Rachel bent momentarily to brush a quick kiss across her brother's dark hair.

''We don't need him, Jay,'' she murmured.

''What are we gonna do, Rae?'' came the query from her other side.

He reached her shoulder, this ten-year-old who looked so much like his daddy that it made her heart hurt to look at him. Her smile was sweet as she met his worried gaze.

''We're going to climb back into our wagon and head out before the sheriff gets his hands on us, Henry.'' As a spur-of-the-moment suggestion, it had as much merit as any other notions she'd come up with in the past day or so. Rachel Sinclair was plumb out of ideas. But standing in the middle of the dusty street, halfway between the hotel and a general store, she had reached a conclusion.

''There's enough food in the wagon to keep us for a while. We've got a barrel of water and two good horses to pull the wagon. It'll be a cold day in you-know-where when we can't figure out some way to keep body and soul together without a bunch of busybodies pokin' into our business. Just hike yourselves into the wagon, boys.''

Her dark hair swung in a long braid down her back and slim legs were briefly exposed as Rachel Sinclair scrambled atop the high seat. Her brothers joined her in seconds, even as a rangy lawman sauntered from his office to head in their direction.

His hand lifted in a silent gesture and his mouth opened, only to snap shut as the trio huddling on the wide seat ignored his beckoning fingers. Shaking his head in puzzled resignation, he watched them go, until they were just a speck on the horizon.

Chapter One

The line of clothing snapped in the brisk west wind. Four small shirts billowed, the sleeves filling like the sails of a boat. Next to them hung overalls, one pair a little larger than the other. Stockings draped over the line in a dark parade, and his gaze followed their lead, beyond the pale assortment of undergarments to where a skirt caught the breeze.

"Damned if there isn't a passel of nesters squattin' on my doorstep!" Talking to himself had long been a habit, and Cord McPherson was more than comfortable with the sound of his own voice.

His hands rested on the pommel of his saddle and he slouched just a bit as he leaned forward to better view the small valley that rimmed the north side of his property.

He'd ridden this far only once this spring, more than a month ago, and nothing unusual had caught his eye. Only the leafing out of the trees along the stream and the greening of the meadows had pleasured his vision. This was another thing entirely.

His gaze narrowed on a small figure just beyond the ramshackle building at the edge of a patch of trees. Dark haired and slim as a reed, a young boy scampered into full view, his voice a piping song.

"Rae! Listen to me! I can whistle just like that bird over there," he called, and then proceeded to do a creditable imitation of a robin.

Cord's mouth twitched, amusement and annoyance vying for a place there. "What the hell is that kid doin', prancin' around in my back forty?" he grumbled beneath his breath.

And then his eyes caught sight of another figure, this one not nearly so reedlike…slender, but well rounded. A female, no doubt of that, he decided quickly, what with the curves that threatened to spill over the front of her petticoat.

"Jay, I sent you to the stream to fill a bucket with water. I need to finish the washing."

She'd turned, coming to a halt with her back to him, and for a moment Cord silently urged her to turn around. He'd thought her to be but a child at first glance, but the sight of rounded hips beneath the clinging petticoat and the memory of curves he'd caught only a glimpse of sent that thought scampering.

"I'm gonna!" the child answered cheerfully. "I just was watchin' the birds for a minute, Rae." The dark head turned, the small face scrunched against the morning sun as he faced the woman, and even from a distance, Cord caught a glimpse of terror in the boy's hurried movements.

"Rae! There's a man watchin'. Over on that rise, there's a big man lookin' at us!" His bare feet were a blur as the boy ran to the woman and she clutched him against herself in a protective gesture, her head bending low over his.

And then she turned. With one hand she swept the

youngster behind her, facing the unknown with a measure of bravery that brought an admiring chuckle from Cord's throat. Even as he eyed her stance, his heels tapped the sides of his big gelding and he sat deeply in the saddle as the horse picked his way down the shallow slope of the hill.

"Go in the house, Jay," the woman said, her voice carrying in the morning air. Low and steady, yet with an authoritative quality he could not miss, her command sent the boy running. She waited, unflinching in the brilliant sunlight as Cord approached, her eyes shaded by the hand she lifted to her forehead.

"Morning, ma'am." He hadn't forgotten his manners, even when faced with a half-dressed female in his own backyard, so to speak. His gaze on her face, he was only too aware of her state of dishabille, and his treacherous eyes narrowed as they widened their focus to include the lush curves she made no attempt to hide.

"What do you want?" She lifted her head as he neared, her eyes remarkable in their fearless daring. Not a twitch of muscle in that suntanned face betrayed her. Nor did her hands tremble as she lowered the right to meet the left at her waistline. Her chin was a bit too firm for his liking, but the mouth that spoke a challenge in his direction was soft and full, her flesh clear, her cheeks flushing a bit as he rode close to where she stood.

"I was about to ask you the same question, ma'am." His words were mild, his senses instinctively lulled by the sight of a defenseless woman and a small child.

She shrugged with deliberate defiance and her jaw tightened. "I'm sure I don't know what you mean. I don't want anything from you, mister. Just to be left alone."

Cord McPherson was a man of few words, but the

ones that came to mind this morning weren't what he could in all good conscience spout in her direction. His hands itched to circle that narrow waist. His body twitched in a too long neglected fashion as he allowed his gaze to openly scan her form.

Not for the life of him could he be so blunt as to tell her she was about three feet from a randy man.

He shifted in the saddle, discomfort a reality now. "I'm wonderin' just what you're doin' on my property, ma'am."

Over her shoulder, a taller version of the small boy she'd sent scampering peered around the corner of the shack.

Cord nodded at him. "Another one of your bunch?" he asked politely. And then his eyes glittered with a dark menace as the youth lifted a shotgun to his shoulder.

"I wouldn't do that if I were you, boy." As far as from dawn to full dark, his voice plunged to a low, growling threat, the affable visage only a memory.

The woman spun about, her head shaking a warning. "Henry, put the gun down!"

The barrel wavered and fell, its weight pulling it almost to the ground, and the boy glared, a passionate threat, unhampered by his compliance. His dark hair gleaming in the sunlight, he waited, as if one movement from the horseman would bring his heavy weapon into line once more.

The young woman turned to Cord again, as if caught between two opposing forces. "He's only a boy and no threat to you."

"Hate to gainsay you, ma'am, but any hand holdin' a gun is a threat in my book. I'd suggest you have him put that shotgun on the ground, or I'll have to see to it myself."

"Put down the gun, Henry. Right now." Without looking back over her shoulder, the woman issued the order, her tone of voice speaking confidence in his obedience.

And he obeyed. Without hesitation, he leaned forward and deposited his weapon on the grass. His mouth twisted in a mutinous grimace and his eyes burned with a thwarted gleam, but he obeyed.

Cord swung from his saddle, dropping his reins to the ground. With two long strides, man and woman were in touching distance and Cord's mouth twitched as he caught sight of the alarm she could not hide at his approach.

She stepped back, her hands rising distractedly to spread across her breasts, a purely female gesture, honed by the instincts inbred in women, and he recognized it for what it was. She'd only now remembered her state of undress, her vulnerability to his masculine strength.

In the heat of the first few minutes of their encounter, she'd been aware only of the danger his presence offered to the young boys she guarded with her very body. Now she was apprehensive for her own sake, and her eyes were wary as she faced him.

"We haven't got anything you'd want, mister. There's just me and the boys. Our pa will be back any time now, but—"

Cord's eyes flickered to the telltale clothesline, strung between two sturdy maple trees. "Not much on that line that'd fit a full-grown man."

Her eyes met his, a defiant look alive in their depths. "I haven't gotten to his things yet." The softness was gone from her lips as the blatant lie fell from her mouth. She swallowed, a visible breach in her composure, and her cheeks flushed crimson as she turned away, her hands moving to spread over the bare flesh above the bodice of her petticoat.

He followed an arm's length behind her, his gaze sweeping over the length of her slim body. The petticoat was too short for fashion, exposing bare feet and ankles and just a suggestion of curving calves. Her shoulders were smooth, creamy and inviting, and his hands clenched as he felt the urge to touch the softness he knew would meet his caress.

"You're on my property," he reminded her. Her shoulders lifted, as if she'd caught her breath at his words, and she halted.

"We didn't know anyone lived here. It was empty and neglected and we..." Her words trailed off and her head shook, a negative gesture. "We can pay a little for the use of the place. We'll only be here for a while, just till we make some decisions."

It was a fair offer. But Cord McPherson was used to doing business face-to-face. Looking at her back was a pleasure, but the memory of what she had become so conscious of in the past few minutes gnawed at him.

"Turn around and look at me if you want to do business, ma'am." His words were low, but unwavering, an ultimatum in any man's language.

"I can't." She whispered her denial of his demand. Her head turned, just a bit, and he caught sight of her rosy cheek, her lashes sweeping its heated surface.

It was enough. He'd managed to embarrass her beyond her endurance, and his good sense took command.

"Go put a dress on and get yourself back out here."

She fled. With slender feet brushing aside the grass, she ran the few steps to the shack, one hand grasping the arm of the watching boy as she turned the corner.

"Rae!" The protest rang out in the silence and was hushed by a soft murmur from beyond his sight.

Cord cast one measuring glance around the empty clearing, then, lifting an empty wooden bucket from his path and leading his horse he headed for the stream.

She'd known it was too good to be true. That they would find an empty house...no, not a house, a shanty really. But sufficient for their needs for now.

She'd cleaned it up, sweeping the dirt floor with her mother's good broom, scrubbing the crude wooden table and chair with an old shirt of Pa's. The stove worked, once she'd carried out an accumulation of ashes and set a small pile of kindling to burning in its depths. The draft worked and the chimney drew well.

The boys had taken over the single bunk, one at each end for sleeping, and she'd been content to roll up by the stove at night, the shotgun placed in front of her. It had almost been idyllic, this three-week stretch of time, with her marking the days in her mother's journal.

Somehow, it was important that she know when Sunday came. And just the other day she'd sat beneath the trees to read from Pa's Bible, knowing the boys would only pay attention for a short while. She'd sung with them, reminding them of the words they stumbled over, yearning for an hour in the white church back home in Pennsylvania.

Home. Her mouth tightened as the word nudged her memories. She bent to find her blue dress in the trunk beside the boys' bunk, her fingers busy as she unfolded it and pulled it over her head. No sense in getting maudlin over the past. This was here and now and she was committed to making the best of things.

The buttons slid easily into the handmade buttonholes

her mother had worked with care one winter's evening. Rachel Sinclair allowed only a moment's grief for that memory as she prepared herself to face the man waiting outdoors.

Crying never did anyone any good as far as she could see. She'd shed her tears when the bodies of the people she loved most in the world were lowered into their graves, each a day apart from the other, more than a month ago, beside the trail in Missouri.

Then she'd gathered up the reins and taken charge. Any grown woman, eighteen years old, had better be equipped to tend to her family these days, or she'd be showing a decided lack of good upbringing, she'd vowed on that day.

And she'd done just that. Taken charge of her brothers and turned her face west. In the direction of her father's dream…a dream she vowed would not die with him.

This shack was only a temporary stopping place. Somehow she'd find a way to continue on, to where she might find a place for the boys to grow and flourish. A place where she might find a man willing to take on a ready-made family.

A man. She blinked at the reminder. *You've got a man waiting right this minute, Rachel Sinclair. You need to go on out there and face him and do some dealing.* The memory of the small nest egg in the bottom of the trunk reminded her of the limits of her bargaining power and she shrugged off the daunting thought.

At the door the boys waited, watching the tall intruder as he walked from their sight, heading for the stream. Preparing to join them, Rachel brushed back her hair with agile fingers as she approached the door, feeling for the braid that hung down her back.

"What's he doing?" she asked quietly. Hastily, she

rolled up her sleeves to just beneath her elbows. He'd already seen pretty near everything she owned. No sense in being overly modest, she decided stoutly.

Washing clothes in her petticoat had seemed safe enough. Besides keeping her dress dry and clean, she'd enjoyed the breeze blowing against her bare shoulders and arms, keeping her cool. She'd scrubbed out the boy's overalls, rinsing them in the bucket and wringing out the water before she hung them on the line to dry.

And then, just as she'd sent Jay to the stream for clean water to wash the rest of her own things, the stranger had come, destroying what little peace of mind she'd been able to find in this place.

She was ready to face him, as ready as she'd ever be, but she hesitated at the threshold. His demeanor had overpowered her, more so than the gun she'd spied behind his saddle, which she was dead certain he could handle with an expert touch.

He'd not threatened her, not bodily, but his eyes had paused to survey every living inch of her, especially the parts the bodice of her petticoat had failed to cover.

She blushed anew at the thought. And so it was that she watched him, reins in one hand, bucket in the other, striding up the fresh path from the stream, worn down only by the repeated steps of Jay and Henry over the past weeks, the grass still green beneath his feet.

He carried the bucket easily, its weight a barely noticed hindrance to his easy gait. His hat was pushed back a bit and she caught sight of dark eyes, their intensity focused on her, his nose flaring just a bit as he came to a halt in front of her.

"I figured you needed water. Thought I'd save you a trip to the stream while I watered my horse."

"Yes, thank you." He'd put her at a disadvantage

already, being nice. She drew in a breath, reaching for the handle of the bucket.

"Let the boy get it." He nodded, his movement a silent command, and Henry eased past her to take the bucket from his grasp. "Take it in the house, son."

"Yessir," Henry said quietly, obviously subdued in the presence of subtle strength. His eyes had lost their challenge, if not their wariness; but as if he sensed no danger for the moment, he turned from his sister to obey the stranger's command.

Rachel buried her hands in the pockets of her dress and faced her visitor. "Can we come to an agreement, mister? Maybe reach a fair price for us staying in this place?"

"Are you dead serious about staying out here by yourself?" The stranger faced her, his expression disbelieving as he surveyed his surroundings. "This shack isn't fit for animals. The door's hangin' by one hinge and there isn't even a floor. You can't tell me you're set on livin' here."

"For now, I am," she answered, her mouth firm as she staked her claim.

"How much you plan on payin' for rent?" His gaze swung back to her as she defied his judgment. "What are you thinkin' to live on?"

Rachel thought of the dwindling supplies she'd stashed with care in the rude cabinets against the wall inside the shack. "We'll make do," she told him proudly. "There's good fishing in the stream and Henry is a good shot."

Her mind worked quickly as she defended her position. "We noticed the berries are ripening up along the stream and there's more greens growing than we can ever eat, even with the rabbits getting their share. We've got plenty of food.''

Plenty, if we dole it pretty thin and the rabbit population holds out, she amended silently.

A nicker from beyond the shack caught his attention, and Cord's gaze shifted from the woman before him. For all her claims of independence, he'd warrant she was barely holding her own out here. And yet, beyond the shelter she'd found, somewhere past the shack, was a horse.

Another nicker joined the first and his gelding answered the challenge, lifting his head from where he'd buried his muzzle in the lush grasses.

''How many head of horses you got out there, ma'am?'' His query demanded an answer, his words delivered with a hard edge.

''The team is not for sale,'' she answered quickly. ''They belonged to my pa.''

''Belonged?'' The single word made mockery of her claim. There was no father about to return. These three were alone here, on the edge of his land, ten miles from the nearest town.

''They're mine now,'' she told him bluntly.

''It's not safe out here for a woman alone, with two young'uns.''

Her eyes flashed defiance. ''We haven't seen another soul, till you came up over that hill.''

''And you might not again. But then again, you might. And the next man to ride up on you probably won't be willing to ride away without giving you some trouble.'' His words were roundabout, but the look on her face told him he'd managed to get his meaning across.

That slim body was tempting enough in its blue covering, the modest dress buttoned up to the neck. Any man worth his salt would have been tempted mightily by the sight she'd presented just minutes ago, prancing around in her undergarments.

That thought alone was enough to give him pause and he silently cursed the urges that ran rampant in his body. Too long without a female wasn't good for a man, and he'd about reached his limit.

"How much do you want for rent, mister?"

Her demand caught his ear and his thoughts returned from their meandering. She waited, watching him, and the cautious hope in her eyes was his undoing. Full-blown, a picture sprang to his mind, and his words gave it life.

"Maybe we can work something out," he said. "Looks to me like you're pretty good at washing clothes, ma'am. How about if you come up to the house and do up the laundry and maybe see what you can do in my kitchen a couple of days a week?"

His lips thinned as he waited for her reply. What the hell was he thinking of? He'd do well to send her and her brothers on their way, or at least take them to town and find a place for them to roost, out of danger. No sense in saddling himself with any more of a load than he already had.

The girl shook her head, denying his offer. "I'd just as soon pay a bit for the place to stay, mister. Maybe till we get our mind made up about what we're going to do."

So much for that plan. Ill formed as it was, he'd decided in a hurry it might be her salvation. That she would be a temptation to every roving cowhand and stray rider in the county was a fact.

Once the word got out, she'd be under siege. Fool woman stood there like an unwary doe just before dawn, with danger all around, and not enough sense to take cover.

"We can come to an understanding, I'm sure," he said, not wanting to douse her hopes. She was so valiant, so willing to do what had to be done for her family. "Let me think about it."

The boys came from the doorway to flank her, lending their mute support, and her arms lifted in an automatic gesture to lie across their shoulders. He suspected she'd lent them her strength on a regular basis over the past few weeks or months. How long they'd been alone was anyone's guess. Maybe she'd open up a little more next time. For now, he figured he'd about gone as far as she'd let him. Further than she'd wanted.

"I'll be back," he said, easing into the saddle with a lithe movement. One tanned, broad-backed hand reached out to her. "My name's Cord McPherson."

She moved toward him, accepting his hand, her own enclosed by his fingers, and he felt its slender strength against his palm. He held it for a moment, silently urging her to reply to his words of introduction. And she complied.

"Rachel Sinclair. These are my brothers, Jay and Henry."

As if she begrudged him the intimacy of knowing her name, she ducked her head, drawing her fingers from his grasp, stepping back.

He tipped his hat and turned his horse away, aware of her gaze on his back as he rode. Her length of dark hair, the braid thick and heavy against her back, nudged his thoughts. She looked good in blue, he decided. Matched her eyes.

But the memory that edged out the others, that haunted him on his ride back across the fields and meadows he traveled, was that of womanly curves, of slender arms and smooth shoulders, gleaming in the sunshine.

Chapter Two

It was a long trip, and her heart beat at a rapid pace as the town came into sight. Coming to Green Rapids was a calculated risk, she knew. The sheriff was bound to see them, unless he should by chance be gone from town this morning.

The thought of a confrontation with the law was far from appealing, although the lawman had probably thanked his lucky stars to have them off his hands. Nevertheless, Rachel had her jaw set and her spine stiff as a ramrod, ready for the encounter should it come about.

Traffic on the dusty road was heavy, probably not more so than usual for a Saturday, but Rachel was counting on the assortment of buggies and wagons to conceal her passage down the main street.

Her eyes scanned the business places lined up alongside the broad, wooden sidewalks. Just ahead, the wooden sign of Green Rapids Emporium and Dry Goods came into view, and she brought the horses to a halt.

Henry jumped from the seat and snapped the lead in place on the harness, then tied the team to a hitching rail convenient to the store. "All set, Rae," he called out, tugging one more time at the leather strap, testing the security of his knot.

"Thank you, Henry. You and Jay come along now, and remember, no treats today. We're only here to buy the things we absolutely need." She spoke in an undertone, ruing the warning she gave, wishing for a hundred pennies to shower on her brothers, with no thought for the expense.

"I know, Rae," Jay whispered on a wistful sigh, his nostrils flaring as they entered the store.

The smell was always the same, Rachel thought, aware of the deep breaths her brothers had taken. Drygoods stores the country over, at least the parts they'd traveled, had that selfsame scent of leather and lye soap, mixed with the starched aroma of fresh bolts of fabric.

A whiff of molasses reached her nose, countered by something freshly baked, perhaps bread or cake. So much temptation, she thought, and so little hard cash to spend.

"Can I help you, ma'am?"

Rachel looked up quickly as the clerk approached, her eyes widening at his elegance. Pomade slicked his hair back neatly, a heavily starched collar clenched his throat and his shirtsleeves were buttoned firmly at the wrist. A genial smile curled his mouth and his eyes were faintly admiring as he nodded a greeting.

"Yes," she answered, fumbling in her pocket for the list she'd written. As if she needed prompting to remember the few items she'd scribbled on the brown scrap of paper: sugar—a pound or two, depending on the price, a bag of cornmeal, a pound or so of lard and perhaps some eggs. Maybe even cans of milk for the boys' oatmeal.

She'd yearned for weeks for the taste of a fried egg.

Not that she could afford that luxury. These, if they weren't too dear, would be used for baking. Jay and Henry had responded to the bribe of a cake, should they do their chores and carry water without complaining.

They'd been more than compliant, she realized, once they were settled in and ready to call the tumbledown cabin their dwelling. They'd followed her lead, straightening and settling in, making a home of the place they'd found.

"We got some new dimity in from St. Louis just the other day," the clerk said, recalling Rachel from her thoughts.

He probably thought she could use a new dress. And he was right. Her smile was grim as she shook her head. "No, we just need a few items today. Some cornmeal to start with."

She read off her short list and watched as the clerk moved efficiently behind the gleaming wooden counter. He filled a cloth sack with her sugar, surely more than a pound, she thought, her eyes narrowing as she watched his deft movements. The lard was next, dealt with quickly, then three cans of evaporated milk.

Finally, wrapping four eggs individually in brown paper, he placed them carefully inside the bag of cornmeal. "That'll keep 'em from breaking if they get jostled," he explained, tying the neck of the bag once more.

He rested both palms on the counter, leaning just a bit in her direction, his smile more eager now. "What else will you have today?"

Rachel's mind moved quickly, counting up her spending against the coins she'd brought with her. Such strict rationing of money was a burden, but one she was willing to assume, given the alternative. There was no way she would give over the care of her brothers to strangers, no matter how well off they might be.

"How much is a small bag of tea?" she asked.

He turned from her without reply, opening a tin on the shelf behind him. From within rose a pungent aroma as he turned with it to face her. His smile was inviting as he scooped out a generous portion into a metal box.

"I don't think I can afford that much," Rachel protested as he closed the lid tightly on the enameled container. Covered with painted roses and green leaves, intertwined over the top and down the sides, it beckoned her, silently tempting her.

"Well, why don't we just call it a welcome present from Green Rapids, ma'am. You're a stranger here, and we like to make newcomers feel at home."

As a gesture of friendship, it was more than she had expected. But from the look in his eyes and the ready grin he bestowed upon her, she suspected he'd taken a shine to her.

"I don't know you, sir," she said quietly, aware of the silence of her brothers as they flanked her in a silent show of support.

"Conrad Carson, proprietor, ma'am," he announced, offering his hand politely. "At your service."

His bow spoke of old-world manners and good upbringing and Rachel was mollified. Her hand felt cool as she placed it against his smooth palm for a moment. Clean, with well-kept nails, it touched hers with assurance.

She was reminded suddenly of the hand she'd taken hold of just two days ago. That hard, callused hand that had held hers with care. A far cry from this storekeeper's.

"Thank you, Mr. Carson," Rachel said, withdrawing

her palm from his touch. She fumbled in her pocket for her small change purse and drew it forth. "How much do I owe you?"

"Well, let's see now." Quickly, he scratched out figures on a piece of brown paper and told her the total of her purchases before he wrapped the bits and pieces together in the heavy paper.

Rachel counted out her coins and breathed a sigh of relief. She had enough and a bit left over. Recklessly, she handed each boy a penny. "You can buy a piece of candy, if you like," she told them beneath her breath.

"Really, Rae?" squeaked Jay.

"Can we afford it?" Henry whispered, standing tiptoe to speak closer to her ear.

She nodded and smiled at the two of them, these dear boys she would defend with her very life if need be. And then she watched as they marched quickly to the glass case that held jars of assorted candies.

He'd give her a week, he'd decided, riding back to the ranch house. He'd let her eke out an existence in the shack, living on fish and rabbits and whatever else she had stowed in that pitiful excuse for a house. And then he'd go back. She'd be ripe by then for another offer.

He lasted three days.

Thoughts of her filled his waking hours. Dreams of that womanly body haunted his sleep, and the pure imaginings of his mind were the impetus that sent him on his way early on Monday morning.

Surely he hadn't been so long without the companionship of a female that he couldn't control his own needs.

Certainly he was capable of running his ranch, tending to his stock and overseeing the men working for him without allowing the memory of a slender woman to take precedence over the operation he was heading.

Derisively, Cord shook his head at his own folly. The slim creature he'd been obsessed with for three days would be merely an ordinary woman when he saw her again. No more and no less than any other he'd run across in his life.

Once he set eyes on her again, he'd be able to vanquish the assortment of urges he'd been fighting for three days.

The miles were long beneath the reaching strides of his gelding. The far corners of his ranch had never seemed so distant before. Maybe he shouldn't have left her alone out here. What if someone had come upon the small family and taken advantage of their pitiful situation?

His heels dug into the sides of his mount and he searched the horizon for the line of trees that rimmed the uppermost ridge of the small valley he sought.

The best approach would be to offer her a job. Not just a couple of days a week, as he'd suggested the other day, but a full-time, everyday job that would necessitate moving her and her brothers, bag and baggage, to his place.

And then there would really be fireworks to deal with, once Jake had his routine disturbed.

He'd have to depend on Sam Bostwick to keep Jake in line and away from Rachel. No sense in scaring her off first thing. The thought of his brother brought a frown and a deep-felt sigh.

Jake wouldn't take well to a female around the place.

The Circle M employed five ranch hands, none of whom was capable of putting a decent meal on the table, as far as Cord was concerned. Finding help had become almost a farce in the past year. The gold strike was a thing of the distant past, but there were always the hopeful ones making their way west.

The fact was, getting decent ranch hands here in Kansas, and keeping them, depended in good part upon the food you put in their bellies.

The gradual rise before him was a sea of wildflowers, topped by a ridge of trees. The sun was brilliant against the horizon. A hawk skimmed the treetops, a silent hunter against the cloudless sky.

And there, kneeling beneath the freshly born leaves of a maple sapling was the slender woman who'd occupied his thoughts for the past three days.

She lifted her head, her eyes wide as she watched him approach. As his horse came to a halt just feet away, she stood. Her dress showed the effects of many wash days, its color nondescript, with faint images of flowers against a faded pink background.

It was too short, even though the hem had been let down, and he felt a quick surge of gladness at that fact, his gaze pausing on the slim ankles and bare feet she made no attempt to conceal.

"Mr. McPherson."

It was a greeting of sorts, accompanied by a slow nod of her head, her eyes wary as he slid from his horse to stand before her.

"Miss Sinclair." He stopped abruptly. Then, as if his senses had deserted him, his tongue refused to speak.

She was watching him in a grave, sober fashion that was not encouraging to his proposal. What he wanted to say would be insulting to a lady, and she deserved that designation.

How could he ask her to gather up her family and come home with him? He could offer no chaperon, no other woman to protect her name while she occupied his home. And yet the desire to be in her company had not eased with the passing of time. His best bet was to put it on a business basis, he decided.

She'd thought about him for three days. And now he was here, appearing at the crest of the long slope, atop his big horse, making his way to where she stood.

"I came out to see if you were needing anything, ma'am."

Rachel considered the man standing before her. He'd been studying her with a penetrating eye, all the way up the hill, as if he could somehow see beneath the wash dress she wore. And then he'd offered a neighborly suggestion.

Did she need anything? Here she stood, fresh from praying upon the highest spot available in the valley, as if the height of the small hill could somehow make her more noticeable to heaven's eye. She'd just asked God's help in stretching her pitiful supply of money. There was about enough left to feed her brothers for another week or so, but not much longer.

With the oatmeal about done for and the flour gone weevily when she made biscuits this morning, she'd had to face the facts. She'd shuddered as she sifted the small brown bugs from her measuring cup, and cast them out the door of the shack. She'd manage to feed the boys a while longer, but even after the trip to town, the end of her supplies was in sight.

And so was the bottom of her small cache of coins.

Now here, as if he bore a message from the Almighty, came the man who'd not been far from her thoughts since Thursday, when he'd announced his ownership of the very spot they'd taken over as their own.

"Do we need anything?" She repeated his words and her voice was alive with wry incredulity. "I suppose I should be polite and tell you that my brothers and I have everything under control, Mr. McPherson."

Vainly, she tried to smile, but the worry of the long night hours had left her without a trace of good humor.

Cord McPherson swept his wide-brimmed hat from his head and slapped it against his thigh. "I'm not looking for niceties from you, ma'am. I'd take the truth over a polite denial any day of the week."

"We can survive for a while," she said finally, her breath escaping in a sigh. "We had enough food to last a month or so, when we got here, with fresh meat and fish to fill in. But we've about reached the bottom of the barrel, and I don't know how many more trips to the store in Green Rapids we can afford."

"Green Rapids? You've been there?"

She nodded. "I wasn't sure I could find the way back there, to tell the truth, but we made it."

He nodded. "Any problems in town?"

"No." She smiled, remembering the welcome they'd received. "The shopkeeper was pleasant. He gave me a tin of tea as a gift."

His brow lifted in disbelief. "Conrad?"

"He seemed very nice," she said primly, her eyes lowered, her cheeks flushing, unable to meet his gaze.

"I'll just bet he did." His words were gruff, and he settled his hands against his hips.

"I didn't expect you back," she said finally.

"I told you I'd come."

Her shrug was answer enough, he decided. She'd probably hoped he wouldn't show up, if he knew anything about it.

"Anybody give you any trouble here?" He looked

beyond her to where the shack huddled in the small valley, the two horses tethered on the other side of the stream, the empty wagon under a tree.

"No." She shook her head. "A man rode up yesterday and looked things over. But he left after a few minutes."

"Probably Moses havin' a look-see. I told him if he got a chance, to check on you."

"Moses?" She rolled the name on her tongue, her quick mind nudging her dormant sense of humor. "Do you suppose he thought he'd discovered the promised land?" The wave of her slender hand encompassed the shack and its surroundings.

His chuckle warmed her. "And here I thought you didn't have a lick of jocularity to your name."

She caught a glimpse of white teeth beneath his dark mustache when he smiled. She'd had little to brighten her days lately, other than meeting Conrad Carson. And even that small bit of pleasure had not been enough to lift her spirits for long.

In fact, until this very minute, she'd about decided life had reached rock bottom.

The small valley had seemed an Eden of sorts for a while. Only when the store of supplies began running out had she faced facts. Eden would soon pale once the cornmeal and sugar sacks were emptied.

"You asked me to come to your place and do your washing, Mr. McPherson. Does the offer still hold?" Unbidden, the words rushed from her lips and she hesitated, her cheeks flushing with her own temerity as she waited his reply.

His fingers gripped the dented top of his hat and he swept it from his head. "Matter of fact, that's the very reason I came out here this morning," he said politely.

Her heart skipped a beat and she felt a rush of warmth flow through her veins. That her prayer should be answered so quickly was surely a sign.

"You want me to go back with you and work on your laundry?" she asked, her mind already speeding ahead to the preparations she must make, were that the case.

His mouth quirked at one corner, and she wondered if he were mocking her eagerness. And then he grinned outright, a smile that carried a welcome message. "More than that, I want you to take on some cooking chores, if you will."

"If there's any great amount of washing to do, it may take the rest of the day," she countered. "I might not have much time left over to spend cooking a big meal for you."

He ran long fingers through his hair, scratching a spot at the crown, as if he pondered her words. Then the big hat went back in place over his dark hair and he set his jaw, as if he had reached a decision and would not be swayed.

"I'd thought you might be persuaded to take on the ranch kitchen. Just to see if you could handle it. It's probably too much of a job for a girl like you to cope with, but—"

"I'm far from a young girl, Mr. McPherson," she said sharply, interrupting him. "I've been cooking and scrubbing out the washing on a board for several months now. I'm sure I can handle cooking for a man and doing his clothes without much effort at all."

Her mouth set primly, she awaited his reply, her pride the issue now. If he thought for one minute she was too puny to be of any use, he could just... Just what? Find someone else for the job? When she so desperately needed the security of cash money in her hand and food for the table?

"Well…" He seemed to hesitate, and she urged him silently, her mouth firm, her eyes intent on his, her breath stored tightly in her lungs, as if she feared to release it before he made up his mind.

"It's not just for me," he told her. "There's my brother, too. Plus four ranch hands and Sam. He's been cookin' for us, but I doubt he'll ever be able to put a decent meal together to save his soul. That's seven men to cook for. The washing is just for me and my brother, but if you wanted to earn more money, I'm sure the men would be happy to get their duds scrubbed out on a regular basis. They like clean clothes come Saturday night, usually."

Seven men! The image was daunting, but Rachel swallowed her urge to spew the words aloud. She caught her breath, her mind in a whirl. If the ranch house was farther than an hour away, she'd spend much of the day driving the wagon back and forth and never have time to do her own work here.

And then there was the question of the boys.

"Can I bring my brothers along for the day?" she asked, her heart beating rapidly as she bargained.

His shrug was casual. "Don't know why not. They can give you a hand, maybe. Or just pitch in with the barn work."

She glanced at the shack, where Jay had just appeared in the doorway. "They'll need to eat, too. If I'm cooking for you, it will be for nine, not just seven."

"Ten," he corrected her. "I'll expect you to share the table with us, Miss Sinclair." His eyes lit with a glow of triumph and she noted it uneasily.

"How far from here is the house?"

"Better than an hour in a wagon," he told her. "Little less on horseback."

"It'll take me a few minutes to get the boys ready and set things to rights here." She brushed her hands against the front of her skirt. "I probably should change my clothes too."

He cleared his throat, looking past her to where Jay stood near the shack. "Why don't you just plan to stay on at the house, long as you're going to be working there anyway?"

She blinked, attempting to digest his suggestion. "You want all of us to move to your house?" The thought was beyond her comprehension.

His nod of agreement stunned her. "Reckon that's what I had in mind, ma'am. Thought you might load up your wagon and follow me back. I'll give you a hand with your things."

"Rae, what'cha doin' up there?" From the shack, Jay's reedy voice lifted on the still air.

Rachel's head turned and she looked down at her small brother, dressed in too-short pants and a shirt he hadn't grown into yet. His dark, stubborn hair stuck up at the crown, ignoring his efforts at the stream to plaster it against his scalp, and one bare foot rubbed against the other as he watched her.

"I'm talking to Mr. McPherson, Jay. I'll be right there. Go get your brother out of bed." Her words carried easily to where the child stood and he nodded agreeably as he turned back to the shack.

"You'll go with me?" Cord asked, and she cast him a knowing glance.

"Look around you, Mr. McPherson. If you were trying to tend two boys and keep them fed and clean and had to worry about where you were going to land once you set out from here, would you turn down an offer like the one you just made me?''

He nodded, his lips parting in a smile of approval. ''I see what you mean. I think you're a smart lady, to tell the truth. Workin' for me will give you time to figure out what you want to do next.'' He grasped his horse's reins and walked ahead of her, down the rise and across the grassy clearing.

Rachel followed in his wake. He sure as the world had it all figured out, didn't he? Her feet dragged as she considered the man striding down the shallow slope before her.

He was taking an awful lot for granted, organizing their lives this way. Pa's vision of claiming land farther west was still alive in her soul and if she agreed to stop here, the boys would never see the West their father had dreamed of.

''Mr. McPherson, why don't we make this a sort of temporary thing, me working for you? Just in case I'm not satisfactory for the job.'' She'd managed to halt his progress with that one, and a small sense of triumph buzzed within her as he paused in front of her.

He hesitated, just for a moment, then swung to face her, his eyes alight with an emotion akin to amusement. ''Oh, I'm sure you'll work out just fine, Miss Sinclair. I'll give you time to learn the ropes, get your feet wet, so to speak.''

He waved expansively at the clearing ahead of them. ''If you can make a home here, with nothin' to do it with, I'll warrant you can run rings around the help I've got in my kitchen now.''

The web he was weaving wrapped around her, its elusive threads beguiling her, and she made one last valiant effort to establish her ground.

"I need money, Mr. McPherson. Not just a place to stay. If this doesn't work out, I'll need a stake to get us where we're going."

He nodded slowly. "I guess that's only fair. Why don't we give it a year's trial?"

"A year!" Her voice lifted, the words a squeal, and the hard-won dignity she'd managed to don like a Sunday dress fell about her feet, leaving her exposed to his dark gaze.

His nod was emphatic. "A year. You can't head west in the autumn. Even if there were any supply trains at that time of year, it would be suicide. And any shorter time than that wouldn't be a fair trial, would it?"

The words sounded reasonable, the way he put it, and she cleared her throat, her mind boggling at the idea of spending a year in the company of this man.

Enough that he was tall and well muscled, his shirt fitting him as if it were tailor-made to cover those broad shoulders. Add to that the very masculine presence he exuded, all tanned and well-put-together, with those dark eyes gleaming as if they knew secrets beyond her comprehension.

He almost frightened her, this benefactor who had given her the choice of eking out an existence on the edge of his property or following him to his home. He seemed kindly enough, but there was about him a power she didn't understand, as if a magnetic field surrounded him and she was being drawn into its depths.

Now he watched her, with a patience she wouldn't have credited him with, as if allowing her to choose. When in reality there was no choice. Behind her was Green Rapids and the sufferance of strangers. Ahead, only the uncertainty of the unknown.

And smack in the middle was Cord McPherson.

"All right, but not quite a year. Come spring, March or April, I'll decide, soon as the first chance to go west comes in sight. I'll have to have enough money on hand to buy a pair of oxen."

Tom Clemons had been right, she admitted to herself. Horses weren't sturdy enough for the rigors of the trail.

She bit at her lip, determined to give the man an honest bargain. "And if it doesn't work out before then, if you find that I'm not suitable for the job, you'll let me know," she offered.

His eyes made a quick survey of her, his broad hands spread wide against his hipbones, the reins trailing from between his fingers as his horse waited patiently.

"All right." He nodded finally, his gaze dark, his eyes holding a subdued excitement. "If you can't make the grade, I'll let you know." His mouth twisted into a shadow of a grin, as if he would not allow any levity to dilute the serious aspects of their agreement.

Rachel wiped her palm against her skirt and offered it in his direction. "Do we have a deal, Mr. McPherson?" she asked firmly, her breath catching in her throat as she realized the enormity of this undertaking.

His lean, callused fingers grasped hers and he held them firmly. "We have a deal, Rachel."

It took less than an hour to load their pitiful belongings into the wagon, close up the shack and be on their way. Cord harnessed the horses, admiring their plump, sleek lines, due probably to the lush grasses of his valley, he surmised with a subdued grin.

He worked rapidly, leading the team to the cabin door, where Rachel waited beside an assortment of crates and boxes. In moments, he had the wagon in place, the reins tied to a low branch of the nearest tree, lest the horses take it in their heads to return to the rich pastureland on the other side of the stream.

"How long you been here?" he asked, satisfied finally that the team was secure.

"A few weeks." She lifted a box he deemed beyond her strength and he took it from her, their hands brushing as he eased it from her arms.

"I can get it!" Her pride glittered from blue eyes that scorned his aid.

He nodded. "I imagine you can, but there's no need."

She turned away, bending to lift one end of a trunk the boys were struggling to shove through the doorway. And then as she stood erect, he was there once more, close behind her.

His big hands gripped her waist and he spoke gruffly against the dark braid she'd coiled on top of her head.

"Stand back, Rachel. I'll tend to this. The boys can help me."

She shivered in his grasp and he heard her indrawn breath. "I'm stronger than you think," she told him, her voice containing a faint breathlessness. And then she lowered the trunk, stepping away to retreat toward the waiting wagon.

"I've not underestimated you, Rachel," he said, lifting one end of the trunk with ease. He waited till her brothers passed the doorway, then, lifting the bulk of the weight, he helped them ease their burden into the wagon.

She watched him warily and her hesitant air amused him. He had her on the run, off balance and acquiescent. Just as he'd hoped, she was going along with his plan. Now if he could keep her moving, he'd have the thing accomplished before she caught her breath.

"This won't take long." With a hand on each of their heads, Cord turned the two boys back toward the shack.

Willingly, they followed his lead and in minutes, the motley assortment of boxes and crates had been loaded. Her mother's rocker and feather ticks, along with her hand-carved dresser, topped the load. Their faces alight with admiration, Jay and Henry watched as the pile was secured with a rope taken from Cord's saddle.

"That didn't take any time, did it, Rae?" Jay's enthusiasm was evident, his cheeks flushed with excitement as he launched himself over the tailgate.

She shook her head, scraping up a smile for the small boy's benefit. "No, you were a big help, Jay."

"You want to take a look in the shack, make sure you haven't forgotten anything?" Cord's husky voice prompted her and Rachel nodded, hurrying toward the doorway.

It was cool inside, only a trace of sunlight slanting across the floor from the single window. She looked around, taking in the dilapidated furnishings, the dirt floor and the dust motes that filtered down from the rafters. Already, the place held a deserted air.

Another few days and the last trace of crumbs on the floor would be eaten by stray critters, the wind would whistle through the broken door at night, and it would be as if they had never been there.

She shivered at the thought and turned away. "I think we're ready," she said, squinting against the sunlight as she passed through the doorway.

Cord set the door in place and gave her his hand, lifting her to the wagon seat. "Let's get on with it, then."

Rachel lifted the reins and looked down at Henry. *He's growing,* she thought. *His head comes above my shoulder now.* From behind her, Jay was making impatient noises, and she cast him a glance of warning.

Cord's big gelding moved ahead of her, leading the way. She slapped the leather straps against the broad backs of her team, urging them to move out.

"He's nice, isn't he, Rae?" Henry's words were soft, meant only for her ears, and she nodded her reply.

The boy reached into his pocket, lifting on one hip to snake the long licorice whip from its depths.

"You've still got candy left?" she asked, smiling at his frugality.

"Yeah. Want a bite?" Gnawing off a length, he offered the treat in her direction.

"No. Thanks anyway." Perhaps he'd have more than a piece of candy now and then, once she managed to save a little money. Maybe she could afford to do better by the boys if this job panned out.

She drew a deep breath, glancing up at the sky, where clouds rode in billowing herds...where the sun cast its muted rays on the earth below. And then that brilliant orb burst forth from behind a cloud bank, allowing the undiluted splendor of sunlight to wash over her surroundings.

As if it were a sign, a prediction of good things to come, she basked in its warmth. Her gaze drawn again to the man who rode before her, she smiled, admiring the straight line of his back, the easy movement of his body as he sat astride his horse.

And wondered at the shiver of delight that coursed through her body as she considered him.

Chapter Three

"**D**amn dog belongs outdoors, Rachel!" Cord's brows were lowered over stormy eyes as he confronted his new cook. The front of his shirt wore a lavish display of hot coffee, and his fingertips held the wet fabric as far away from his chest as possible, as he roared his disapproval.

Rachel's lips were pressed tightly together and her eyes widened with dismay as she beheld her employer's anger. "I'm so sorry, Mr. McPherson. The boys gave Buster a bath when they got up. They let him in the house so he wouldn't roll in the dirt. I had him shut in the pantry during breakfast. He must have gotten out when I was clearing up."

Cord's fingers worked at the buttons of the shirt he'd donned, fresh from his drawer, only an hour ago. Undoing them and stripping the wet garment from his body, he muttered his thoughts aloud regarding the mutt who watched from behind the pantry door.

"Rules are rules, Rachel. Dogs belong outdoors." He handed her the gray shirt and she reached to grasp it.

"Let me get some butter to put on the burn," she

offered, her gaze intent on the flexing muscles in his upper arms as he moved. "It will take out the sting."

"A cold cloth will do as well," he told her. She turned to the sink where a dish towel was pressed into service as she pumped water to wet it before wringing it out. Rachel handed it to him, watching as he spread the cool cloth against his flesh.

He was tall, well muscled, his arms and shoulders seeming more powerful without the covering of a shirt. Her gaze was drawn by the width of his chest, her eyes fixed on the curling dark hair that centered there. He was big. There was no other word to adequately describe the man. His arms were long, thick with muscles and pale above the elbows.

She clenched her hands, fearful that the urge to touch him would somehow gain control of her, that her traitorous fingers would reach to flex against the flesh he bared to her eyes.

"Will you go up and get me a clean shirt?" He motioned to his boots, dusty from the barn. "I don't want to track on the carpets. My room's the one at the head of the stairs."

She'd paid scant attention last night, once she'd put together a meal for ten. Though only nine had been around the big table in the kitchen. Cord had muttered something about Jake eating later and Rachel could only be relieved at one less to wait on.

The men had made short work of her fried ham and mashed potatoes, scraping every last smidgen from the bowl. Jay and Henry had eaten their share, silent for a change as they attempted to follow the fast-paced conversation. Rachel had only held her breath in hopes that the men's monstrous appetites would be satisfied before the food ran out.

"Rachel?" Cord waited, hands on hips as his low-voiced reminder prodded her into action. "The shirt?"

She nodded, feeling a flush paint her cheeks as she dropped her gaze, hurrying from the room. He'd think she was foolish, gawking at him that way. As if she'd never seen a man's chest before! Pa had often stripped to the waist to wash up before a meal, in front of the sink in the kitchen.

But he'd never looked like Cord McPherson, she admitted to herself, her feet flying up the stairway as she hurried to do his bidding.

Matter of fact, she'd never seen a sight anywhere to match the man downstairs.

She opened his bedroom door and paused for a moment. It was a man's room, no doubt about it, with no frills to be seen. A huge bureau sat against the far wall, between the two windows. She slid open the first drawer, only to find short stacks of undergarments. Her cheeks ablaze, she slid the drawer shut and opened the second.

Success. His shirts were folded neatly, four altogether, still bearing iron marks where the hot sad iron had imprinted itself.

Even fresh from the ironing board, they bore his scent, an aroma lye soap could not overcome. She'd noticed it on the shirt she held in her hand, that smell of leather and fresh air, the faintly musky odor that had caught her nostrils at the supper table as she served the food.

Snatching at a neatly folded shirt, she closed his bureau drawer and scurried toward the doorway. If he should see her standing like a dolt, staring at his belongings, he'd likely send her packing. The man had offered her a job in his house, not the right to moon over him like a...

She shook her head against the thought. Whether or

not she admired the sight of Cord McPherson's body, he was her employer, and she'd do well to remember it.

Her feet skimmed the stairs as she hurried to where he waited and then she slammed to a full stop as she caught sight of him once more.

He was facing the sink, his back to where she watched at the kitchen door. His hands were occupied with wringing out the cloth he'd held against his reddened flesh and his skin stretched tightly across his back as he lifted his hands to apply the cooling towel once more.

Rachel's gaze was caught by the exposed flesh, her eyes widening as she viewed the pale stripes crisscrossing his body. A sound of despair she could not recall slipped from her lips and she lifted one hand quickly to cover the lapse.

He spun to face her, his eyes dark and threatening as he scanned her wary stance. "You might have let me know you were there," he said, lowering the towel he held in one hand. "Give me the shirt." He reached for it, his palm outstretched, and she moved to obey.

He clasped the soft fabric and in the doing managed to grasp her fingertips. She'd gripped the fabric tightly, so stunned by the sight of his scarred flesh she'd been unable to release her hold. And then the warmth of his palm enclosing her fingers brought her to her senses and she murmured a soft sound of protest as she freed herself from his grasp.

He slid his arms into the sleeves and rolled them up, an automatic gesture that bespoke his usual mode of dress. His fingers worked the buttons rapidly, and then his mouth twisted in a dark, mocking grin that brought a flush to ride her cheeks.

"Would you like to turn your back while I tuck it in?" His hesitation gave her the moment's grace she required and she spun to face the doorway, aware of the sound of his denim pants being opened, the brushing of his hands against fabric as he completed the donning of his shirt.

"I'm sorry, I didn't mean to be rude," she managed, aware of his gaze upon her, straightening her shoulders as if she must assume a cloak of dignity before she turned to face him again.

He cleared his throat. "No, I'm the sorry one, Rachel. I embarrassed you, and I apologize." His hands rested on her shoulders and he turned her to face him.

The vee of his neckline was before her eyes, a few strands of dark hair curling against the gray cotton and she felt stunned by the intimacy of it. He held her inches from his body, just a finger's touch from his flesh, and from his skin rose that faintly musky scent she yearned to inhale.

"You've been hurt." The whispered words were all she could manage.

His shrug was a mute dismissal of her concern, even as his fingers slid to tighten against her upper arms.

She trembled in his grasp and rued the emotions that ran riot throughout her. Sorrow, that he had been hurt. Anger, at the culprit who had damaged him so badly.

And most of all, fear, for herself, for the woman she'd become in these few short moments.

Cord McPherson held it within his power to ruin her, her mind proclaimed, the knowledge quickening her heartbeat. His strong hands could tug her against his body and she would go, willingly. His mouth could lower to hers and she, who had never known a man's caress, would welcome the touch of his lips.

She'd made an unwise choice, coming here. An even graver error in judgment, pledging her presence in his home until springtime next year. With only the weight of his hands against her shoulders, he'd been able to melt her store of resistance to his greater strength.

With just a look from those dark eyes, he could send her insides churning in a whirlwind of emotion she had no ability to guard against.

From girl to woman, she had turned the corner in these few minutes of time, and her heart ached with the knowledge of her own vulnerability to this man.

"Rachel? Are you all right?" His hands shook her, clasping her firmly as if he would support her entire body by the hold he had taken on her upper arms.

She blinked, roused from her soul-searching, and met his gaze with what she grimly hoped was a sensible smile of accord.

"I'm fine, Mr. McPherson. Just fine." Her spine held her erect as she stepped back from him, her flesh cooling as his hands slid to his sides.

She was too tempting by far, this piece of womanhood he'd brought into his home. Cord's mouth tightened as he considered his folly, not to mention his carelessness in shedding his shirt in her presence. And so his measuring glance was harsh, his words a warning.

"They're old scars, Rachel. Too old to worry about now, and none of your concern."

She lowered her lashes until she could no longer see his upper body, and she concentrated on his words, as if unwilling to meet his gaze any longer. "You're right. I made a fuss over nothing. I'll tend to my own business from now on."

She watched his hand clench into a fist, there at his side, and then his fingers flexed and he rested his palm flat against his thigh.

"You'd better soak that shirt or the coffee will stain it," he said, grumbling the order as he turned away.

"Yes..." Her whisper followed him, as did her bewildered glance, looking up from the clean, wide boards of the kitchen floor as he allowed the screen door to slam behind himself.

A clod of dirt received a swift kick, his hat was mercilessly swatted against his thigh, and words his mama had never taught him spewed forth from Cord's mouth in a muttered litany. Each stride was a thudding release of the anger he directed at himself, jarring his teeth as he clenched his jaw.

"Shamus!" The roar was almost enough to rattle the rafters in the big barn. From inside, a growling reply met Cord's ears and he halted in the wide doorway.

"You needn't scare the bejabbers out of the mare, McPherson." Bending over a hind hoof, Shamus Quinn spoke around the nails he held between his teeth. Beyond him, the mare turned to look at the noisy intruder, her placid manner belying the fright attributed to her by the man fitting her with the last of her new shoes.

Cord cocked one hip, his fist resting against the angle, his abused hat tugged low over his forehead. "When are you gonna learn who's boss here?" he snarled, his jaw jutting fiercely.

Spitting the nails he held in his mouth into his palm, Shamus dropped them into the front pocket of the leather apron he wore. Lowering the mare's foot to the earthen floor, he eased his back, stretching to one side, then the other.

"Don't know as I've got a problem with that, McPherson." His sandy hair was a riot of curls atop his head, and one hand rubbed slowly over the thick mat as he eyed his employer. His bowlegged stance and sun-leathered skin proclaimed him a horseman, but the ease with which he handled the mare added credence to that title.

"Thought I told you to see to the new stud next." Cord's words were harsher than he'd intended, his ire easing as he watched the man who'd been his friend since childhood.

Shamus nodded. "So you did." Moving back to the mare's side, he lifted her foot and rested it against his leg.

"Hold still, girl," Shamus murmured to the horse. "We're about done with you." With ease, he worked at the shoe, fitting it carefully, his pliers nipping at the exposed nails.

"I'm wanting to ride him today." Cord's voice had resumed a normal volume and Shamus cast him a side-long glance.

"He's ready for you. I took care of him first thing when I got up. Before breakfast in fact." Easing the mare's foot to the floor, Shamus stepped back. "You sure hirin' that gal on was a good idea?"

Cord's eyes narrowed. "What does Rachel have to do with anything?"

The other man shrugged. "Dunno." He peered at Cord, a grin edging his mouth. "Seems like you been on edge ever since she got here yesterday. Havin' a fe-male around ain't good for you. It makes you ornery. S'pose maybe you need a trip to town?"

Cord's glance was fierce, his demeanor defensive. "We needed a cook. Sam's got his hands full with Jake." He frowned, thinking of his brother. "I haven't taken time to see him yet today. Right now I need to get the rest of the calves penned up for branding this afternoon.''

He thought of the woman he'd left in the kitchen. To beat all, he'd snarled at her and stomped off in a fit of temper. He didn't need a woman fussing over him, even though the thought of Rachel's slim fingers brushing against the old, silvered scars he bore made him shiver involuntarily.

Just as well he'd snapped at her. She was too good a cook to lose, and if he let his urges loose on her, she'd be hightailing it up the road, sure as the world.

Shamus was on his way to the back of the barn with the mare, and Cord followed him. ''Bring me my saddle from the tack room,'' he called, halting before the big box stall enclosing his new stallion. The horse eyed him cautiously, then bobbed his head and approached, stretching out his neck and flaring his nostrils.

Cord's big hand snagged the leather halter and drew the animal closer. ''Remember me, boy?'' His voice was low, his movements easy. ''We're gonna get on just fine, you and me.''

Easing open the door of the stall, he led the stud through the opening, snatching up a bridle from a hook on the outside of the enclosure.

His hands were deft as he exchanged the halter for the bridle and bit, dropping the reins to the ground as he worked. From the rear of the barn, Shamus whistled tunelessly inside the tack room. And then the door closed behind him as he headed back up the broad aisle to where Cord waited.

''Buck and Jamie been sortin' out the last of the calves. I think that holdin' pen's about full already. They've been at it a while now, since right after breakfast.''

"I'll check it out," Cord answered, swinging his saddle to rest on the broad back of the stud with a lithe movement.

"Jake under the weather?" Shamus's question was carefully casual. "He wasn't around for supper last night and Sam didn't mention him this morning."

"Just a bad spell," Cord muttered. "He gets in a mood and won't eat. Sam just has to let him get past it on his own."

"What does your new cook think about takin' care of him?" Shamus asked guardedly.

Cord lifted into the saddle. "She doesn't know about him yet, and she won't be doin' the takin' care of anyway. I'll talk to her at dinnertime."

Shamus grunted his displeasure. "You better hope he doesn't take to havin' a tantrum in there." His head nodded at the big house. "She'll be skedaddlin' to town faster than you can blink."

His chuckle was low and his eyes lit with humor. "Damn, that gal sure can bake up a good pan of biscuits, McPherson. You better hang on to her."

His stallion sidestepped in a skittish dance as Cord cleared the barn door and he held the reins firmly, his voice low as he spoke to the animal. Beside the corral fence, Rachel's brothers watched, wide-eyed as the big horse vied for control with the man atop his back.

"You boys lookin' for a job to do?" Cord called out.

Henry nodded. "Yessir, we can help out. Rachel said we were to pitch in."

"Go inside the barn and tell Shamus I sent you. He'll put you to work gatherin' the eggs and tendin' to the chickens."

Henry's smile lost its shine. "I thought maybe we could help with the horses, sir."

"Start with chickens and work your way up, boy. Your sister won't have time to tend to them this morning."

"I brushed down my pa's horses," Henry said quietly, unwilling to be relegated to tending the hens.

Cord's eyes narrowed as he took in the boy's stance, shoulders back and chin uptilted. "Take care of the hens today, and I'll let you give a hand tomorrow morning with the yearling colts."

Henry's eyes brightened with excitement and he nodded quickly. "Yessir, that'll be just fine. Me and Jay can sure learn how to feed chickens in a hurry."

Jay nodded his agreement, standing almost behind his brother. "Yessir, we can do that."

Cord jerked at the brim of his hat, forcing it firmly against his forehead. "Don't get into trouble, now."

Two small heads swung in unison. "Oh, no sir, we won't," Jay warbled, poking at his big brother. "Did you hear, Henry?" he asked in his clear treble voice. "We get to be in the barn tomorrow."

Cord's stallion moved out quickly, and he watched as the two boys scampered toward the barn door, Henry calling for Shamus as they went.

Across the yard, Rachel stood on the back porch, shaking the dust a dozen feet had deposited before breakfast on the small braided rug she held. Her hair gleaming in the morning sunshine, she watched as he rode past the corral, meeting his gaze across the grassy expanse.

"Probably ought to take time now to talk to her about Jake," Cord muttered to himself, regretful that he hadn't said something last night.

From beyond the barns, a shout caught his attention and he swung in that direction, where a cloud of dust bespoke activity. A spiral of smoke from a fire caught the breeze and he sniffed at the scent of burning wood. The men were setting up shop without him, it seemed.

With a nudge of his heel, the horse beneath him turned in the direction of the holding pen, and within minutes Cord was enmeshed in the branding of his calves.

Setting a pot of beef to simmer on the back of the stove, Rachel surveyed her kitchen. Though it belonged to Cord McPherson, it had become hers the moment she donned an apron yesterday afternoon.

Already, she had rearranged the pantry shelves to her liking, adding her own meager stores to the bountiful supply of tins and sacks gracing the shelves. That any one household should be so blessed by an abundance of foodstuffs was almost beyond belief.

A thrill of anticipation brightened her eyes and lightened her steps as she gathered the ingredients for the beef stew she planned for the noon meal. The meat was cut up and browned right after breakfast, with several onions adding a tangy scent. She'd found a sack of sprouting potatoes and upended them in the sink, sorting and scraping at the lot.

Somewhere outdoors, she decided, there must be a cellar where the garden produce had been stored for the winter.

The pantry held cans of peaches and she determined to make a cobbler, with sweet biscuits crusting it. Then she'd discovered the jars of home-canned applesauce and her eyes had widened at the sight of such luxury. Traveling from Pennsylvania had inured her to the prospect of dried and unpalatable fruit, not to mention the absence of fresh meat, except for the rabbits her father had managed to shoot along the way.

Her heart sang with the pleasure of putting roses in the cheeks of Jay and Henry once more, too long fed with oatmeal and cornbread, a handful of greens and an occasional fish. Henry had brought down a few rabbits, but she'd had a hard time cleaning the small specimens he'd managed to bring home.

Her mind wandered as she peeled potatoes, setting them aside in a pan of water to wait for the stew to be ready, her mouth shaping the words of a song as she sang beneath her breath.

The memory of a piano she'd spied in the front parlor yesterday afternoon entered her mind, and she thought with longing of the music hidden in those black and white keys.

Cord McPherson had walked her past those open double doors guarding the formal room at one side of the house, affording her but a glimpse of the beautiful instrument. Perhaps she could just take another look, maybe even open the other doors on that long hallway.

A house of this size was a wonderment. That Cord McPherson was a man of means had been a given. After all, he owned the ranch. That his home should be so fine was a pleasure beyond her imagining.

Wiping her hands on the dish towel she'd tucked into her apron, Rachel looked around the kitchen. Midmorning sunshine splashed across the pine floor, too strong to be stopped by the streaked windows.

She'd do well to get out a keg of vinegar and wash them, instead of considering poking her nose into the nooks and crannies of Cord McPherson's home, she thought virtuously. And then with a twirl of skirts and a girlish laugh stifled with her open palm, she left her apron behind and set off down the hallway.

The parlor was magnificent, with a plush sofa much

like the one that had graced their own parlor in Pennsylvania. The library desk beneath the window held an assortment of pictures and small ornaments that beckoned her invitingly.

She paused beside the mantelpiece, admiring the brass figures and marble pieces gathered there for display, then hesitated in the middle of the room to turn in a full circle. Coming to a halt, Rachel faced the piano, her mouth opening, a soft, yearning sound passing her lips.

Her feet moved soundlessly across the carpet in the center of the wooden floor, her soft-soled shoes a whisper. With reverent fingers, she lifted the lid that covered the keys and eased it to its open position. One finger touched white ivory, and she tilted her head as she heard the clear tone of hammer striking string within the instrument.

"Ohhhh...!" It was more than a whispered exclamation of delight. From the depths of her soul, the yearning of her hungry heart expressed itself.

Music. The gift that eased the longings of her spirit, that fed her, nourishing her with beauty beyond bearing.

The temptation was more than she could resist. Rachel slid onto the bench, yielding to the attraction of the sounds held captive within the depths of the instrument before her. Lifting her hands, she placed them on the keys.

A melody flowed with liquid beauty from beneath her right hand, the fingers of the left adding a counterpoint of chords and running trills. Her eyes closed with the sheer ecstasy of it and she bent her head, her ear attuned to each note.

From the hallway a roar of disbelief sounded, a bellow of rage that halted her hands in their melodious pursuit.

She spun on the bench, one leg half-bent beneath her as she looked over her shoulder.

Framed in the wide doorway was a man, sitting in an invalid's chair. Empty pant legs hung lankly to the foot rest, only one knee curved over the seat. His hair hung to his shoulders in dark disarray. Bearded and hunched, looking like a beast set on ravishing the cause of his anger, he leaned in Rachel's direction.

"I'm so sorry I disturbed you." It was barely more than a whisper, spoken from between trembling lips. Her hands were clenched between her breasts, her heart beating a rapid cadence beneath her fists.

But he paid her apology no attention, his whole being seemingly bound by the furious rage that impelled him. His hands gripped the wheels and he spun them, sending his vehicle surging in her direction. Dark eyes, narrowed and blazing with an unholy anger, stopped her breath in her throat as she met his gaze with dismay.

And then he halted, midway across the room, and snarled a curse that fell on her ears and caused her to draw an unbelieving breath. He spun the wheels once more and the chair bumped against the piano bench, jarring her from her frozen pose of horror.

One hand reached toward him, as if to fend off his attack, and he cast the trembling fingers a look of such scorn as to cause them to fall back in her lap.

"I beg your pardon, sir…" The words were stronger this time as her mind raced, seeking an answer to the appearance of this creature before her.

And then he spoke, the words spaced as if uttered in the presence of an idiot, to whom he must make himself clearly understood.

"Who the hell are you?"

Chapter Four

Rachel caught her breath with a shuddering gasp, her words barely a whisper. "My name is Rachel Sinclair." She swayed where she sat, expecting to be shunted from her perch momentarily.

The rolling chair backed a few inches and thumped again against the padded seat, jarring her. Her hand grasped for purchase and she caught her balance, her long, slender fingers clutching at the arm of the chair.

Horror-stricken, her eyes fastened on the man before her and she flinched as he plucked her fingers from his chair, dropping them from his grasp with contempt. He brushed his palm against his patchwork lap robe and her gaze was drawn to the gesture.

Long, elegant fingers, pale with winter's flesh, wiped her warmth from his skin. It was an insult she could not ignore.

"I beg your pardon. I wasn't aware that I was disturbing anyone with my playing, sir." Pleased at the even tenor of her words, she lifted her chin to face the disheveled intruder.

Beneath lowered brows, his gaze was fierce, his voice

rasping. "Who gave you leave to be in here? This piano is not to be touched. Not by anyone."

Rachel lowered her leg to the floor and slid from the bench, easing beyond the end of the keyboard. Retreat seemed to be in order. "Mr. McPherson didn't say... I'm afraid I've overstepped, sir."

The doorway looming over his shoulder was wide and inviting. Rachel eyed it, wondering if he would attempt to stop her should she scamper past him. His agility in the chair he'd maneuvered so easily gave her pause as she considered.

"What are you doing in this house?" His query was forced between taut lips, his flaring nostrils adding to an air of fury that was punctuated by the spacing of his words.

"I'm the new cook," she managed. "Mr. McPherson hired me to do the laundry and fix meals."

And if Cord McPherson knew what was good for him, he'd have a dandy explanation for this little episode.

The intruder's snort of derision was accompanied by the spinning of wheels as he turned his chair about and headed for the double doors of the parlor. "Out of my way, Sam," he directed, rolling past the bewhiskered man who watched from the hall. "Cord's brought home a play toy." His glance back in her direction was mocking. "Take a gander."

Rachel's cheeks burned at the slur as she lifted one hand to cover her mouth, lest she let loose the response that burned to be spoken. How dare he? To insinuate such a thing was reprehensible, a grievous smear against her honor.

"Sorry, ma'am." Sam Bostwick's head bobbed as he tendered his apologies. "Jake's been out of sorts for a couple of days now."

"That's Mr. McPherson's brother?" Her eyes widened at Sam's nod. "I thought..." She shook her head. What had she thought? Perhaps that the elusive brother was an invalid?

And apparently he was. But a more hateful man she'd never met. Her back stiffened as she considered the words he had flung at her.

He'd called her Cord's play toy. She, who'd been a churchgoing woman all of her life, who had been above reproach in all things, had today been referred to as a man's... Her mind could not even form the thought.

Surely she could no longer stay in this house, not when her reputation was in danger of being dragged through the mud of scandal.

"Ma'am, I'm sure sorry Jake took on thataway," Sam said quietly, his sad eyes fastened on Rachel's countenance. "I knew Cord shoulda told you about him last night at the supper table. But, honest to God, Mr. Jake's not usually so downright mean."

Rachel brushed her hand against Sam's sleeve. "He just wasn't what I expected, Mr. Bostwick." She edged past him, heading for the kitchen.

"Damnation! Just when we got ourselves a decent cook, things gotta blow around here." Disgust was in Sam's voice as he watched the young woman's hurried escape. Behind him doors slammed, and the sound of breaking glass caused him to wince as he turned to trudge reluctantly back to the rear of the house.

Rachel was primed to blow. Her eyes met Cord's as he walked through the kitchen door, and a sense of dread slowed his steps. Quickly, he scanned the kitchen, breathing easier when he caught the aroma ascending from the steaming kettle on the stove and noted the platter of biscuits in the center of the table.

A crock of butter and a bowl of jam nudged the plate, and he set his jaw as he considered the young woman who was noisily scattering silverware and plates down the length of the bare table.

"Smells good, Rachel. Want me to call the men in for dinner?" That they were already washing up at the pump was obvious, their raucous joking audible through the kitchen window. Rachel ignored his offer, turning to the stove to fill thick crockery bowls with beef stew.

"Heard tell you had a fuss in the parlor this morning." Cord was beside her as he spoke, his big hands taking the bowls as she filled them, setting them in place on the table.

She cast him a sidelong glance. "You didn't tell me your brother was a madman, Mr. McPherson."

His face reddened at her choice of words, his nostrils flaring as he inhaled sharply. "I don't know as I'd call him mad, Rachel. That's a pretty strong statement."

She handed him the last bowl. Her look was direct, her face flushed with remembered embarrassment. "You weren't there."

He cleared his throat. "Sam told me what happened. Seems Jake took offense at you playing the piano."

"Your brother insinuated you had brought me here for your—"

"I heard about that," Cord cut in quickly. "I'll set him straight."

"You could have told me about him. You could have warned me not to infringe on his territory. And you could have let me know about his vile temper."

Cord's shrug acknowledged her accusations, his nod accepting blame. "I wanted you to see the house and give you a chance to look things over first. I thought knowing about Jake would put you off. Putting up with his moods is enough to discourage a saint.''

''And I ain't anywheres near a saint,'' grumbled Sam Bostwick from the kitchen doorway. ''I've about had it with that brother of yours, Cord. If I hadn't known the man before the war, I swear I'd never spend another minute takin' his guff.''

''He calmed down yet, Sam?'' Cord asked.

''Yeah. But he sure was a sight to behold, goin' after this young'un. It's a wonder she didn't hightail it outta here.''

''Would you like to take him some dinner?'' Her innate sense of courtesy nudged Rachel into making the offer as she filled another bowl with stew.

''Thank you, ma'am,'' Sam said, taking a wooden tray from atop the cabinet near the stove. Scooping up silverware from the table, he piled several biscuits on a plate, dolloping jam and butter on the side.

''I'll be back out here to eat with y'all presently,'' he said, carrying his laden tray from the kitchen.

''Doesn't your brother ever eat at the table?'' Rachel asked.

''Once in a while. Not often.''

She glanced at Cord, her ear attuned to the bleak response. ''Is he always so fierce?''

His grunt of laughter was without humor. ''That's a good word for him. Fierce. Maybe bitter would describe him more accurately. He hasn't found much to laugh about in the past years.''

Not like this bunch coming in the door, Rachel thought, an unbidden smile twisting her lips as the noisy cowhands invaded the quiet kitchen. Jostling for position, they fit through the doorway, finding their seats at the long table.

The stew was an apparent success, devoured with much lip smacking and accompanied by praise from the hungry men. They laughed and joked and ate at a rapid pace, as if racing to a finish line.

Indeed, Rachel had barely begun eating when chairs were shoved back and the crew took their leave. Cord watched her assessingly from the other end of the table, his own meal half-consumed.

"It seems you've got a job, Miss Rachel," he said with satisfaction. "Old Sam said he hadn't had such good food in a month of Sundays."

Rachel's spoon halted midway to her mouth. "I don't know how you could hear him, with all the noise. Did he take your brother any coffee? I think he went on out with the rest of the men."

Cord grinned, leaning back in his chair. "Why don't you trot on down the hallway, and find out for yourself. Jake's in the library, last room on the right. Makes it handy, with the wheelchair."

"I don't think so," Rachel said quickly. "My last encounter with your brother Jake didn't give me a taste for a second helping."

Cord's smile faded and he allowed his chair to settle on all four legs. "He's a handful to deal with, Rachel. We all know that. In fact, it's almost too much for Sam these days."

"And you want me to stick my nose into that room and get it cut off?"

"He's probably cooled down by now. The piano playing was what set him off."

Rachel's brow furrowed. "He doesn't like music?"

"That would be a mercy. Music was his life, before

the war. He'd trained in New York City to be a concert pianist, and then when the war broke out, he felt compelled to join the army.''

He laughed, a mirthless sound. ''We were all so worried about his hands. Instead, he lost his legs. One above the knee, the other below.''

Rachel nodded, shaking her head as she acknowledged the loss. ''He can't play because he can't use the pedals.''

''Exactly.'' Cord rose from his chair and walked to the door, looking through the screen to where Henry and Jay hung over the corral fence. ''He wanted to have the piano burned at first. Then, when he'd thought better of it, he decided to give it to the church.''

''Why didn't you?'' Rachel asked.

''It wouldn't go in the door. We measured every which way and it wouldn't make it.''

''And so it sits and gathers dust. What a loss.''

Cord turned to face her. ''I hear from Sam that you play well.''

She shrugged. ''Well enough, I suppose. I certainly worked hard enough at it. We had to sell my piano when my folks decided to come West.''

''It must have broken your heart.''

Rachel shook her head. ''No, it broke my heart when I buried my mother and father two months ago. Selling the piano was small potatoes compared to that.''

''They died two months ago? On the trail?''

She nodded. ''Pa collapsed one day after we crossed a river. The horses were in trouble and Pa was done in when he finally got them up the bank. His chest began hurting and then he collapsed. We buried him there. The doctor in the next town said it was probably his heart.''

''What about your mother?'' Cord asked.

Rachel's voice was thick with the unshed tears she hoarded within herself as she whispered the tragic words she still found hard to believe as the truth. "Mama wandered off the next night while we were sleeping in the wagon and got bitten by a rattler. The scout found her the next morning."

"My God, Rachel. How did you bear up under it?" Cord asked in a strained voice. He shook his head, as if he groped for words.

"I can see where the loss of your piano wasn't nearly so important anymore," he said finally.

"I wish I had it now," Rachel whispered. "Music soothes the soul."

"Maybe…" Cord hesitated, then gestured at the coffeepot. "Give it another try, Rachel. I'd be willing to bet Jake enjoyed his dinner. Pour a cup and take it in to him." His lips curved as he tried on a grin for her benefit.

"If he throws something at you, duck. Chances are he'll just grouse for a few seconds. Jake enjoys nothing in this world more than a cup of coffee."

Her chin jutted as Rachel listened unbelievingly to his instructions. She glared at him, her mind torn from the sorrow she'd been reminded of for a few moments. "You owe me, Cord McPherson. I didn't bargain for catering to an invalid, but I've a notion that's exactly where I'll be heading, once Sam Bostwick sees me waiting on Jake."

Cord lifted his shoulders in a helpless shrug. "Maybe you can deal with him, Rachel. God knows no one else gets anywhere."

"I'm not taking him on, Cord." Her mouth set in a determined line as she plunged both hands into her apron pockets. "I'm your cook, and I'll wash your duds, but ducking every time I open your brother's door is out."

"Not even once, Rachel? Just one cup of coffee?" The teasing grin was gone.

The vision of the unkempt man who'd so rudely interrupted her few moments of joy burst inside Rachel's mind, and she shook her head. "I doubt he'd welcome me, even with a cup of coffee in hand."

Cord's mouth twisted in a wry grin. "Can't blame me for trying, Rachel." He reached for a heavy cup from the cupboard and filled it from the blue-speckled pot. "I'll deliver it myself. Send in the troops if I don't come back in five minutes."

Breakfast was barely devoured the next morning when Cord stepped back into the kitchen, hat in hand. "Rachel, I'm going to town to the emporium. Anything we need for the house?"

She turned from the dishpan, wiping her hands on a towel. "Do you think I could go along? The boys need some boots if they're going to be working in the barn, and I thought I could get them each a pair."

"I can pay you for your first week here, if you need the money," Cord said.

She shook her head. "No, I have enough, so long as I know I'll be earning some right along. Shamus wants me to do up his laundry every week, and Buck and Jamie asked if I'd iron them each a shirt on Saturdays."

He laughed. "That's so they'll look pretty when they go into town Saturday nights." He shook his head. "You won't make much cold hard cash ironing two shirts, Rachel. Better charge them a pretty penny." He turned back to the door. "Come on ahead, then, if you're riding along."

She untied her apron and hung it on the hook in the pantry, running back to the stove quickly to check the black kettle where a stewing hen was simmering. With a practiced eye she gauged the bubbling liquid and slid the pot toward the back burner, clutching the handle with a heavy flannel pad.

"I'm ready," she announced, her hands quickly smoothing back her hair. "I just have to run up and get my money."

"Five minutes," Cord said, heading out the door.

Jay and Henry were kicking their heels on the back of the wagon when Rachel crossed the porch, her bonnet strings trailing from her fingers.

"Mr. Cord said we could go along," Jay piped up.

"He said you were gettin' us some new boots." Henry's voice rose at the end of his sentence, as if he questioned the validity of such an idea.

Rachel nodded, her heart lifting as her brothers poked at each other with delight. She could even spare them each a couple of pennies for candy again, she thought, imagining their delight.

"Can we get high tops, Rae?" Henry asked wistfully.

"We'll see," she answered doubtfully, unsure of the cost of such a luxury.

"Looks like you need to get them some britches to go along with the boots," Cord said, lifting himself to the wagon seat.

"Theirs have a lot of wear left in them," she put in quickly. "Maybe next week we can look at new over-alls."

Cord reached down a hand to her as she peered up at him. "Let me give you a hoist up," he offered.

Accepting his broad hand, she placed her foot on the wagon hub, and he lifted her to sit beside him. "They'll be happy with boots,'' she told him, settling her skirts around her.

He bent to her, watching as she tied her bonnet in place. Then, following an urge he'd resisted more than once in the past few days, he brushed at a stray wisp of hair that clung to her face.

She flushed at the gesture and turned her head, her fingers rising to spread across the rosy surface of her cheek. His touch had been gentle and unexpected, his fingertips a bit rough from the calluses he bore.

''Rachel?'' He reached for her again, this time to cradle her chin within his grasp, turning her to face him.

''We need to be on our way,'' she mumbled, unwilling to meet his gaze, flustered by his attention. ''I can't be gone all day with dinner cooking on the stove.''

''Look at me.'' It was a command, delivered in a low, yet forceful voice, and she obeyed.

''You have no reason to fear me, Rachel,'' he said firmly. ''I'm old enough to know my place and decent enough to remain there.''

''I'm not afraid of you,'' she whispered, her voice catching in her throat.

It was a lie. There was about him something she feared, some unknown threat he offered that caused a trembling in her belly.

The level look he sent in her direction across the kitchen sometimes was enough to set her heart scampering, and his kindness to her brothers gave her a warmth deep inside, and made him tall in her sight.

''Aren't you?'' His eyebrow quirked as if he doubted her brave words, and then he flicked the reins against the backs of his team and they set off for Green Rapids.

There was no doubt about it. Mr. Conrad Carson was more than taken with Miss Rachel Sinclair. Cord watched from his post next to the cracker barrel as his cook chose boots for her brothers. And all the while, Conrad smiled and joked as he offered one pair, then another for her approval.

Kneeling before the boys, he took their measure, then tried on the boots Rachel pointed out. With only a moment's hesitation, he assured her that her limited resources would be sufficient to cover the cost of two pair, and then his gaze rose, his eyes meeting Cord's with a trace of warning in their depths.

"I'll handle the difference, if she runs out of funds," Cord said, his mouth twisting in a parody of a polite smile.

Conrad flushed a bit. "Miss Rachel can choose what she pleases, Mr. McPherson. I'm sure we can work something out."

Rachel's eyes widened as she looked first at one man, then the other. "I thought—"

"You have enough money for the boots," Carson cut in smoothly. He grinned at the two boys, who were stomping their feet and marching up and down the aisle, admiring their new footwear. "Probably even enough for a couple of licorice whips for each," he added, counting Rachel's meager funds into his cash drawer.

Jay's head turned quickly at the mention of candy. "Can we, Rae?" he asked hopefully.

"We got boots, Jay," Henry reminded him quickly, as if he would relieve Rachel of the burden of refusal.

Cord cleared his throat. "I expect my two new hands have enough wages coming to them to buy a bag of candy, Conrad. See what they want, will you?"

Rachel's gaze met his and she bit at her lip. "I don't

want you putting any more money out than is right, Cord.''

She was more than a temptation, he thought. And too much woman for Conrad Carson.

Cord took two long strides to where she waited by the counter, one hand rising to rest on her shoulder.

''They've been a help, Rachel. I'm sure at least a nickel's worth each.'' He raised his voice, catching the attention of the trio who were intent on the contents of the candy jars. ''Give them each a bag and let them choose five cents worth, Conrad.''

The younger man looked up, nodding, and then halted, his eyes narrowing as his gaze swept over Cord to Rachel, fastening on Cord's possessive gesture. He'd gotten the message, Cord decided with satisfaction. Rachel was not up for grabs. His fingers tightened for just a moment, squeezing the narrow bones beneath her supple flesh, and she looked up at him in surprise.

''We need to be getting back as soon as I help Conrad load my supplies on the wagon,'' he told her.

She nodded. ''All right. I'll have the boys change back to their old shoes and we'll be right out.''

''Let them wear the new ones, Rachel. They can save the others for mucking out the chicken coop and cleaning stalls.'' His mind traveled back quickly to childhood memories.

''There's nothing like a new pair of boots to set a boy's heart to thumpin' real good,'' he said with a grin.

He'd carried out nails and a roll of wire, come back in for the can of kerosene and met Conrad at the door, his arms wrapped around a wooden crate of fresh vegetables.

''You don't have a garden growing, Cord,'' Rachel put in quickly. ''Conrad gave me a good price on the peas and carrots. He'll have fresh beans in by next week, he said.'' Her explanation was hurried, as if she worried over his reaction, and Cord shook his head, watching as Conrad settled the crate on the back of the wagon.

"You buy whatever you want, Rachel. The men are sick of canned stuff. Maybe it isn't too late to put in a kitchen garden. I'll ask Conrad for seeds.''

"I've already told Miss Rachel I'd make up an assortment for her to plant,'' Conrad said from the doorway. "I'll bring them out to you tomorrow afternoon, if that's all right,'' he added, his gaze hopeful as he stepped into the store, watching the young woman for a sign of her acceptance.

"I'd appreciate that,'' she answered, a tentative smile touching her lips. "I'll save you a piece of pie.'' Her look at Cord was tinged with defiance as she turned to leave the store, and he grunted his own goodbyes.

"Put everything on my bill, Conrad. I'll pay up at month end,'' he instructed harshly, casting one last look at the jaunty smile the storekeeper wore.

Cord made a production of helping Rachel into the wagon, lifting her to the seat before he circled to the other side to take his place beside her.

"I could have gotten up alone,'' she said quietly, turning to him with a puzzled look.

He lifted the reins, cracking them briskly over the backs of his team as they moved out at a smart pace. "Conrad's wanting to court you, Rachel.'' He hadn't planned on being so blunt, but the words had come unbidden. "If you're not thinking along those same lines, you shouldn't encourage him.''

"Encourage him?'' Her voice rose sharply on the words. "I was polite, no more. If the gentleman wants to be accommodating and is willing to make a trip to bring out the garden seeds, I can surely offer him a piece of pie. That's only being courteous, Mr. McPherson.''

Beneath lifted brows, her cheeks bore rosy flags and her mouth was firmly drawn. Rachel was upset with him.

He hid a smile as he took inventory of her. Stiff and unbending, she rode beside him, her fingers retying the strings of her bonnet, her mouth primly closed. The deep breaths she took as she fanned the flames of her anger lifted her bosom in an enticing fashion and he allowed the smile to widen as his gaze rested there for a moment.

She could fuss all she wanted. Rachel Sinclair would be his, perhaps not as quickly as he'd like, but sure as the summer brought longer days and shorter nights, Rachel would belong to him.

In all of his years of considering the females he'd come in contact with, he'd not found one so pleasing to the eye as the young woman sitting beside him.

Others might have been more beautiful, more voluptuous, clothed with silks and satin, but the fresh innocence of Rachel Sinclair, garbed in a faded cotton dress, spoke to him in a way he found he could not resist. Despite his words of assurance, he was not certain he could keep his place without more effort than he was willing to expend to that end.

With her gentle curves and creamy skin, her blue eyes, her dark vibrant hair that tempted his fingers to its depths, she was exactly what he had been waiting for.

Now he only needed to persuade her in that direction.

Chapter Five

Baking pies was a tremendous waste of time, Rachel decided, as Cord's crew of hands devoured two pies between them in less than three minutes. Jay and Henry watched, their eyes wide in awe as the men scooped the golden crust and juicy berries onto their forks in rapid succession. The boys' modest pieces were eaten more slowly, perhaps due to the forbidding frown on Rachel's face.

The rest of the third pie was hidden on the pantry shelf, covered by a clean dish towel, each piece already apportioned. One to Jake, should he want dessert, one to Conrad Carson, should he show up with her seeds this afternoon, one for herself, and the last set aside, in case Cord came in late, looking for something to tide him over until breakfast.

"Wonderful pie, Miss Rachel," Buck Austin said respectfully, licking the tines of his fork.

"Best raspberry pie I ever ate," added Moses, the eldest of Cord's men.

Rachel nodded her appreciation of their words, watching as their chairs emptied like the outgoing tide, men flowing past the doorway in a rush as they returned to work.

"You're a good cook, sure enough," Cord said, lifting his coffee cup to drain the contents. He watched her over the edge and she shivered under the heat of his gaze.

Ever since they'd come back from town yesterday, he'd given her the same sort of look, as if he were peering beneath her skin, investigating the very thoughts that ran rampant in her mind. Their eyes met and he lowered his cup, the trace of a smile curving his lips.

"I've been thinking maybe you need someone to give you a hand here," he said. "You're about workin' yourself to a frazzle, cooking and cleaning, let alone trying to keep up with the washing."

"I thought I'd tackle that again this afternoon," Rachel told him. "I've heated two buckets full of water on the stove already. I just need help lifting them down. I can dip and carry from the reservoir myself."

He nodded. "I noticed. That's why I was wondering if we hadn't ought to find somebody to help out."

"Who helped out before I got here?"

He laughed, a short, derisive sound. "It was pretty much every man for himself. Sam cooked, I pitched in when I could, and everybody scrubbed out their own duds. I had a neighbor come over once a month or so and wash up the sheets and such."

"And the house got a lick and a promise," Rachel said dryly.

"If that much," Cord admitted.

"The piano was clean," she said quietly. "In that whole parlor, only the piano wasn't dusty."

His eyebrows lifted in surprise. "I guess I didn't notice that. Not that I spend much time in there anyway.

It's about all I can do to find my bed at night, some days.''

"Where's that neighbor? The one who washed the sheets?''

"Still livin' down the road a couple of miles,'' he said. "Alice Claypool's her name. I guess we could ask her to come, but I doubt she'd do it. She's got a family of her own to take care of.''

"Any widow ladies who need some extra money?'' Rachel asked.

Cord looked thoughtful, his fingertips meeting as he propped his elbows on the table. "There's someone....''

"Who?'' She'd settle for any warm body, Rachel thought, so long as she knew how to scrub on a board and use a carpet beater. The rugs in this house were in pathetic condition.

"Miz Claypool's daughter, as a matter of fact.''

"Is she a widow?''

He shook his head. "No...but she might as well be.'' He pushed back from the table and stood abruptly. "I don't think that would work out at all. We'd better stick with Sam taking care of Jake and lending you a hand when he can. For now anyway.''

"Who were you talking about?'' Rachel asked insistently. If he was serious about getting her some help, she was willing to take what she could get.

"Before the war, Jake and Lorena Claypool were keeping company,'' Cord said reluctantly.

Rachel's heart skipped a beat. "And after the war? Did she change her mind about him?'' If so, Lorena Claypool would not be welcome in this kitchen, she decided without hesitation.

Cord shook his head. "No, just the other way around. Jake didn't want anything to do with her. Said he wasn't a man any longer and he wasn't about to waste Rena's time.''

''And she just gave up on him?''

''No, she came around two or three times, asking to see him, and he turned her down flat. You could hear him shoutin' from here, cursing and carrying on like a madman.''

''I've heard that same routine. Just the other day, in fact,'' Rachel said, her mouth twisting into a sad parody of a smile.

''Rena left that day, more than three years ago, and hasn't been back since.''

''My mama used to call that 'cuttin' off your nose to spite your face,''' Rachel said quietly. ''Seems to me if the woman loved him enough to come to him, he'd ought to have given her a chance.''

''He's a man, Rachel. A proud man, lacking the legs to hold him upright. Too proud to expose himself to anybody, let alone a woman he cared about.''

''Well, I'll warrant she's a proud woman, with enough gumption to face that fact. I don't even know her, but I'll bet she's tough enough to—''

''I doubt she'd set foot on the place again, Rachel,'' Cord said, shaking his head.

''Well, if you want the kind of meals you've been getting, and clean clothes to boot, it might be worth your while to find out.''

''Is that a threat?'' His eyes gleaming with laughter, he rounded the table, tugging her from her chair, his big hands firm against her shoulders.

She laughed, feeling a sense of power as he asked the question. She'd proved herself here. In the short length of time she'd been running Cord McPherson's house, she'd become a necessary part of his life, and she knew it. Except for those times when he looked somber and all withdrawn, as if the world was sitting heavy on his shoulders, he acted as if things were looking up in his life.

"No, I don't make threats to big cowboys," she said teasingly.

"I run a ranch, Rachel. I'm not a cowboy." He tightened his grip, turning her to stand within inches of his muscular frame. She stumbled a bit as he placed her firmly in his grasp, then sucked in a quick breath when his arms slid around her to meet at the back of her waist.

"Take it back," he growled, his gaze warm as it moved over her face.

"What?" She felt the flush creep up from her throat to cover her cheeks. His hands were wide, spreading from her ribs to her spine, and she felt each fingertip like a branding iron through the layers of fabric she wore.

His teasing was tinged by more than a touch of arrogance. "You called me a cowboy, Rachel. That's not a word we use around here. My men are ranch hands. I'm known as a rancher. I own the place. Half of it anyway. Jake's name is on the deed, right next to mine."

"Let go of me," she gasped, her teasing laughter cut short by the apprehension overwhelming her. Leaning from his hold, she shivered as the formidable masculinity of Cord McPherson surrounded her. Forgotten was the simple joy of teasing the man, swallowed up by the temptation of his embrace.

It would be so simple to allow the powerful appeal of this man to overcome the teachings of her early years. So easily could she lean into his embrace and succumb to the lure of his smiling lips and dark, devouring gaze.

Cord's arms tightened, his teasing demeanor transformed in a heartbeat to that of a needy male creature. She'd asked for her release from his arms and his reluctant good sense echoed the demand. Only the immense pleasure he was gaining from the soft curves he'd managed to capture kept him from complying with her plea.

"In a minute," he growled. She was about as tempting a morsel as he'd ever held. A dimple hid within each rosy cheek; he'd seen them deepen with her smile. Now he yearned to touch their hiding places with the tip of his tongue, to taste the firm texture of her skin. Her lips were barely parted, her breath audibly passing between their soft surfaces.

And suddenly, it was more temptation than he could resist.

He saw her eyes squeeze shut as he leaned to her, heard the sound of her gasp as she caught her breath, felt her hands pushing against his chest in a futile attempt to free herself, and then he caught her mouth with his own. His lips enclosed hers, his tongue yearning to touch and plunder.

Too soon...too soon... His mouth released her and he tilted his head just a bit, returning to the damp surface of her lips, a prize he'd only begun to relish, his mouth gentle as he offered her a more chaste caress.

It was almost too much to hope that this woman could be his. He didn't deserve her innocence, her honesty. He feared the darkness dwelling within him, darkness that would swallow up all the joy she contained, leaving her empty, should he claim her as his own.

Against his chest, her hands curled into fists and in her throat a whimper was born. She sagged against him and he lifted his head, his narrowed gaze seeking hers.

No use. Her eyes were closed and from beneath her

lashes a single tear slipped to roll slowly down each cheek.

"Ahh...damnation, Rachel. Don't cry!" He hugged her. Then, fearful that he might be holding her too tightly, he held her away from him, one big hand cupping her chin as he bent to snatch the salty drops from her face. His lips inhaled the tiny specks of moisture and he savored the flavor.

She sniffed in a less than elegant manner and he grimaced, reaching for the handkerchief he kept in his back pocket. It was brand spanking clean, fresh from his drawer, and he tucked it into her small fist. "Please, Rachel. No more tears. I've never felt guilty for wanting to kiss a woman before."

She blinked, glancing down at the white square of cotton she held, then lifted it to blot her eyes and wipe her nose. "Thank you." It was a prim little response and he forced a smile.

"I'm sorry, Rachel. I took advantage of you, and to top it off I reckon I frightened you."

She shook her head. "No."

"I didn't scare you off?" His smile broadened.

She met his gaze, her blue eyes shiny with the tears she had not shed. "I liked the kiss. I just didn't think it was proper, with me working for you, and all. I can't stay here if you intend to..."

"I won't take you to my bed, Rachel."

Her quick look was skeptical. "I don't know much about men, Cord McPherson, but my mother told me that when a man takes a kiss, he usually plans on... Well, anyway, she said I should be sure that a man has honorable intentions when I let him kiss me."

"Ah...there's the hitch, honey. You didn't let me. I just went ahead and stole the kiss without permission."

His gaze was filled with the wonder of her, the glowing color she wore like the armor of a virgin bride, the trembling of her bottom lip as she attempted to control it with the touch of her teeth against the soft surface. Her hair, escaping the confinement of the simple braid she wore, curled around her face, and her eyes shone with guileless beauty.

If it weren't so soon, if she'd had time to settle in better and know him longer... Even at that, he'd run the risk of hurting the girl.

Shattering his thoughts, a shout of youthful laughter came from the yard as Jay called out a greeting. Cord bent just a little, peering past the curtain to where a horse and buggy had pulled up to the hitching rail. From within, a dark-clad figure dropped to the ground and Jay approached at a run, skidding to a stop as he beamed at the visitor.

"Here's your young man, come to visit from town, Rachel," Cord said, his words stilted and forbidding. "I'll carry your washwater out for you. Hope it doesn't take all afternoon for him to deliver those seeds he promised you."

It took only an hour. An hour during which the washwater cooled in the big washtub, an hour during which Cord McPherson had already made two trips back and forth from the barn to the house, scraping his boots carefully each time on the edge of the porch.

Conrad sat on the porch swing, an appropriate six inches from Rachel's skirt, telling her in great detail how to plant the seeds he'd brought her. She should put in a new planting of the green beans every two weeks, ensuring a steady supply until cold weather. A flat box of tomato plants, for which she was most appreciative, graced the porch, and she had listened attentively as he gave his instructions for their planting.

"I'm sure I can handle getting everything into the ground, Mr. Carson," she said politely, watching as Cord made another foray from the barn.

"If there's ever anything I can do to help you feel welcome in the community, I'd surely be willing to make the effort," Conrad told her earnestly. "In fact, if you would be agreeable, I'd like to come calling one evening next week, Miss Rachel." He held his empty plate carefully, every crumb of pie having disappeared in short order.

She glanced at it with a smile, then, noting the color ridging his cheeks and the appeal in his dark eyes, her heart twinged with compassion. The man was looking to court her, and she didn't have it in her to turn him down, not today anyway, when he'd made such an effort, coming to visit.

He'd had to find someone to keep the store for the afternoon, and surely he'd gone to a lot of trouble to locate the plants and seeds he'd brought.

"I'd enjoy having you come out to visit, Mr. Carson," she answered, taking the plate from his hands, certain she heard Cord in the kitchen as she spoke the words.

Heavy boots stomped across the doorsill. Cord's glare caught her broadside as he made his way down the steps and across the yard for the third time.

Conrad moved uncomfortably in the swing. "Perhaps Mr. McPherson wants you to resume your duties, Rachel. I'm taking up a lot of your time, I fear," he said apologetically.

She breathed a sigh of relief, rising from the swing. "I have laundry to do this afternoon. It's a good thing the wind is up. Perhaps everything will dry by sun-down.''

Conrad said his goodbyes, holding his hat carefully in place with both hands as he nodded his head, thanking Rachel for her company.

''How shall I pay you for the things you brought?'' she asked as she walked him to his buggy.

''I'll bill Mr. McPherson's account.'' He climbed into the vehicle, gathering the reins in his hands.

Rachel smiled. Ever the businessman. And that was not all bad, she thought. She watched him leave, aware that she'd just been the object of a man's desire. Conrad Carson was courting her, and the thought was a daunting one.

What would she do if he should ask her to marry him?

How could she say yes when her mind was so filled with the presence of Cord McPherson?

''You got a beau, Miss Rachel?'' Sam asked, feigning innocence as he brought Jake's empty tray into the kitchen.

Rachel shook her head, casting him a forbidding glance. The supper table was silent, as if someone had demanded the attention of the gathered crew, and Sam grinned, his eyes twinkling as they narrowed in pleasure.

''That young man is a right fine catch for any young woman, ma'am,'' Sam said, nodding his head. ''You might want to consider lookin' him over real good.''

''Miss Rachel just got settled in here,'' Shamus Quinn spoke up. ''She's not goin' gallivantin' off with the storekeeper. There's half a dozen good men right here who can marry her if she's of a mind to get hitched.''

Rachel's face blazed as the table fell silent, each man

looking to another as if they sought verification of Shamus's words.

"I'm not in the market for a husband," she said after a moment. "Mr. Carson is a fine gentleman and a friend. I'll thank you all to respect my privacy."

The plate of cookies she carried thumped onto the surface of the table with a resounding clatter, and eager hands reached to snatch at the resulting cascade of baked goods.

"You can stay here forever, Miss Rachel," Buck declared, three cookies in one hand, another halfway into his mouth as he rose from his chair.

Jamie Callahan followed him, nodding his agreement, his share of dessert safely cupped within his big palm.

"They like you, Miss Rachel," said a soft voice from behind her as the last man left the table, leaving only the two small boys behind.

"Jay and Henry! Take your dessert and go put the chickens up for the night," she said briskly, ignoring the man whose presence was causing her heart to beat at a rapid pace.

"We all like you, Rachel," Cord said, amending his earlier statement.

She circled the table, breathing easier as she left him standing near the stove. Her hands gathered up the silverware, stacked the plates and scraped the scant leftovers into a bowl for the dog's dinner.

"Rachel?" He was unmoving, a tall, unsmiling presence in her kitchen, and she turned to him as she finished clearing the table.

"I don't mind being teased, Cord. I'm getting used to it. You don't have to speak for the men."

He shook his head. "I'm not. I'm speaking for me. I like you, too, Rachel."

Flushed with the heady success of her day, Rachel poured a cup of coffee and pressed it into Cord's hands. "Take this to your brother, Cord. He didn't get cookies on his tray. Take him some."

"Coward." The word was softly spoken, but a dare nonetheless.

"I'm not," she said staunchly.

"Are, too."

With suddenly trembling fingers, she took the cup back from his grasp and held it gingerly, pausing only to gather up four cookies before she turned to the kitchen door.

"Go do your chores, McPherson," she said crisply. "I have a kitchen to clean, and laundry to fold. You're in my way."

Her steps were rapid as she headed down the hall, past the parlor and the formal dining room. Past Cord's office and on to where the library doors were rolled almost shut.

She rapped with one knuckle, careful not to crush the cookies she carried. Then with the tip of her shoe, she eased the door open, rolling it on its hidden wheels, sliding it within the wall.

"Mr. McPherson, I've brought you dessert," she said quietly, her gaze veering neither left nor right. From one side, she saw a movement and then the wheelchair rolled into her path.

"Ah...Cord's lady friend, come to visit."

The cup shifted in her grasp, the coffee sloshing to the very edge before she righted it. Her breath caught in her throat as she lifted her gaze to meet that of the man who watched her.

"I thought you might like coffee." Ignoring the slur

he'd offered, she extended the cup, watching as his long fingers grasped it, claiming it. "I baked cookies."

His mouth twisted and his eyes were dark beneath lowering brows. "Trying to tame the beast, Miss Rachel?"

She shook her head. "No, just being polite."

He reached for the cookies. "A peace offering?"

She considered that thought, a new one to be sure. And then deciding it might be well to use it to her advantage, she nodded. "I invaded your territory the other day. I must apologize. I wasn't aware that the parlor piano was off limits to me."

He ate a cookie in two bites and swallowed it down with a gulp of hot coffee, his eyes intent on her. "It was a week ago, Miss Rachel. And if my memory serves me, you already apologized, very nicely."

A second cookie followed the first, and then Jake rested the cup on the arm of his chair, watching her in silence.

She cleared her throat. "Was the first one accepted? I can't recall, to be honest." Her voice barely wobbled. He hadn't thrown the cup at her. Hadn't even raised his voice, in fact. But the words he spoke were cutting and curt.

"You can dust the finish off the parlor piano, as you call it, Miss Rachel. Just don't lift the lid. I don't want to hear your feeble attempts at making music."

The chair spun away from her and she was given the back of his head, long hair spreading in a mantle across his shoulders. Clean and combed today.

"Get out, *Miss Rachel.*" He spoke her name in a parody of politeness, emphasizing the syllables as if he mocked the title given her by Sam Bostwick.

She backed to the doorway, her footsteps silent on the

carpet. The dusty carpet, she noted, her quick eye taking in the streaked windowpanes and the cluttered dresser.

Nudging the rolling door closed, she fought the lump that had somehow lodged in her throat. What a waste. What a pity that a man of his obvious talent and intelligence should spend his life within four such dingy walls. The shelves of books had looked to be untouched, and yet he must do something with the long hours.

Rachel entered the empty kitchen, unaware of Cord, watching from the half-open parlor door. Her movements were slow, her mouth working as if she pondered much, and she neither sang nor hummed as she washed up the supper dishes.

Silent steps took Cord to his office, and he listened in vain for the soft sounds he'd grown accustomed to during these moments after the evening meal.

She was all right. He'd seen to that, listening carefully, lest Jake should attack her with harsh words and accusations. She'd dodged his opening sally very nicely, actually ignoring the insulting phrase.

"'Cord's lady friend,'" he repeated softly. Not an insult actually, only Jake's tone had made it so.

"I want more from you than friendship, Rachel," Cord muttered to himself, sorting out the receipts he must enter in his ledger.

And still he listened for some sound from the kitchen, some sign that the woman he wanted was there, beneath his roof.

Chapter Six

"Hello in there. I'm Lorena Claypool." Tall, golden-haired and garbed in a gingham dress, the woman stood on the porch, just outside the screened door.

Rachel hurried to open it wide, waving her visitor into the kitchen. "It's awfully warm in here, I'm afraid," she said apologetically. "I'm baking this morning."

She reached for coffee cups in the cupboard as she spoke. "Won't you sit down?"

Lorena pulled out a chair, her smile transforming her face from a quite ordinary set of features to a classic vision of beauty. "I take it I'm welcome?"

Rachel nodded vehemently. "As the flowers in May!" Placing the cups on the table, she filled them from the blue-speckled coffeepot. "Do you want cream or sugar?"

"Just a little cream," Lorena answered. She made a quick survey of the kitchen, nodding her approval. "You've made your mark, Miss Sinclair. The last time I was here, this place was a shambles."

"Oh, call me Rachel, please!" Carrying a plate of fresh cinnamon rolls with her, Rachel came back to the table and sat down across from her visitor. "I'm so glad to see you. Did Cord send for you?"

Lorena shook her head. "No, Sam Bostwick came by to see my father and told us about you. I've been wanting to stop by for the better part of a week, but I thought I'd let you get settled in first." She glanced at the kitchen doorway, down the long hall that extended the length of the house.

"He's fine," Rachel said quietly, discerning the direction of the other woman's thoughts.

Lorena flushed, lifting one hand to press against the warmth of her cheek. "I didn't come here to cause a fuss. It would be better if he didn't know...."

"You don't want to see him?"

Lorena dropped her gaze, nodding her reply. "You'd think I'd have gotten over him by now, wouldn't you?" Her laugh was forced, a mockery of her emotions. "I thought I could come here and visit with you and not let it bother me."

Rachel reached across the table to clasp the other woman's fingers within her own. "I don't think you ever forget your first love."

Lorena looked up. "Have you?"

Rachel's laughter was a peal of denial. "I've never loved a man, except my father, and I'm sure that's not what we're talking about here."

"No, fathers are a different thing altogether," Lorena agreed, her smile coming readily. "Now, tell me where Cord ever found you. How did he talk you into coming here to work?"

An hour flew by, Rachel rescuing her bread from the oven in the nick of time, her heart light as she talked of her childhood and life in the East, her sadness finding release in tears as she told of the death of her parents. And she listened.

Rena—she'd asked Rachel to shorten her name soon after arrival—was hesitant at first. Then, as she drank her second cup of coffee, she spoke haltingly of her romance with Jake McPherson. In whispered words, she mentioned their courtship, her desire to be married before he joined up, and her utter devastation at the news of his injuries.

"I was so sure that he still loved me, that we could somehow make a life together."

"Cord said Jake wouldn't see you."

Rena shook her head. "He shouted at me through the door. He told me he wouldn't have me feeling sorry for him because he was a cripple."

"He's still shouting," Rachel said dryly.

"At you?"

Rachel nodded, then quickly changed her mind. "Well, not really. I took him coffee and cookies after dinner a couple of days ago and he was almost civil. But then, yesterday I suggested I might clean his room and he chased me out."

"He did?" Rena's eyes widened as if she found it hard to believe such a thing.

"He wheels that chair around lickety-split," Rachel said. "I gave up that idea for a while. I thought I'd try again in a week or so."

Rena emptied her coffee cup and pushed away from the table. "I suspect I'd better leave. Mother will be waiting for the groceries I brought from town."

She cast a speculative glance at Rachel as she pushed her chair into place. "I talked to Conrad Carson. About you."

Rachel felt the flush creep up from her neck to cover her face. "Did you? What did he have to say?"

"He's sweet on you, Rachel. But I suspect you knew that already. Has he come courting yet?"

Rachel nodded, then shook her head. "No, not really. He brought out some tomato plants and onion sets and seeds for the garden. We spent an hour discussing planting them. I'm not sure you can call that courting."

Rena grinned. "Give the man time. He seems quite smitten. In fact, he mentioned the dance at the grange hall next week. I'll bet you any money he's planning on asking you to go with him."

"I can't," Rachel said quickly. "I've got my brothers to watch and a job here to tend to. I can't be gallivanting off to dances."

"I'll just bet you could find someone to look after them if you really wanted to go. Maybe Cord would even take you, if Conrad doesn't ask first."

"No, I don't think so," Rachel answered. Her head tilted as if she heard music from afar. "I'd love to attend, though. I haven't danced in a long time."

"Did you do square dancing back East?"

Rachel shook her head. "Some, but mostly we waltzed or danced the Virginia reel. I even learned to polka."

"They do some pair dancing, but everyone likes to square dance hereabouts. You ought to go, even if you don't get invited by Conrad. We could pick you up on our way to town, if you like." Lorena's face was bright with anticipation as she awaited Rachel's reply.

And in that moment Jake McPherson's angry shout sounded from the long hallway. "Rachel! Who's out there with you?"

Lorena stepped hurriedly toward the back door. "I'd better leave."

Rachel's mind went back to an evening several days ago and one word slipped from her lips.

"Coward."

"You bet!" Lorena whispered, eyeing the kitchen doorway to the hall as she backed away. Pale as alabaster, she was visibly trembling, and Rachel's heart was stung with the depth of emotion apparent on the young woman's face.

"Wait for me," she whispered. "I'll be right back."

Her feet flew as she went down the hallway, heading for Jake's room. He was in the doorway, frowning and peering the length of the hall, his querulous words aimed in Rachel's direction.

"Who's out there with you? I heard a woman's voice."

Rachel pulled up short, her heart beating double time as she felt indignation rise within her. The man was beyond rudeness.

"Were you wanting company, Mr. McPherson?" she asked with cutting sarcasm as her gaze swept over his wrinkled clothing and unshaved face. "I'm not sure you're fit for a lady to come visiting. Maybe if you made acquaintance with your razor and put on a decent shirt, we could find you someone willing to…"

His anger overflowed. "Just you shut your mouth, Miss Rachel. Women are only good for one thing, and when I want a damn female to come visiting, I'll do the inviting. You and your kind are not welcome in my room."

Rachel's face flamed with color and she leaned against the wall, afraid her trembling knees would fail her.

Never had a man spoken such words to her. The insinuation was more than insulting.

From the kitchen came a shriek of outrage, and through the kitchen doorway a whirlwind of feminine indignation raced full tilt toward the man in the invalid's chair.

"You ungrateful, miserable cur! How dare you speak to a lady in such a manner! I'm ashamed I ever knew you, Jake McPherson!"

Lorena Claypool pulled up short as her knees collided with the metal wheel of the chair and she lost her balance. Muscular arms rose in an automatic gesture and she was enclosed in the unwilling embrace of Jake McPherson.

"What the hell are you doing here?" he shouted. He shook her, his big hands clutching at her, one against her hip, the other gripping her shoulder. His face was a terrible mask of anguish, lips drawn back, nostrils flaring, eyes glaring with an emotion Rachel could not put a name to.

And then as suddenly as his roar had filled the house with its violent outburst, quiet descended, enshrouding them in a cocoon of unearthly silence.

Rachel slid to the floor, crumpled against the wall. What had her smart mouth accomplished this time? she wondered bleakly. How had she managed to allow such a fiasco to take place?

For no matter how she sliced it, the fault for this episode was hers, and hers alone, to bear.

The back screen door slammed and heavy footsteps pounded across the kitchen. Cord stood at the end of the wide hallway, leaning with one hand on the kitchen doorjamb. His index finger pushed on the brim of his hat and he shoved it high on his forehead.

His gaze rested on Rachel, then swooped to the unmoving pair occupying the rolling chair in the doorway of the library. "You all right, Rachel?" he asked quietly.

She nodded, lifting herself to her feet, brushing at her skirt with trembling hands. "I'm sorry, Cord. This is my fault. I yelled at Jake and made him angry, and then Rena heard the fuss...."

"So did I and half the men on the place." Leaving the kitchen door, Cord moved quickly down the hall, his hand reaching for Rachel, tugging her to stand next to him.

"Let me loose," Lorena whispered tightly, stiffening in the embrace Jake had not deigned to relax.

"I didn't invite you to start with," the big man growled, his hands tightening for just a moment, then freeing the woman who sprawled inelegantly across his lap. His eyes swept over her slender form as she stood next to the chair, and as Rachel watched, a darkness descended over his features.

"Leave me be." The chair rolled backward into the room and he disappeared from view, one push of his hand rolling the door into place.

"Jake!" Cord rapped sharply on the oak panel, only to be met with silence. "Jake, I want to talk to you!"

"Not now, Cord," Rachel said quietly.

He glanced down at her, searching her face. "He needs to apologize to you."

She shook her head. "I antagonized him. I was impatient and I—"

"Nothing you could have said to him gave him leave to shout insults in your face."

Lorena stepped carefully toward the pair. "I'm the one at fault. I never should have come here. I'm so sorry, Rachel. I wanted to meet you." Her hands spread wide in a gesture of helplessness. Tears filmed her eyes and she brushed at them distractedly. ''I'll go now. I'm sorry, Cord. I never meant to cause this kind of a fuss.''

Cord took off his hat, brushing it against his thigh. ''You don't owe anybody an apology, Rena. Maybe this whole mess will work out for the best, yet.''

He turned Rachel toward the kitchen and waved Lorena to follow her, turning back to the library doors with a last pondering look before he traced their footsteps.

''Rae, Mr. Sam said I could ride one of the horses today if it was all right with you.'' Henry was poised in the kitchen doorway, anticipation alive in his every movement. ''Please, Rae! I'll be so careful, you won't even know it's me on that horse!''

''What about Jay?'' she asked, peering over his shoulder in an attempt to locate her younger brother.

''He's out in the barn with Mr. Sam, helpin' to saddle the horses we're gonna ride.'' Henry shifted from one foot to the other, his excitement barely contained as his sister hesitated over her decision.

''They'll be fine, Rachel.'' Behind her Cord's reassuring words were a low rumble in her ear.

She shivered, an automatic reaction as the warmth from his body radiated to the long line of her spine. He'd come up behind her unaware and she closed her eyes for a moment, containing the response his presence engendered.

''Please, Rae?'' Henry uttered the coaxing words in a whisper, standing on tiptoe as if he readied himself for her word of approval.

''Yes, all right,'' she said, her thoughts on the man behind her. ''Cord says it will be fine.''

The boy turned and raced for the barn, and Rachel called after him. "Look out for Jay!"

Cord laughed, an indulgent sound. "They'll be all right, Rachel. Sam is going to take Jay up in front of him for this ride. He's looking for a small horse for the boy. Says we don't have an animal quite the thing for Jay yet."

"You're going to buy a horse, just for my brother?" she asked. Turning to him, her gaze swept his face. His mouth was slanted in a half smile, his eyes narrowed, gleaming beneath heavy lids.

It was a look of intent. Innocence did not preclude awareness, and as if she scented the desire he made no attempt to hide, her nostrils flared and she inhaled sharply.

His chuckle was subdued, his gaze focusing on her mouth. "If my buying your little brother a horse that suits him manages to put that look on your face, I'll tell Sam to bring home a whole herd and stick them in the corral, Miss Rachel."

She blinked, shivering again as his arms circled her waist, drawing her into the circle of his embrace. Her breath caught in her throat and she swallowed against the obstruction, then took another shuddering breath as he tugged her more firmly against his body.

Firm and ungiving, his chest did little to cushion her breasts, and she whimpered as he brushed against the fullness. She felt swollen and sensitive, and was, for the first time in her life, truly aware of the dimensions of her bosom.

She'd accepted that she was well endowed. Mama had always allowed extra material across the bodice when she sewed her spring and fall wardrobes, back in Pennsylvania.

Now, she was aware, again for the first time, of the sensations those feminine parts were capable of. The movement of his chest across hers was producing a most exciting sensation within her.

Deep inside, in a part of her body she had seldom considered food for thought, a warm, churning commotion came to life. She wiggled her hips, attempting to ease the tension, and in the doing managed only to butt against his groin.

"Judas Priest, Rachel!" The words were muttered with vehemence, resembling an oath to her ears, and she stiffened in his embrace. He shifted against her and his body jolted in response.

"Let me go!" As demands went, it was not as vehement as she'd have liked. Her words were slurred, her eyes half-closed as she attempted to withdraw from his embrace.

She might as well have remained silent. Had her mouth been closed, his might have merely brushed against her lips. As it was, he took the opening she gave him, his tongue sweeping the edge of her bottom lip with assurance, easing its way past her teeth to brush against the roof of her mouth.

He claimed her, his lips and tongue eager as he kissed her with a passion she had never been aware of in her sheltered life.

She flinched from him, at once horrified at the liberty he took and startled at the pure pleasure its sensation produced. Her moan of protest was swallowed up by the groan he uttered, his arousal finally finding ease against the softness of her belly.

Rachel jerked away, her lips swollen and damp, her eyes filling with tears of fright. "Cord, let me go!" The words were whispered, accompanied by a sob he could not mistake for anything else than the distress of the young woman he held.

His grip softened, and he bowed his head, his forehead resting against hers. "Ah, hell, Rachel. I'm sorry."

And he was, as sorry as any man had ever been, he decided. He'd not only scared her half to death with his openmouthed assault, he'd managed to push his manhood against her like a rutting stallion with mating uppermost in his mind. And all of that in broad daylight in the middle of his kitchen.

"Please, Rachel." His murmur whispered against her ear as he bent to bestow a multitude of gentle kisses against her cheek and throat. "I'm sorry. I didn't mean to scare you like that. Look at me, Rachel, please." He lifted his head and with one finger tilted her chin, gently forcing her to turn her gaze upward.

Her eyes shiny with a glaze of teardrops, her face a rosy mask of confusion and embarrassment, she drew in a deep breath. "I never...no one ever..."

Her words ran together as she whispered her innocence.

If ever Cord McPherson had felt shame, it was now. That he could have so forced himself on the girl was unforgivable, and yet, he must have her pardon for the act. Otherwise, they could not continue on in this relationship of ranch owner and...and what? Cook? Housekeeper? The question seemed to be in what capacity he was willing to place Rachel Sinclair.

Right now the only place he could think of that would suit his state of desire was his bedroom. And that would involve a ring and a wedding, two things he had been more than adept at evading for several years.

Perhaps the time for evasion was at an end. She was what he wanted in a woman; he'd decided the first time he spotted her, living in that shack on the north end of his ranch. Even then, in a petticoat that barely contained her lush charms, he'd recognized a purity, an innocence he could not deny.

Whether or not he deserved the happiness she might bring him, he felt the yearning of his soul for her presence in his life.

So be it. Rachel would be his.

"Rachel?" His voice was gruff, harsh in his own ears, and yet she opened her eyes to meet his gaze without hesitation.

"Forgive me. I didn't mean to frighten you. It won't happen again." Not until he had her in his bed, at any rate, his honest heart reminded him.

She nodded hesitantly, her blush fading as his words assured her. "I must seem awfully young and foolish, Cord," she said hesitantly. Her eyes met his with an honesty in their depths he could not doubt. "No one has ever kissed me before, except for a man on the wagon train." Her nose wrinkled in a gesture of disgust that brought a smothered chuckle from his throat.

"Why did you let him kiss you, Rachel?" Although he certainly didn't blame the hapless fellow for trying.

"I didn't!" she said indignantly. "He just grabbed at me and slobbered all over me. He had a passel of children, his wife was dead, and he wanted me to marry him."

"And you turned him down?" Cord asked with amusement.

Her head nodded firmly. "You bet I did. I don't blame her for leaving him in the only way she could. I'll bet he'd have given her a baby a year from now till forever."

"She died in childbirth?" His face was sober now at

the thought of such suffering during the harsh rigors of a wagon trip across the country.

Rachel nodded. "I wasn't about to take on the job, and I couldn't have stood him kissing on me. I just said I wasn't interested, thank you."

Her prim recital of the facts made him smile, her mouth pursing as she considered the kiss she had received at the hands of her would-be suitor.

"And I kissed you that way and reminded you of him?"

"Oh, no! It was nothing like that. It just made me...I just felt so strange...inside where..." She stopped, obviously helpless to describe the beginning stages of desire, and Cord nodded, accepting her words.

"Desire is not determined by our minds, Rachel. Our bodies are strange things. We can feel a need for another person without rhyme or reason. The way I kissed you is the way a man and woman who are going to make love might express their feelings."

"We're not going to make love," she blurted. "I'm your cook, Cord!"

"For now." He eased the firmness of his hold on her, moving her to arm's length as he shifted his stance. Distance would ease the discomfort he felt, a bucket of cold water over his head might even ready him for a day of hard riding. Right now, mounting his horse would guarantee him a pain he wasn't about to look for.

She cocked her head and he drank in the beauty she seemed so unaware of. Her hair had loosened from the simple plait she formed every morning, falling in loose tendrils about her face. Her eyelids were damp, lashes stuck together in a frame that enhanced the dark blue of her eyes. The dimples were almost in evidence as she offered a half smile, and he watched for them as he might have sought the rising sun in the morning.

He was sure enough smitten, he decided, his sigh a recognition of the fact. "I've got work to do, Rachel," he told her, setting her farther from him. "Sam will keep a good eye on your brothers. Don't worry about them. Just fix me a good dinner, will you?"

Unable to resist, he leaned forward to snatch a quick kiss from the pink softness of her mouth, his lips closed and firm against hers.

She looked a bit bewildered, he thought as he strode from the house. And well she might be. He'd made a complete ass of himself.

"I'm going to speak to Lorena and see if she'll come to work for us," Cord announced. Rachel was drying the last of the supper dishes and she turned to him, towel in hand.

"What about Jake? Will he pitch a fit, do you think?"

Cord shrugged. "What can he do?"

"Make her life miserable. She loves him, Cord! What do you think it will do to her to have him shout and carry on the way he did yesterday?"

"The way he carried on yesterday told me he still cares about the woman, Rachel. He's my brother and I love him. If having Rena here brings him back to life, I'm all for it."

"She'll be hurt!" Rachel twisted the towel between her hands, her eyes dark with concern for the young woman.

"Better her to bear some wounds than for Jake to live and die in that room." Cord's words were fierce, whispered in a savage tone that sealed the decision. "I'm going over there tomorrow to talk to her. She'll know what she's getting into, and I'm willing to lay money that she'll come.''

"All right,'' Rachel conceded, aware she had lost this battle before it began. "I can use the help, that's for sure.'' Her smile broke through as she considered the idea. "It will be good to have another woman here. I think I'll let her clean the library, first thing.''

Chapter Seven

The burn pile was located far from the barn, an equal distance from the house. Sam watched it with an eagle eye. With the sun shining brightly for the third week in a row, and no rain in sight, the chance of fire spreading was great.

The household trash from a week or so was there, along with an assortment of papers and old periodicals dragged from the library yesterday.

Rachel smiled to herself as she recalled the vision of Lorena tugging three boxes of assorted rubbish from Jake's hideaway. He'd stayed stubbornly by the window, after the first set-to. His gaze had focused on some faraway spot, only occasionally turning to watch the determined woman who had set herself to cleaning up the room he lived in.

From the doorway, Rachel had peeked in, more than once, willing the man to unbend, yet realizing it was far too soon to expect him to change the habits of years.

"Good morning, Rachel." Lorena entered the kitchen, rolling up the sleeves of her dress to the elbow, her hair pulled back in a neat snood at the nape of her neck.

Rachel cast a brilliant smile in the young woman's

direction. It was like a gift from heaven, having her here. After just one day, she'd proved herself to be efficient and industrious, both qualities Rachel could only admire.

That her own work would be lessened by Lorena's arrival was a fact. That her company would be a joy and a delight was a bonus she was prepared to take advantage of.

"After breakfast, we need to shuck peas, and then we have to work in the garden," Rachel told her, pulling cinnamon rolls from the oven. She'd set them to rise for the second time last evening and put them in the hot oven first thing upon awakening this morning. The men would be pleased, and pleasing the menfolk in her life seemed to be the focus of her days, she reflected.

Lorena's hands were full, distributing plates the length of the table. "I can pull weeds while you shuck peas on the porch," she offered, as if willing to do the more menial task.

Rachel laughed as she cracked eggs into a crockery bowl. "Not a chance! I've been wanting someone to talk to for weeks, and I'll be jiggered if we're going to separate to do chores. We'll do them together."

Lorena's smile lost its sparkle for a moment, and her voice lowered. "I want to talk to you, anyway. About Jake."

"Wait until we're outdoors," Rachel cautioned in a whisper. "He was in the hallway yesterday while you were cleaning the parlor. He manages to get around without even a whisper of noise, and neither of us wants him listening while we discuss him." Her eyes glanced at the kitchen door several times as she spoke and then she placed a finger against her lips.

Lorena nodded her understanding, her hands busy sorting out the silverware for breakfast.

In a few minutes the men began finding their seats at the table and Rachel spooned out scrambled eggs onto their plates. Lorena pulled a steaming platter of sausages from the oven, and in moments the kitchen was filled with laughter and the sounds of men preparing for a day's work.

"He wouldn't let me in the library this morning," Lorena said quietly as she ran her thumb down the length of a pea pod. It split open and seven round specimens rolled into the bowl she held in her lap. The pod was discarded in a pail by her side and another pea pod picked up and disposed of in the same manner.

"You're showing me up," Rachel said, her own movements slower.

"I've been doing this all my life," Lorena answered. "My grandma taught me how to shell peas the summer I was five. We used to sit on the porch by the hour, her telling me stories and me just following her lead."

"We had a cook back home," Rachel confided. "I only learned to put a meal together after we started on the wagon train. Mama was sort of sickly and I did the cooking for our family every day."

Lorena popped a pea into her mouth. "These are nice and tender, Rachel. Did Conrad sell them to you?"

Rachel nodded. "He sent a mess of green beans home with me, too. He said they were the first ones to come in. I washed them up and put them on to cook before breakfast."

"What else did he say to you? Did he ask you to the dance tomorrow night?"

"He asked, and I said no."

"For pity's sake! Why don't you go with him? He's

a fine catch, girl. He has his own business and he's an usher at church.''

Rachel shook her head. ''I don't know why. I just felt like it would be leading him on to accept and have him come all the way out here to pick me up.''

Lorena grinned. ''I'll bet he wouldn't have cared. Chances are he was looking forward to the long ride back out here afterward.''

''If she goes to the dance, she'll go with me,'' Cord said from the other side of the screen door.

''Land sake! How did you get in the house?'' Rachel asked, twisting in her chair to look at the tall rancher.

''Came in the front door,'' he said. ''My horse is out front waiting on me. I needed an extra kerchief to tie over my mouth.''

''My pa is ready to start cuttin' on the young bulls next week, so he can get them out in the far pasture for the summer,'' Rena said.

Cord cast a look at Rachel, hesitating a moment. ''We're gettin' to that, Rena. We're done with the branding.''

''You going to the dance, Cord?'' the woman asked with a sly look at Rachel.

Cord slid his hands into his pockets, rocking on his heels as he considered the two young women on his back porch. ''Might,'' he allowed. ''It all depends.''

Rachel's face flamed as the conversation flowed past her. With a sigh, she poured the peas she'd shucked into the bowl Lorena held and rose from her chair.

''I'll be in the garden,'' she said brightly. ''Those weeds will be getting away from me, and all the effort Conrad put into bringing those tomato plants out here will have been in vain.''

She ran lightly down the porch stairs and moved

quickly toward the garden patch, a small fenced area between the house and the chicken coop.

"Why don't you ask her, Cord?" Lorena asked, giving him an impatient look.

"I don't do much dancin'," he muttered.

"Don't let her get away. You'll be sorry if you do."

"I don't need to take her dancin' to court her." His voice held a trace of stubborn pride.

"It wouldn't hurt any."

"You think she's takin' Conrad seriously?" Cord's gaze was fastened on Rachel, down on her knees in the garden.

Lorena smiled, her face bent to the pan of peas in her lap. "I'm sure there are a dozen women hereabouts who'd give their eyeteeth for a chance at Conrad Carson. Why should Rachel be any different?"

Subduing her amusement, she lifted her head to meet Cord's gaze. "He's a real catch, Cord. If he asks her to marry him, she'll be a lucky girl."

His snort was immediate and expressive. "Lucky? To be tied to a stiff-collared, pale-faced storekeeper? Rachel needs a man in her life, not a grocery clerk."

"You got anybody in mind?" The query was softly spoken, her glance sidelong.

"Damn right, and you know it, Rena Claypool!"

"Then do something about it. I've got to finish up in the library." Picking up the pan of shucked peas, she rose, facing the man in the kitchen doorway.

His palm slapped the wooden frame and the door was flung open, banging against the house siding. He stepped across the sill and in three long strides had cleared the porch and steps. Hat at a jaunty angle, he slowed his pace, heading for the garden patch.

Rachel's slender form was bent low, her arms stretching as she reached for the weeds before her. Piling a handful in the basket she'd designated for the purpose, she rose, gathering her skirts as she moved forward another three feet or so. Her ankles and lower calves were nicely outlined against the fragile green of the waving carrot tops, and Cord's eyes were drawn to the sight. She'd obviously scorned wearing stockings, working as she did in the garden, and had kicked off her shoes at the edge of the row. Her toes were pink against the dark soil and she curled them into the dirt, as if she relished the coolness hidden there.

He halted, his breathing a conscious effort as he watched the young woman kneel. Like a penitent, she gazed up at the sky, narrowing her eyes to shield them from the sunlight, and a faint smile touched her lips as a robin flew overhead, landing just a few feet away from her.

My God, he thought in a reverent manner that had almost escaped him over the past years. What if he hadn't found her? What if he'd missed out on having Rachel Sinclair in his life?

She glanced to where he stood and her eyes widened as she met his gaze. "What do you want, Cord?"

He swallowed the words that would have stunned her with their boldness. "Thought maybe you'd consider..."

From the field beyond the apple trees a shout of distress ended his question. His body was poised for action as he turned on his heel to face the danger inherent in such a call. Jay and Henry danced about in a frenzy, and Sam was leaning forward, his shirtsleeves ablaze.

Henry halted suddenly and snatched up the pail of water Sam had carried to the burn pile. Stumbling, water splashing from the pail as he moved, he poured its contents over Sam's hands and arms.

"Rachel...Mr. Cord...come quick!" the boy called, his thin reedy voice rising above the frantic cries of Jay, who had succumbed to tears.

Cord was already on his way, halfway to the tableau before him, and Rachel stumbled to her feet, following quickly. Sam was white-faced, his hands beet-red from the heat of the blaze. His shirtsleeves were blackened and wet, hanging from his forearms.

Thankfully, the water had done the trick, and Cord blessed the quick thinking of Henry Sinclair. Sam's arms were reddened, but the skin had not turned black. Blisters were rising above his wrists and his mouth poured forth a steady stream of cuss words.

"Help me get him to the horse trough, Rachel," Cord ordered, his shoulder easing beneath the old man's armpit.

"Yes, of course." Breathless and frantic, she followed Cord's lead, and between them, they hustled Sam to the pump.

He knelt against the trough and Cord shouted instructions to the boys, who were only steps behind. "Pump fresh water, Henry. Jay, go in the house and get towels, a couple of 'em."

"Yessir!" Jay's feet flew as he obeyed Cord's instructions, his fingers scrubbing at his eyes, dirt marking his efforts to halt the tears.

Henry gave his full strength to the pitcher pump and water cascaded from its mouth to pour in a cold gush over Sam's hands and arms. Cord stood behind him, his muscular thighs gripping the old man's shoulders, submerging him upright on his knees. His long fingers gripped Sam's elbows, holding his hands just under the surface of the water.

"Damnation! You'd think I was a greenhorn," the old

man muttered between grunts of pain. "Gettin' in too close to the fire like that."

"The wind caught up a piece of paper and it snagged on his shirt," Henry said, panting with his efforts. "It flared up before we could do anything. Mr. Sam was brushing at it and it caught the other sleeve on fire, too."

Cord nodded. "You saved the day, Henry. You used your head."

"I'm so proud of you," Rachel said, her own tears flowing in a steady stream.

"Told you the boy was a winner, didn't I?" Sam grumbled, swaying as he spoke. His face had paled, his eyes feverish with pain as he viewed the blistered skin on his arms.

"You're headin' for the spare room, Sam," Cord told him, his tone offering no room for argument.

"Hell, the bunkhouse is good enough. I'll be up and around tomorrow. Just need a little salve and an old sheet torn up to cover the blisters."

Rachel drew in a quick breath, but Cord beat her to the draw. "You'll come to the house and let Rachel tend those burns, Sam. I don't need to have you out for weeks with infection."

"Do what the boss says or hit the road? Is that the way it goes?" the grizzled cowhand asked, his words slurring as he stumbled to his feet.

"You can take it any way you like, Sam Bostwick. I'm runnin' the show around here. I'm telling you this is the way it's gonna be." Cord stated the facts, his voice gruff but his hands gentle as he guided Sam to the house.

Rachel wrung out the wet towels, draping them over Sam's hands and arms as he passed her. "They'll keep down the burning," she said, her touch careful as she tended him.

"Thank you, ma'am." Courteous to the core, Sam bobbed his head, then stumbled. Cord's arm tightened around him and he half lifted him up the steps.

"I ain't dead yet, McPherson. Leave me be." Wrenching himself from Cord's grasp, Sam made it to the door, then inside the kitchen, where Rachel pulled out a chair for him to sit on.

"You'd better keep an eye on that fire, Cord," she said, kneeling to better assess the damage to Sam's skin. "I'll take care of this."

"We'll help, Rae," Jay piped in.

"I'll get Sam a drink of water," Henry said, fetching a cup from the pantry shelf.

Cord, satisfied that Rachel was in control, went out the door, pausing on the porch to look in his kitchen. No, he amended silently, Rachel's kitchen. And as quick as he could make it happen, he'd have her there permanently, right where she belonged.

"Who's making all the fuss out there?" Pulling the curtain aside, Jake peered toward the back of the house, his expression fierce, recognizing his inability to see past the corner of the side yard.

He rolled his chair through the center of the room, scarcely glancing at the woman who had just set about dismantling the kerosene lamps that provided light for the library.

Gently, she placed the slender glass chimney on the table and rose. "Everything was quiet out there a few minutes ago. I'll go see what's happening, Jake."

His chair moving swiftly put him through the doorway and she followed him down the hall toward the kitchen. He came to a halt there, his gaze drawn to the side of his chair. Lorena Claypool stood inches from his shoulder, and his gaze was filled with the comely vision.

Her bosom was on a level with his eyes and he felt a stirring in his depths as he allowed himself a stolen glance. Her hair, scooped back into a soft swirl at the nape of her neck, was golden in the light from the kitchen window, and waving tendrils had fallen to rest against her temple.

Damn, the woman was more than he could cope with! She'd plowed her way into his life again, ignoring his protests, paying no mind to his settled way of doing things.

"Cord and Rachel are bringing Sam in from the burn pile," Lorena said, her words rushed. "Oh, Jake! I think he's been hurt bad!" She lifted her hands to cover her mouth as she peered past him.

He wheeled back from the doorway, affording her space to enter the kitchen. "Go find out what's happened."

Jay raced onto the porch and threw the screen door open. "Miss Rena, we need a couple of towels!" Halting before Jake's chair, he watched as Lorena hurried to the linen closet, off the dining room.

Wide-eyed, the boy investigated the rolling chair, taking in the rubber-treaded wheels at each side, and the small one in back, barely looking at the man who rode on the caned seat.

Lorena hurried back, pressing two towels into the child's grasp. "I'll find bandages and the medical supplies," she murmured, backing from the sight of the figures huddled around the water trough.

"Top shelf of the linen cabinet," Jake said gruffly, maneuvering his chair to watch as the young woman raced through the dining room doorway. She left his range of sight as she turned sharply to the right, where a passageway led past the household linens and dishes.

He could envision her there, where he'd hidden during childish games of hide-and-seek, amid the shelves and in the corner where long-handled dusting tools, carpet beaters and brooms were stored. Almost, he could hear Cord's voice calling him, the younger boy's fear keeping him from the dark nooks and crannies of the long closet.

His memory went to another time, when the slender form of Lorena Claypool had been held in his embrace, his arms an eager cradle for her lissome charms. With painful clarity he recalled the soft, curving length of her pressed against him.

"No more, Jake old boy," he muttered, his frown dark as he pushed the memory to the back of his mind. Having her here had brought to life a multitude of pictures, flashing through his head with the rapidity of a repeating rifle.

"I ain't dead yet, McPherson!" From the kitchen, where Sam was being helped to a chair, the old man's querulous voice reached Jake as he sat within the shadows of the hallway. He watched as Cord left with reluctant steps, noted the care taken as the older of Rachel's brothers brought a cup of water to Sam. And then Lorena was there, at his side, a box of medical supplies in her hands.

Too bad nothing in that fully equipped kit would make a dent in the cage he lived in, he thought, his bitterness coming to the forefront as he rolled his chair with swift precision back to the library.

The door slid closed behind him and he faced the room that was his prison.

Watching the sunset took Rachel's mind from the blistered skin on Sam's arms, and she drank in the sight with hungry eyes. The horizon stretched beyond the fields and meadows, broken by a line of trees where a stream played within shallow banks.

She'd walked there early one morning, while the biscuits baked. It was a brisk ten-minute walk, the last few hundred feet of her return done at a quicker pace, lest the oven be too quick, burning the big biscuits.

It was becoming home, she thought, this whole place, from the big ranch house to the far reaches of Cord's property. Cattle were abundant in all directions, except for the western fields, land he had decided needed to lie fallow for a year. There, a meadow of wildflowers greeted her gaze, daisies and clover thick against the grass.

"Looks like you won't have to water your garden tomorrow." Cord's voice broke her reverie as he sat on the step above her.

She scanned the sky. "Think it's going to rain?"

"Yep, sure looks like it to me. Can't you smell it in the air?" He leaned back, his elbows on the porch, and she glanced over her shoulder, meeting his gaze head-on.

"Nope. Smells like sweet meadow grass to me." She frowned at his grin. "What are you looking at?"

"You."

She wiggled uncomfortably on the step. "What about me? Do I look different from the back?" Her voice took on a sharp edge, and he laughed in a teasing fashion.

"I guess I never paid much mind before to the way your hair looks when you let it down. I always see it braided up in that long tail you wear every day."

She reached to brush back loose strands from her face,

her cheeks warmed by his regard. "I washed it after supper and I've been brushing it dry."

His voice lowered and he lifted one hand to tangle his fingers in the flyaway waves. "I'd like to see it…kind of spread all over your pillow, dark against the pillowcase."

She jerked from his hold and he grasped her shoulders, holding her in place. "I want you, Rachel." His breath was warm against the back of her head as he spoke, and she shivered. "Don't pull away from me."

His fingers lifted the weight of her hair and he allowed it to sift from his hands, murmuring words she could not decipher as he held her prisoner with the force of his will.

She was captivated, not by the masculine strength he was capable of, but by the lure of his gentle hands and caressing words.

Her eyes closed and she responded to the soft tugs he exerted as he turned her to face him. "Look at me, Rachel."

She hesitated, knowing that obeying his command would place her in his power, that Cord McPherson had the ability to blind her to her surroundings.

His arms had held her, his mouth had possessed hers, his fingers had claimed the curves of her hips and the straight line of her spine. If she allowed it, he could break down the inhibitions her mother had set firmly in place through the years.

If she let him, he could talk her into most anything.

She wasn't ready for that. She had choices to make; even though her body leaned in the direction of Cord McPherson, she had two brothers to consider. She owed it to them to consider the suit Conrad Carson was more than likely to offer.

She owed it to the memory of her father to think about the future, to remember her vow. Come next spring...she'd made the promise. Would it be so simple now to forget the dream of moving west, of finding paradise over the horizon?

"Rachel?"

Never had her name been tinged with that tone of dark urgency.

"Rachel?" Again he spoke the syllables that called to her, like the first robin of spring or the cry of a hawk circling overhead. Setting free within her a yearning she could not describe, and asking from her a gift she was not yet willing to offer.

"What do you want from me, Cord?" It was a whispered plea, attended by an involuntary shiver as his hands turned her, then slid again into her hair to hold her head at an angle for his kiss.

"Just this." His mouth was warm against hers, his lips brushing the soft surfaces without demand. His lips opened a bit, barely enough to give voice to his throaty growl of satisfaction.

"Your mouth tastes like strawberries in May," he said, the whisper spoken against her throat.

"I ate jam on my bread...."

His chuckle was rich with amusement. "If I tell you your hair smells like the rain coming in from the west, will you tell me you rinsed it from the rain barrel?"

She nodded, just a bit, her tongue snaking a trail across her lips. She tasted the flavor of his mouth, the coffee he'd drunk and a stronger tinge, like the medicine bottle of whiskey Pa had kept in his trunk.

"You taste like whiskey." She licked at her lips again, as if determining the flavor she found there.

"Call it Dutch courage," he said, his grin lifting one corner of his mouth.

"I wouldn't think you were the kind to look for bravery in a bottle."

"Maybe you scare the bejabbers out of me, Rachel." His grin was gone and his eyes were dark and shadowed in the twilight. He leaned forward the few inches it took to touch her mouth with his, and she closed her eyes.

He was circumspect, brushing a series of kisses across her face, holding her with an easy touch. "Will you go to the dance with me tomorrow night, Rachel?"

She leaned away, opening her eyes, drinking in the masculine beauty of his face, the dark intensity of his gaze. "I think I told Lorena I'd ride into town with her and her folks."

He nodded. "All right. I don't do much dancing, but will you save me a couple of dances?"

"Yes...but I'll warn you, I'm not very good at square dancing."

His smile was back. "I'm a good teacher."

Chapter Eight

Conrad's shirt collar was making ridges against the flesh of his throat. His cheeks were rosy, his breathing rapid and he held Rachel with a possessive air, dipping and turning, forging a trail around the perimeter of the dance floor. Against her back his hand was damp, causing her dress and undergarments to stick to her skin between her shoulder blades.

She'd worn her fanciest chemise, her only good corset cover and the dress her mother had stitched up for the Autumn Jamboree last year. It was blue, the sweetheart neckline edged with a wide ruffle of imported lace.

She'd tugged at the snug fit of the bodice, bending to the mirror, blushing as she noted the faint rise of her bosom above the fine lace ruche. It had fit better last year, she thought, but there was nothing to be done. It was the best she owned, the only dress fit for such an occasion.

Conrad had gulped visibly as he approached her for the opening dance. To her relief it was a waltz, at which she was adept. When it was over he'd led her back to her place with Lorena and her mother, bowing deferentially over her hand.

"May we walk outdoors, later?" he'd asked quietly, his suddenly somber gaze making him look older, more mature.

With a nod, Rachel dismissed him, turning to the women, who watched her expectantly.

"You dance beautifully, Rachel," Lorena said, her eyes sparkling with delight. "You're going to be the belle of the ball, so to speak. The menfolk can't seem to take their eyes from you." Her face beamed as if she were personally responsible for the newcomer's popularity.

The single men of the community had swarmed about Rachel as if she were queen bee and they the workers who were only existing for her benefit. Young and old, they paired her for the dances, frequently cutting in on each other with possessive glances. The younger men were somewhat awkward, their eyes staying circumspectly above her throat, the clean-shaven cowhands from the area more bold in their surveillance of her charms.

Cord watched from the edge of the room, after just twice spinning a partner across the floor. And even then, he could concentrate only on the young woman whose feet seemed to barely skim the wooden boards, whose face was flushed with pleasure, whose eyes gleamed with a victorious light.

He stood it as long as he could. Then, with a boldness of purpose that brought attention his way, he strode onto the dance floor and claimed Rachel from the red-faced cowhand she was endeavoring to keep up with.

Giving a sigh that might have been relief, she relaxed into his arms and Cord nudged her a bit closer, his hand widespread against her waist. "You're gonna have sore feet tomorrow, Miss Rachel," he murmured against her ear, turning her deftly as he evaded Buck Austin, who was squiring Lorena Claypool in a lively fashion.

The sight of Lorena sobered him for a moment, remembering other dances in this place, when Jake had escorted Lorena in and out the door, spending most of the evening in her company.

Never again. It was a daunting thought, and he gripped the woman in his arms a bit tighter, spinning her until she gasped, laughing with delight.

"I'm dizzy, Cord! You dance like a whirlwind."

He'd waited for this waltz, unwilling to partner her in a square dance, much as he'd wanted to be the one to teach her the steps. It meant relinquishing her to another man's arms throughout the dance, and he was feeling selfish tonight. It was enough that he had to watch her go from one to another.

Perhaps she'd danced her last with the men of the community for this night. Maybe…

The fiddle and piano ended their offering with a shivering crescendo and the room broke out in applause. Rachel looked up at him and her smile was trembling. "You're quite a dancer, Mr. McPherson." Her head tilted to one side and he thought he detected a flirtatious gleam in her eyes. "I thought you were going to teach me to square dance."

"Thought maybe I'd teach you something else, Rachel," he said, putting her from him, lest her nearness leave him with an embarrassing problem. Later on, he could allow his desire to overcome his good sense. Not here. Certainly not now.

Her brow furrowed as she considered his words. "A different dance?"

His smile twitched a bit and he swallowed the chuckle that bubbled in his throat. "You might say that." Over her shoulder Cord could see Conrad approaching, his step firm, his head held high. Looked like a man coming courting, Cord thought, all starched and buttoned up to the brim.

"Miss Rachel. Have you forgotten your promise?" The storekeeper bowed a bit, offering his hand, and Rachel looked up at him, her brow still showing signs of puzzlement.

Then the fair skin smoothed, her smile came readily and her hair bounced as she shook her head vigorously. "No, of course not, Mr. Carson. The next dance will be yours." Turning from Cord, she took the proffered hand and walked away, her hips twitching just a bit, as if she knew his gaze would be focused on her every move.

And it was. A glass of lemonade was probably going to do little to cool his ardor, but Cord headed for the refreshment table anyway.

Let Carson have his say. Let him court her all the way around the dance floor. When time came to leave, it would be square on the seat of Cord McPherson's buggy that Rachel's little bottom would be planted.

"Can we walk outside, Miss Rachel?" Conrad waltzed her past the door and then drew her to a halt, his arm still around her back, his other hand holding her fingers in a damp grip.

She nodded. Carson seemed determined to spend a few minutes in the moonlight, and she was not averse to hearing what he had to say.

They walked past the line of buggies and wagons, under the shade of tall maple trees to where the road turned both to the east and west. To their right lights flickered in the windows of the buildings in town. The barber shop and emporium were dark, the bank building an imposing structure against the night sky, with its facade rising high.

The hotel was ablaze with light, a golden glow spilling through its double doors, open wide to catch the night breeze. Rachel tilted her head back, dizzy as she scanned the starlit sky.

Conrad's arm rested across her shoulder as she swayed. "It's enough to boggle the mind, isn't it, Miss Rachel? To see the universe spread over the sky, making you wonder what's beyond the edge of forever."

"Why Mr. Carson, I believe you have the soul of a poet," she exclaimed, truly pleased by his words.

"I have the soul of a man who has found the woman he wants to spend his life with, Miss Rachel." He turned her to face him, his touch respectful, his hands at her waist.

"I can offer you a good life, and I'm willing to support your brothers, too. They can work in the store to earn their keep, and I'll be fair with them."

Her tongue hesitated, as if unwilling to squelch his enthusiasm, her tender heart touched by the words he spoke. So like the practical man he was, to already have put Jay and Henry to work in the store. A vision of her brothers, with suspenders and starched-collars, entered her mind and she smiled.

Perhaps the lure of Rachel's curving lips gave him hope. Perhaps the softening of her eyes as they gazed into his led him to believe she was accepting his suit. Whatever he saw in the woman before him, it was enough to push him into a rash action.

His hands slid to encompass her waist and he tugged her forward, taking her off balance so that she fell against his chest. Without hesitation his head dipped, his mouth taking possession of hers. His lips were cool, dry and sterile against her own, his kiss less of an offense than a disappointment.

Rachel drew back, gaining her balance. Using the full force of muscles honed by hard work, she pushed him from her. "I think you are overstepping, Mr. Carson."

Even in the moonlight, his flush of embarrassment was obvious and she softened her tone. "I appreciate the offer. I really do. I just don't think my brothers would do well in town. They're too full of life and energy. Besides, I can't consider such a move right now. I'm bound to work for Cord McPherson until next spring. Beyond that time, my future is unsure."

"Next spring?" His tone was incredulous as Conrad stepped away from her, his face frozen in a mask of horror. "Why did you ever let yourself get in such a bind, Miss Rachel? Is the contract..."

"There is no contract, only my word. I promised him I would stay that long." She took a deep breath, her fingers twitching, her mouth feeling the need of a drink of water. Conrad had left her dry and empty, and the disappointment was harsh. She'd really thought....

In her daydreams she'd considered what life in town might be. What it would be like to be part of a small community, perhaps married to one of the leaders of the town, to watch each Sunday as he ushered folks into church and carried an offering plate.

It wasn't enough. With sudden certainty, she recognized the barren life she would lead, a life in which Cord McPherson would play no part.

"Let's finish this dance inside, Mr. Carson," she said quietly, turning toward the brightly lit building behind them.

Her foot was on the wagon wheel when she was gripped from behind. "You're coming home with me."

Cord's voice in her ear was not totally unexpected, and she smiled in the darkness. Her foot slid to the ground and she turned to face him.

"Is there a problem?" Her voice sounded breathless to her ears, and she swallowed, wishing for another sip of lemonade.

"None that I can't handle," Cord answered. "I'll be taking Rachel home," he told Lorena, who stood with her parents just beyond the tailgate. In the back of the wagon the Claypool boys were wrestling, tossing hay back and forth, ignoring the adults who played out a silent scene.

Mr. Claypool nodded his understanding, his wife and Lorena exchanging glances. "We'll see you Monday morning," Cord said to Lorena. "Maybe you'd better think about bringing your things and spending nights at the house. There's plenty of bedrooms upstairs. You can pret' near have your pick."

"I'll think about it," Lorena answered, slanting a look of promise at Rachel.

Cord's arm circled her waist and Rachel was spun around with ease, her feet headed in the direction of the McPherson buggy, tied beneath a tree next to the road.

"I have a notion you were standing not far from here when Conrad made his pitch," he told her, lifting her to the high seat.

She looked down at him, watching as his hands tucked her skirts inside the buggy. "Were you spying on me?"

He moved soundlessly around the heads of the team, untying the horses from the metal ring that had been drilled into the tree. It wasn't until he was seated beside her that he deigned to answer her accusation.

"I watched from outside the door." He flicked the

reins over the horses' backs, making a sound with his tongue and teeth that set them on their way at a slow trot. His look was all encompassing as he turned halfway in the seat.

"You're my responsibility, Rachel. You work in my home and I'm planning on marrying you."

Her mouth opened and then closed. If she'd thought it dry before, it was an arid desert now. Such nerve. That he would consider her a package, bought and paid for.

"I don't remember accepting a proposal from you," she said finally, looking straight ahead into the night.

He shrugged and she felt the movement against her shoulder. She shifted in the seat, unwilling to touch him in even this small way, so angry at his assumption she could have screeched her fury to the stars.

"You let me kiss you, Rachel. More than once, in fact. I talked to you about living on the ranch. I thought we had an understanding of sorts."

She stiffened. "Conrad kissed me, too. That didn't make me his intended."

His snort of disgust was immediate. "That was no kiss! The man barely touched you. And now that I think about it, he had no right to do even that. He's not man enough for a woman like you, Rachel."

She turned to face him, peering at the sharp line of his profile. His nose was a little too big, his jaw a little too firm for her liking and his hat was drawn down, hiding his eyes from her view.

"A woman like me? What does that mean?"

Cord halted the team and in an instant he'd spanned her waist with his hands, tugging her against him. Giving no quarter, he scooped her slender form into an embrace that allowed her no leeway, his head bending to her face. The bonnet she'd tied with such care was unfastened with two fingers, long, lean fingers that tugged at the strings and then removed the saucy little impediment with a careless gesture.

His own hat was tossed to the floor, and as Rachel's mouth opened to protest his high-handed actions, his lips covered hers with a determination she could only accept, given no alternative but to submit to the heated passion of his mouth.

He kissed her as if she were a drink of water and he had been without sustenance for days. His mouth opened over hers, his teeth rubbing at her lips, gaining entrance as she gasped her protest.

As if he allowed passion full sway, he kissed her. No teasing touches, but a thorough, sweeping inventory of the secrets she held within the damp recesses of her mouth. He traveled the ridges beneath her tongue, searched the tight channel between teeth and cheek, vied with her for entry beyond the roof of her mouth and subsided only when she sagged against him.

"I haven't got an ounce of civilization in me tonight, Rachel. Seeing you with all those men, dancing circles around every other woman in the place… Damn! I'm about as randy as I've ever been in my life." He shook his head, his mouth attempting a smile and failing miserably.

He leaned to her, whispering in her ear, his words an apology. "I should be kissing you like Conrad did, with some amount of gentility. Let me try it again."

He was gentle as his lips touched hers again, and she allowed the caress. "We're going to have to get married, Rachel. You're in my blood and that's a fact!"

His voice was like buggy wheels on gravel. "I want you in my bed so bad it's a wonder I don't cart you off there tonight."

She wiggled against him, her hands pushing against his chest. "There you go again! Damn you, Cord McPherson! Just who do you think you are?"

He put her aside, his hands trembling with the effort. Taking up the reins, he set the horse in motion, his jaw set.

"I'm the man who's going to marry you, and don't think for one minute you can change my mind. You can try to lead me a merry chase, but I won't give you much of a lead line, Rachel. There'll be no more kisses in the moonlight with Conrad Carson, no more dances with every man Jack in the county."

"I may be your cook and housekeeper, Cord McPherson, but I'm not your wife yet, and if I were you, I wouldn't bet the ranch on it ever coming to pass. You're about the most arrogant, hardheaded man I've ever met." She spit the words in his direction, her heart beating a rapid pace, whether from anger or the kisses he'd pressed upon her, she didn't know.

She only knew that this man could raise her ire faster than lightning and at the same time churn her insides into a rushing river of desire with just the touch of his hands and the heat of his kisses.

Right now the angry lightning was way ahead of the desire he'd stirred into being. With trembling hands she lifted her bonnet from the floorboards and tied it into place.

The kitchen, already warm with the morning sun, was dense with the heat of Rachel's anger. Cord felt it to the core of his being as he watched her from the doorway. She'd heard his ultimatum last night and wrenched herself from his hold, sitting stiff and unbending by his side until the buggy drew up to the house.

Her exit had been rapid and awkward, her skirts pulling up to expose her legs as she slid from the seat. She'd spent only seconds regaining her dignity before she stomped up the steps and into the house.

He'd watched from the buggy seat, dead certain that he'd botched the whole thing, his lips still flavored with her taste, as the woman he'd chosen as his own flaunted her denial of his claim.

This morning she was still operating on a full head of steam, and he bade his tongue remain under control, lest he add fuel to the flame of her anger.

"Good morning, Rachel."

She muttered a sound that might have contained an epithet. Her hands were fierce in their strength, beating the bejabbers out of a bowlful of eggs. The sound of sizzling butter in the big skillet apparently was a signal, for she poured the contents of her bowl into the pan.

"Breakfast will be ready in five minutes." Clipped and cool, the words were aimed at the high back of her cookstove and she reached to open the warming oven there, exposing a platter of pancakes ready for the table.

A flat griddle on the stove bore four more, and Cord grinned his delight. Apparently a temper hadn't damaged her cooking skills.

He stepped out onto the porch, catching sight of men inside the barn, hearing their voices in the clear, early-morning air. His indrawn breath caught the scent of honeysuckle vines at the end of the porch, and a vision of his mother sprang to mind.

She'd planted those vines, more years ago than he wanted to count, the spring before she'd died. The anger old Harvey McPherson had lived with from that day forward was a memory that had almost blighted Cord's soul. He shook his head.

Even Pa would not cast a blemish on this day. He might wear the scars, but he refused to allow them soul-deep.

The sound of Rachel within his house lifted his spirits, and he reached for the bell rope hanging just beyond the railing. A quick tug on it caught the attention of the men working in the corral and within the depths of the barn. A wave of acknowledgment from Buck and Shamus was his answer, and he turned back to the kitchen door.

The table was covered with a long piece of checkered oilcloth, an addition Rachel had made during her first week at the ranch, looking to him for approval before she'd had Conrad cut it to length at the emporium. Easier to keep clean than the wooden tabletop, she'd said.

The plates were centered between a knife and fork, a glass jar of spoons in the middle of the table. Thick cups awaited the coffeepot, and Rachel turned with a platter of pancakes in each hand, setting them on the table as he entered the door. The skillet of eggs steamed at the back of the stove and she lifted it to dump the contents into a crockery bowl.

She was strong, this woman he'd chosen, and he gloried in the knowledge of her, that he knew the depth of her courage, the width of her determination. Her gaze met his across the table and she lifted her chin, defiance alive in her blue eyes.

"I'll be taking my wagon to town this morning. I'm going to church," she announced. "I'd appreciate it if one of the men could harness my horses after breakfast."

He rocked back on his heels. "You gettin' soft, Rachel? Forget how to harness the team?" It tickled him to watch the flush of anger creep up her throat and blend with the rosy hue caused by the heat of her oven.

"I've not forgotten anything, Mr. McPherson. I

should have remembered that you're not a gentleman. I can take care of it myself, thank you.''

"We'll go to church in my wagon, Rachel. The boys can sit in the back."

She opened her mouth, and her eyes swept to the doorway, where Moses and Jamie were edging each other past the screen door. Her look in his direction was a challenge as she spun in place, reaching for a plate from the cupboard, her hands busy as she filled it with an abundance of hot food.

It clunked onto the tray she'd readied beforehand and she picked up the weight of it, careful not to spill the cup of coffee she'd poured for Jake. Her skirts swished against the doorjamb as she left the kitchen, and Cord sat down to devour his share of the breakfast she'd prepared.

The library door was partway open, and she nudged it with her toe. "Jake? I have your breakfast." Her eyes took in the dim shadows of the room, and she headed for the bed.

"You still asleep? The morning's half-over," she said brightly, unwilling to allow her anger with his brother to spill over onto the man who occupied this room.

"I'm here, Rachel."

She blinked, settling the tray on a smooth corner of the bedding, and turned to the sound of his voice. Stepping to the window, she pulled aside the heavy draperies and fastened them with the ties he'd undone the night before. She turned, willing her lips to curve into a smile, and then discovered it was not a chore to do so.

He'd shaved. Sometime between yesterday afternoon and this morning, he'd managed to use a razor, revealing a mouth that twitched a bit at her wide-eyed response.

His chin was strong, jutting forward, putting her in mind of Cord's profile last night in the buggy.

"Well, you look presentable for a change," she said, her brow lifting just a bit. "Do you want to eat at the table?" Carrying the tray, she obeyed his nod, arranging his plate and silverware as he rolled the few feet to where she stood.

"The food's been worth cleaning up for," he said, casting a sly glance at her. "Thank you."

She stepped back. Perhaps the shaving had been done for her benefit, but somehow she doubted it. More likely, though he might deny it, Lorena Claypool would be the true beneficiary of his foray into civilized behavior. He was being polite this morning, a new side of his character, to be sure, she thought as he placed the napkin across his lap.

"I'm quite a hand with barber scissors," she told him, stuffing her hands in her apron pockets.

He glanced in her direction, a forkful of pancakes midway to his mouth. "Don't try to reform me all at once, Miss Rachel." His words held a tinge of sarcasm and he chewed slowly as he watched her.

"Far be it from me to take advantage of your good mood, Mr. McPherson," she said, bending to pick up a pillow that had fallen from the bed. She pulled the sheets into place quickly, ignoring the vigilance he turned in her direction.

"Have you thought about attending church? Since you're spiffed up and all?"

"Don't push it, ma'am." He drank from his coffee cup, thumping it back on the tray with an angry gesture. "I've allowed you into my sanctuary. I've even been polite. Don't cause me to revert to my normal behavior by offering to haul me off to sing hymns and play the hypocrite.''

"Would spending an hour in church be such a chore?'' Rachel fluffed his pillows and replaced them against the high headboard.

"I no longer find it plausible that a benevolent heavenly father would allow such inhumanity to be inflicted on his servants as I saw take place on my journey through the great war.''

Rachel frowned at his statement, taken aback by the derision of his words. "Men fought the war, Mr. McPherson. It was a choice of the North and South. I doubt God Almighty had much to do with it.''

His brow lifted and his head cocked to one side. "And yet both sides held that they fought for a divine reason.'' He lifted his fork once more and waved it in her direction.

"I fell for that twaddle, madam. I left a promising career to join up with the Union army, set on freeing the slaves and making my mark, vindicating my presence on this earth. And for what? What did I accomplish? What did any of us accomplish? The South is in shambles, men are dead and buried, or even worse....''

Rachel felt an overwhelming sense of shame as she heard the outburst from the man before her. So little had she really known about the war. She, with her pampered beginnings, her sheltered existence.

And yet, within her was the sure and certain knowledge that even Jake McPherson could gain some measure of comfort from the house of worship. "I can only tell you that there is a God, Jake. For I believe in Him and know that He can comfort in times of distress. I know that He gives me courage when I have none of my own, that He gives me strength to do what I must and that He gives me joy when I enter His house and listen to His word and sing His praises.''

He bent his head. ''I bow to your right, Miss Rachel. Trot yourself on to church and sing your songs. I, for one, have no taste for music in any form these days. Nor have I the need for a church full of pious townsfolk staring at me.''

''Call me when you've finished your breakfast,'' Rachel said politely as she turned to leave the library. Her heart was heavy with the sorrow she sensed dwelling deep inside the soul of Jake McPherson.

His shaggy head lifted, his eyes pinning her where she stood, and his arrogant bearing once more descended upon him like an enveloping cloak.

''You can take the tray now. I've finished.''

''You and Jake had quite a talk this morning, Rachel.'' Cord glanced at her, his silence broken for the first time since they'd set out for Sunday worship.

''You listened?'' she asked, her eyes on the road ahead.

''I came down the hallway to say good-morning to him and overheard a bit. It seemed impolite to intrude.''

Rachel bit at her lip. ''He's a bitter man, Cord.''

''He has a right.''

She looked at him quickly. ''You share his bitterness?''

He shrugged. ''A little, I guess. It's easier to be philosophical about the outcome of the war when you can still walk around and function as a man. But I'm reminded every day of the thousands of men who will spend their lives without purpose, tied to a bed or a chair.''

"Don't you think Jake could have more of a life than he has now? If he truly wanted to be more than he is?"

"Don't take him on like a charity case, Rachel. He won't appreciate it."

She looked away, her heart heavy with the knowledge that, in his own way, Cord McPherson also carried the wounds of the war. Perhaps even a certain amount of guilt, every time he looked at his brother.

"It's not your fault that Jake was wounded and you came out of the conflict unharmed," she said finally as the wagon drew up in front of the small church building.

Cord dropped to the ground and turned to face her. "I didn't fight in the war, Rachel. I chose to stay at home, and after my father had a fit of apoplexy and dropped over, there was no one else to run the ranch."

"Your father died during the war?" Her words were a whisper as she watched Cord tie the team to the hitching rail. The boys dropped from the rear of the wagon and slowly approached, as if they sensed the gravity of the conversation of their elders.

"You comin', Rae?" Jay asked in a cautious voice.

She gathered her skirts and stood. "Yes, of course."

Cord held out his hands and she bent to him, allowing him to lift her from the wagon. As if aware of eyes watching their arrival, he stepped back, offering his arm, and she accepted the gesture. Behind them, the two boys followed.

"Brush the hay from your pant legs, Jay." Henry gave his instructions quietly, and Rachel turned to find him tending to the younger boy.

The duty of one brother to look after another, she thought, her gaze scanning the two boys, her fingers smoothing Henry's cowlick as they prepared to enter the church doors.

Chapter Nine

The piano beckoned her, its keys silent beneath the heavy lid, its music an unheard melody in her heart. Rachel dusted the top, moving the family portrait of Cord, Jake and their parents. The two boys were stiff and solemn, almost of a size, she thought, standing back, the better to see the comparison.

It was a formal pose, done, according to Cord, by a photographer who'd come through town, talking most everyone who had two nickels to rub together into having a portrait done.

Lorena laughed aloud from the doorway, and Rachel spun to face her, startled by the sound.

"There's one almost like that in our parlor at home," she said, strolling across the room, her gaze taken in by the framed memento. "Only ours has seven people in it, quite a challenge for the poor man, as I remember."

"They looked alike, didn't they?" Rachel asked, her eyes measuring the two boys who had donned Sunday best for the occasion.

"Still do, if you look close." Lorena's hand reached out, fingers almost touching the figure that was Jake Mc-

Pherson, her expression tender as if she sought something of the man within the boy he had been.

"Cord's father was quite strict, wasn't he?" She was prying, and Rachel knew her questions would not be appreciated by either of the men who owned this house.

Lorena nodded. "Strict might not be the right word. He was harsh with Cord, maybe because they were so alike. He softened toward Jake, after their mother died. I think he sent him to New York because it was what his mother wanted for him, not because Harvey had any great love of music himself."

"Was that before you and he…"

Lorena voiced a low sound, perhaps a chuckle, Rachel thought. "I've loved Jake since I can remember. I used to sit on the ground outside that window and listen to him practice when I was a girl."

"And Cord? Weren't you ever sweet on him?"

Lorena shook her head. "He's been like a brother to me since we were kids. He used to look out for me and my sisters in school."

"My fingers are just itching to get at this piano," Rachel confided, lifting the lid to brush with reverence against the ivory keys.

Lorena smiled wistfully. "This house needs music. Contrary to what Jake says, music would be good for him. But if you play, you're taking your chances with his temper."

Rachel folded the lid back completely, her dustcloth forgotten for the moment. "Slide the doors closed on your way out," she said, her thoughts already on the notes she heard inside her head.

"Why'd you close the doors? We could use a little cross draft in here, Rena. It's hotter'n Hades this morning.'' Jake rolled his chair with swift movements toward the sliding library doors as he glared his frustration at the woman who was making up his bed for the day.

"Just habit, I guess.'' She moved to the opposite side of the bed, watching as he set one door in motion, sliding it into the wall.

"What the hell is she doing?'' His eyes darted to Lorena, then back to the hallway.

"Sounds to me like she's playing some Bach or something down in the parlor,'' Lorena ventured.

"She's making hash of the 'Moonlight Sonata,' and Bach never wrote a single note of it, Rena.'' His heart was pumping, his face burning with a frustrated anger he hesitated to vent.

"Jake?'' Lorena's whisper of his name brought his attention back to her as she crossed the room to him. "Don't have a fit over this, please.''

"Having fits is what I do best, Rena. Hasn't anyone told you about the cripple who carries on like a madman?'' As if caught in a cross fire, he listened to Lorena's words and at the same time allowed the notes from the parlor to be written on the pages of music he played over and over again in his mind.

"Damn, she's got that part all wrong!'' He tilted his head as a measure was repeated. Then the music paused and Rachel backed up to pick up the melody again.

"I told the woman to stay away from that piano. I told her pretty near the first day she was here. But would she listen? Fool girl thinks she can handle Beethoven, and I doubt she's even tackled Schubert's 'Serenade.''' He rolled the wheels to and fro, the chair marking time as he pushed open the other door, allowing the music from the parlor full sway.

His head bent and he winced as Rachel halted in her rendition, stumbling over a phrase, then beginning anew.

Jake's growl was deep in his throat, the emotion too deep for words as he spun his chair into the hallway, sending it to rest against the parlor doors.

He pushed them open, one hand on each, and the resounding clatter as they banged inside the walls brought Rachel to a halt. She swung around on the bench, and for a moment Jake was taken back to the day he'd first seen her there. Now she met his gaze without a trace of fear marring her face, her blue eyes steady as they watched his approach.

"I botched it, didn't I?" she asked, and her grin was unapologetic. "I'm real good at Mozart, honestly. But for some reason I've never been able to do justice to—"

"*Do justice?* You butchered it!" Jake's roar filled the room, and he wheeled himself closer to the piano. "If you can't handle that simple little..."

Rachel shook her head firmly. "It's not a simple little anything, and you know it, Jake McPherson. Beethoven wrote music that looks simple on paper, but only in the translation does it attain its full beauty."

"Your hand is too heavy on the bass, Rachel. It must be solid, but it's only the underlying foundation for the melody."

She looked at him, her gaze meeting his, her blue eyes issuing a challenge. "Show me." She rose, lifting the bench, and moving it to the right, then sat down just to the center of the piano, her hand poised over the keyboard.

"Show me, Jake. Wheel your chair up here and play the bass. I'll do the pedal and the right hand."

At the doorway, Lorena waited, her face pale, her eyes pleading with the man in the chair. He glanced at her, and a memory of the last time he'd seen her before the war filled his mind. She had looked at him so that day, when he'd left for New York.

Jake turned to the piano, his teeth gritting together, his thoughts uneasy over the plot Rachel had hatched with him in mind. That she had deliberately set him up for this was as certain as the sunrise. He scanned her face, spotting a glimpse of uncertainty behind the innocence of her blue eyes.

His chair rolled to a stop and he leaned to the right, his hand braced on the bench behind Rachel. It was an awkward position, but if the girl truly was not aware of the discrepancies in her technique, he'd better set her straight.

"Play."

She glanced at him and opened her mouth. Then, as if thinking better of it, she bit at her lip.

"From the beginning, Rachel."

Her hand touched the keys and she began the sonorous melody.

Jake's fingers cramped as he spread them to form the octave and he lifted them from the keys, clenching his fist several times. He cleared his throat. "All right, try it again."

The first notes came slowly, the minor key not lending itself to anything more than that. Rachel bent forward a bit, and her toe rose and fell from the pedal as she played. His fingers spread wide, his eyes closed, Jake touched the keys. The bass notes reverberated beneath the repetitious rolling chords she played, and their hands formed the beauty of the sonata.

His head bending forward, he felt the flex of muscles in his forearm, felt the music flow from his fingers to the tiny hammers in the wooden form of the instrument, faithfully carrying out the message he sent.

From deep within, a chill barrier he'd set firmly in place began to thaw. He took a breath, unwilling that the warmth spreading throughout his body should melt that cold expanse in its entirety, leaving him exposed.

At his right side, Rachel played, her fingers agile against the keys, passing the troublesome spot she'd stumbled over only minutes before.

"You're a fake, Rachel Sinclair." The accusation, softly spoken, bore not a trace of anger.

"So are you, Jake McPherson." Without losing a beat, their hands played in tandem until he ceased, drawing back from the piano, rolling his chair backward until it halted next to where Lorena had kept watch.

"Now, play for me, Rachel. From the beginning."

She moved the bench back to where it belonged and looked at him over her shoulder. "You really don't mind?"

He was touched in some indeterminate way by the unconscious plea in her voice. Did she beg his pardon for the farce she had set up for his benefit? Or was she truly bereft by the loss of music in her life?

"I mind. More than you know," he said gruffly. "But, play anyway."

She began, her body erect, her hands flowing with the beauty of the composition she had obviously been more than competent at in times past. And as she continued, developing strength and intensity, she bent to the keys.

Beside him, Lorena lifted her hand to grip his shoulder. Jake leaned his head to the side, pressing his cheek against the back of her fingers, leaving a damp residue.

"Sam is moving back to the bunkhouse."

"He'll be fine, Rachel," Cord said. He leaned back

in his chair, watching as she opened the oven door.

"I know, but..." She turned with the roaster in her hands. "Put my breadboard on the table, Cord, will you?"

He complied quickly, adding a hot pad for good measure.

The lid was lifted, fragrant steam rising from the pot roast. "You can cook for me any day of the week, Rachel," Cord said with great emphasis, inhaling deeply.

She cast him a sidelong glance, lifting the tender roast from the pan with two huge spatulas. After placing the meat on a big platter, she removed the roasting pan to the stove top. "I already do, McPherson. Every blessed day of the week."

"Are you wanting Sam to take over again with Jake? Is that why you're concerned about him going back to the bunkhouse?" he asked.

She shook her head. "No, Jake and Lorena seem to be getting along well together. He won't let her do for him the way Sam did, and Rena says he keeps his distance for the most part. I just don't want Sam to get infection in his burns, Cord. He's not a young man, you know, and he'll try to keep up with the younger ones."

Cord folded his hands over his stomach, leaning back in the chair once more. "I'll keep an eye on him, Rachel. By the way, I heard you played the piano yesterday."

She grinned. "It was wonderful. Jake came in like a roaring lion and left like a lamb." Sparing a look at the hallway door, she lowered her voice. "He even sat beside me and played the left hand for a bit. I was so excited, I—"

"Rachel! Rachel! We got company." From the yard,

Jay's reedy voice piped the news, and Rachel bent to look out the kitchen window.

"My word! It's the preacher's wife," she said, recognizing the woman from Sunday church. Hurriedly wiping her hands on her apron, she brushed back stray tendrils of hair.

Cord stood up quickly. "I'll let you two have at it, and I'll just lend a hand out back."

Rachel frowned at him. "You told me you had an hour free, in between horseshoeing and working with your new horses."

He moved toward the door. "I really shouldn't be sittin' around in the middle of the day, Rae. The quicker I get that little pinto tamed down good, the quicker Jay will have a mount of his own."

His boots clattered as he ran down the porch steps and his hat lifted, a ready grin on his lips as he greeted the woman climbing down from a buggy. "I'll tie your horse, ma'am," he offered, taking the reins from her hand.

"I'll be most obliged if you come back into the house after you do that task, young man," Wilhelmina Bryant said firmly. "I need to talk to you and the young lady you have working for you."

"Yes, ma'am," Cord answered, his look resigned as he glanced back at the house, where Rachel waited at the door.

She opened it wide, a smile of welcome curving her lips, her eyes anxious as she glanced quickly at Cord, then back to their visitor. "Won't you come in?"

The stout lady made her way to the porch, climbing the steps with thumping feet. "I was taking a chance that you'd be home, but I needed to talk to both of you."

Rachel stuck out her hand, checking it quickly for

stray bits of roast beef. "I know we met at church, but perhaps you've forgotten. My name is Rachel Sinclair. I'm the cook and housekeeper and..." She paused. "Well, I do most everything here."

The older lady's eye was sharp, obviously taking inventory of the slender girl who claimed to run the McPherson household. "That's what I'm afraid of, young lady."

Rachel blinked, aware that she'd missed something in the brief conversation. "Afraid?" She waved at a kitchen chair. "Won't you sit down? Or would you rather step into the parlor?" She flushed, embarrassed at having such a lapse in manners. The minister's wife would expect to be given the courtesy of a chair in better surroundings than the kitchen had to offer.

"This is fine," Mrs. Bryant said sharply. She leaned to wipe her gloved hand over the kitchen chair and then settled her considerable bulk on it.

Rachel looked past her at the door, where Cord was making his way back into the house. He took off his hat and hung it on a hook, then waited by the window.

"I come on a mission that gives me great concern and sorrow," Mrs. Bryant began briskly.

Privately Rachel thought the lady looked anything but sorrowful, her sharp eyes missing little in their perusal of the neat kitchen.

"What seems to be the trouble, ma'am?" Cord drawled.

"There appears to be a considerable amount of talk about this young woman living in your home, Mr. Mc-Pherson, without benefit of chaperon."

He stood erect, his eyes glittering from beneath lowered brows. "Well, it just so happens that that situation is about to be remedied, ma'am,'' he said, with a warning glance at Rachel.

"Also,'' the lady continued, as if Cord's words had gone right over her head, "I understand that Miss Sinclair appeared at the dance on Saturday night wearing a dress that could not be considered modest by the standards held in this town.''

"Now wait a goldurned minute.'' Cord stiffened, taking a quick step toward the visitor.

"It's all right, Cord,'' Rachel broke in. "The neckline was a bit low. I hadn't worn the dress in almost a year and I guess I...'' She waved her hand in silent explanation, her cheeks flushed with mortification. That the preacher's wife thought she hadn't been dressed suitably for a dance! She'd never be able to show her face in town again!

"I didn't see anything wrong with Rachel's dress. And since she's my intended, my opinion is the one that counts. Not some...'' Cord halted at the offended look on Mrs. Bryant's face and Rachel's equally horrified features.

"Cord, we haven't—'' she began, just as the older lady sprang to her feet.

"Well, I never...'' Mrs. Bryant spouted, tugging at her gloves.

"Please, please wait, Mrs. Bryant,'' Rachel begged, stepping in front of the lady, who was obviously on her way out the door. "This can all be explained. I'm working here for Mr. McPherson, and he is allowing my brothers to help out around the ranch. All that in return for a wage and a place to stay until we can move on west in the spring.''

Mrs. Bryant's head swung in Cord's direction, her

eyes narrowed, her lips pursed. "I thought you said she was your intended."

He nodded, his jaw clenched. "She is. Yes, ma'am, she surely is." His look in Rachel's direction was daunting. And then at the dismay written on her face, he stepped to where she stood and placed his arm around her waist. "We haven't announced it in a general way yet. Rachel is busy making plans for the wedding, though, aren't you, honey?"

Cord's fingers clamped against her waist and she winced at the warning. "Getting ready for the wedding," she repeated blankly, looking up at Cord, bewildered at the fast-moving events.

"Yes, ma'am. I'm plannin' on having your husband out here before too long to do the ceremony for us."

"You're not going to have a church wedding?" the woman asked, her hand flying to her bosom, as though shocked by the very idea.

Cord shook his head. "My brother is unable to get around much. We'd like to be married here, where he can be a part of the ceremony."

"He's in an invalid's chair, I understand," Mrs. Bryant said, her stern features softening as she spoke of Jake.

"Yes, ma'am. A wounded war hero." Cord's voice was filled with pride, and Rachel looked down at the floor. Jake would be madder than a hornet if he heard his brother giving him hero status.

"Well, I can certainly carry the message to town with me if you like, Mr. McPherson." Mrs. Bryant's face broke into a smile. "My husband will be delighted to hear the news. I'm sure he'll be happy to squelch the gossip that's been going around lately."

She leaned over the table, her voice barely audible.

"Why, I heard just yesterday that Miss Sinclair had danced every dance and turned down three marriage proposals last Saturday night."

"Most every unmarried lady there danced every dance, ma'am," Cord said, his voice carrying an admirable amount of restraint, Rachel thought, his hand tightening on her waist as he spoke.

"Well, be that as it may," the woman said sternly, shaking her index finger in his direction, "it isn't good for a woman alone to be talked about. It gives people ideas, and you wouldn't want Miss Sinclair to be food for speculation."

Cord shook his head. "No, ma'am, I surely wouldn't. I'd better not hear of anyone hereabouts speculating one little bit about my intended." His words resounded in the kitchen, his voice harsh.

"Well, I'll be leaving." Tugging more firmly at her gloves, Mrs. Bryant stepped to the door, looking back at the couple behind her as she gained the porch steps. "I think Mr. Bryant has this coming Saturday free. Will that be a good date for you?"

Cord cleared his throat. "How about a week from Saturday? That'll be more in line with what we had planned."

Wilhelmina Bryant eyed him warily, then nodded slowly. "All right. Might as well have time to get the girl a decent dress."

Rachel's strangled gasp was evidence of Cord's heel weighing heavily against her toes. A decent dress? Next Saturday? She was to be married on Saturday next, and all Cord could do was nod and preen like the rooster in the chicken yard? She watched as their visitor took her leave, Henry untying the reins for her and handing them up into the buggy.

By the time Cord reached the porch, Mrs. Bryant was ensconced in the buggy's seat, and he nodded his thanks at Henry as the boy waved a cheery farewell.

"Cord McPherson." Rachel had finally caught her breath, wiggling her toes to assure herself they had not been more than pinched beneath Cord's weight. "What do you think you're doing, planning a wedding for me, when I haven't even said I'd marry you?"

"You want me to lay out the possibilities here, Rae?" he asked bluntly. "To tell you the truth, your choices are kinda limited at this point. Either you marry me and keep on doing the same thing you're doing now, except for the fact that we'll be sharing a bedroom. Not to mention that you and your brothers have a home for life. Or you live and work here, and pull out next spring with a year's wages in your pocket, to head for who knows where!"

"Are you telling me I can't make a success of taking my brothers west, of fulfilling my father's dream?"

He stepped to where she stood and his hands gripped her shoulders. "I didn't say that. But as long as we're on the subject, listen to what you just said. It was your father's dream, Rachel."

His hands gentled against her, and she drew in a shuddering breath. "Rachel..." He held her more firmly, and for a moment she was tempted by the breadth of his chest, lured by the comfort his arms offered. "Ah, sweetheart, I'm sorry. I didn't mean to throw all that at you," he murmured, his mouth warm against her forehead, his big hands spreading across her back.

She cast aside his embrace, even as her hungry heart yearned for his touch. "The only difference I see is that I won't be making any money at this, once I agree to be your wife, Cord. I'll just be trudging around here from morning to night, and then trotting off to bed with you like a good girl.''

''Rachel! That's not what I said. If you marry me, you'll have a *home* here and I'll take care of you and your brothers.''

She waved her hands in the air, no longer lured by the promise of his embrace, her temper at the breaking point. ''We're gonna have to talk later, Cord. Part of my duties in your house involve making gravy and mashing potatoes. It's almost time for supper. The men will be hungry.''

''I'll help you, Rachel. Let me mash the potatoes.'' Cord snatched up a dish towel from the cupboard and tucked it into the waistband of his trousers. ''Are these ready?'' He lifted the lid of the big kettle she'd filled an hour earlier and she leaned past him to poke at a potato with a fork.

''They're about done. You can drain them into this pan.'' Every word was bitten off as if she rationed them.

His brows lifted as he looked down at the empty pan she'd designated. ''What are you gonna use the water for?''

Her sigh of aggravation was accented by a look of scorn, tossed in his direction. ''Gravy, for one thing. I'll mix some of it with the dog's dinner and the rest with the chicken mash.''

''We never did that before,'' he said, following her instructions.

She tossed her head. ''You never had me here before.''

''Well, you're right there,'' he agreed. Rolling up his sleeves, he began wielding the metal masher. ''Where'd you learn all this stuff?'' He halted for a moment as she poured milk into the pan, and added a chunk of butter.

"I did my homework in the kitchen back home and watched the cook. I possess a fair amount of intelligence, and some things stuck with me."

His mouth curled at one corner, then, his head bent low over the potato pan, he nudged her on even more. "You had a cook, and lived in a nice home. Yet your father set out on a wagon with not enough money to put in your eyeball? Seems to me he'd have considered your mother a bit more than that."

Rachel paused, her knife lifted over the roast she was slicing. "He lost his business, Cord." Her chin rose proudly. "I think he was ashamed to stay in town after that, and Mama was certain she would be shunned by the ladies she'd been friends with for all the years of her marriage."

"Some friends!" The words were mumbled beneath his breath, but her quick ear caught them.

"She was lost without her ladies' club and the circle at church. Our house was sold out from under us, and the bank took most everything. Folks with money tend to set a lot of store by the things money buys, Cord."

"How about you, Rachel?" He stilled, his gaze intent. "What do you set store by?"

Rachel rapidly cut the meat into slices, then slid the platter into the warming oven. She was silent for a few minutes, checking the kettles filled with vegetables, filling the cream pitcher and putting out a new comb of honey.

"Mostly the people I care about," she said finally. "My brothers, for sure. Lorena, for the past little while." Her mouth tilted in an unwilling smile. "She's been a good friend."

"How about me?" As if he feared her answer, he turned from her, spooning out the steaming potatoes into a crockery bowl. The sound of his spoon scraping the sides of the kettle went on for some time.

"You're going to scrape the enamel right off that pan," Rachel said quietly, her features softening as she watched him.

Cord stuck the spoon into the potatoes and carried the pan to the sink. He turned back to her, wiping his hands on the dish towel, drying them carefully. His eyes met hers and the question was alive in their depths. *How about me?*

She relented, unable to hold him at a distance. "Maybe you most of all right now, Cord. My brothers are my responsibility, and I love them something fierce, but what I feel for you is different."

"Are you saying you love me, Rachel?" His cheeks wore a ruddy hue, his nostrils flaring as he approached her.

"I don't know...I know I care about you. Even after the way you acted the night of the dance, and that's saying something," she said smartly. "You make me so mad I could spit sometimes. But I like it when you hold me in your arms."

She felt the flush rise to cover her face and she looked away. "I get all flustered when I think about you hugging me, Cord. You make me shaky inside."

His laugh was rusty, as if he forced it past a lump in his throat, and she frowned. "Don't laugh at me!" She lifted her hands to cover her cheeks. "You asked me, and I'm trying to tell you."

"I'm not laughing at you, Rae." His hands were firm as he pulled her into his arms, holding her in a gentle fashion. "I'm just pleased that I fluster you, and you likin' me to put my hands on you is gonna help a lot."

He looked over her head, out the door and into the yard, where men were beginning to gather at the pump.

"We're gonna have a kitchen full of hungry hands in a minute or so, Rachel. I think we'd better finish this later."

She spun away from him to look out the door. "Oh, my word! Let me get the plates on the table." She reached into the cabinet, looking over her shoulder at him.

"Call Lorena, will you? She's turning out the linen closet."

He gained her side in two steps, his hands framing her face. "After supper, Rachel. We'll talk tonight."

"I'll have to talk to the boys," she said as the thought popped into her mind. "And if I decide to marry you, I'll have to have a new dress."

Cord looked blank for a moment. "A new dress?"

"For the wedding, Cord! The only thing I have that's good enough is the dress I wore to the dance, and the preacher's wife would have a fit if I got married in that."

"*If* you decide?"

"Maybe you're right," she said softly. "Maybe I don't have a choice."

Chapter Ten

"...I now pronounce you man and wife." The kindly preacher nodded at Cord, his smile a benediction in itself.

Rachel watched as the man she had just sworn to love, honor and obey leaned toward her, his arms enclosing her in a loose embrace.

The love part bothered her. She'd never known another man who could set her head spinning like Cord. She'd begun to crave his presence and the touch of his hands, not to mention the pleasure of his kisses. If feeling as though she were walking in sunshine whenever he looked her way was akin to being in love, then perhaps she was well on her way to that state of being. If not, then love would come with time, she was sure.

Honor was the easy part. Cord McPherson was an honorable man. Obey might give her a little trouble.

With all that I am, I promise to be a good wife. Your happiness and well-being will be ever uppermost in my mind and heart, Cord McPherson.

She sighed as Cord's mouth touched her, his lips circumspectly pressing a chaste, but firm, kiss against hers. It was for sure that this part of being married wouldn't be a problem. She was managing to become more than fond of the habit, and at that thought, she suppressed a nervous giggle that threatened to erupt.

Cord's mouth lifted from hers and she blinked as her vision cleared. His full lower lip was twitching, as if he held back a chuckle, and the corner of his mouth held a small dimple. All spiffed up, hair brushed back and his jaws freshly shaved, he was a fine figure of a man. He smelled like mint and bay rum soap, like the barber shop when the door was open and the breeze was blowing through.

He smelled like a man set on bewitching a woman.

"Hello there, Mrs. McPherson." One big hand brushed against her cheek, his eyes narrowing as he surveyed her from her throat to the top of her circlet of honeysuckle blossoms. "You look like a bride."

I promise to keep that shine on your face, Rachel McPherson. I'll do my best to keep every promise I've made to you today.

She tried to smile, felt her lips tremble and pressed them firmly together.

"It's all right." He bent to her again, whispering in her ear. "We'll feed them and send them all on their way, quick as a wink, honey."

She nodded, blinking away the tears that insisted on welling up. Her mother should have been here. It was her wedding day, and the only family she had was the two small boys who'd stood behind her as she took her vows. Now she turned to them, Cord releasing his hold as Jay and Henry spoke her name.

"Are you really married, Rae?" Jay asked, wonder alive in his eyes.

"Of course she is," Henry said scornfully. "Didn't you just hear the preacher say so?"

Rachel bent to hug them, holding them fast for just a moment. "Bless your hearts! I love you to smithereens!" she said, kissing first one rosy cheek, then the other.

"Aw, come on, Rachel!" Henry pulled back, looking about, embarrassed at being kissed.

"You're still gonna be our sister, aren't you?" Jay asked, looking first at Rachel, then at the man she'd just married.

Cord squatted, ignoring the gathered guests, the preacher and even his bride. "Sure she is, and I'm gonna be your new brother, Jay. I'll take care of you and Henry and Rachel, all three of you. You belong to me now, just like she does." His hand almost enveloped the child's shoulder as he drew Jay closer, looking up into the boy's face.

"Will you be like our pa?" Henry asked quietly.

Rachel's heart did double time as she watched the three male creatures she was duty-bound to care for. Hope, fear and something akin to love washed over their youthful features as her brothers awaited Cord's reply.

"Maybe more like a big brother," he said finally. "But I'll love you like your pa did, same as Rachel loves you like your mother did."

"I guess it's okay then," Jay announced, a grin banishing the doubtful look he'd borne. "We like livin' here, don't we, Henry?"

Henry nodded, his cheeks red as if he sensed the full attention of the wedding guests behind him. "Come on, Jay. Let's get out of the way." Tugging at his brother, he backed from the makeshift altar, moving to where the ranch hands stood watching.

Lorena had taken the long bench from one side of the kitchen table, covering it with a linen tablecloth and placing it under an arbor of honeysuckle near the apple trees. There, beneath the summer sun, Rachel had met her groom, Jake at his side.

They'd wheeled him out, Buck and Jamie wrestling the chair over the meadow grass, Sam pacing at one side, delivering instructions.

Jake had been remarkably good-natured about the whole thing, Rachel thought. Facing the neighbors and several of the townsfolk had not been his first choice, given his isolation for the past few years. But Cord had asked him to witness the wedding, and Jake had only hesitated for a few moments before giving his assent.

The neighbor ladies had brought food for the occasion and spread it on the big kitchen table, Lorena taking charge. Now Cord raised his voice, calling for attention, inviting everyone to head for the house.

"You, too, Mrs. McPherson," he said quietly, watching as the hands began the task of delivering Jake back indoors.

"I don't know if I can eat anything," Rachel told him. "My stomach has been churning since breakfast."

"Well, just have a bite of cake and shove the food around on your plate a little. Those women outdid each other, tryin' to put on a spread for us."

"All right." She held her skirt above the grass, unwilling to stain the fragile fabric.

"You look beautiful, Rachel." She stumbled, taken aback by his words, but he caught her up in his embrace. He lifted her high, her skirts enveloping him as he strode across the meadow.

"Cord!" It was a shriek of surprise, met with a rousing round of spontaneous applause by the ranch hands.

All about her, the guests laughed and clapped, the men whistling and cheering him on as Cord carried his bride.

Rachel felt a warmth she could not fully blame on the sun, staining her cheeks and throat.

The pressure of Cord's right arm was firm beneath her thighs, while his other arm embraced her back. His hand almost touched the side of her breast, and she shivered at the intimacy. She clung, her arms circling his neck, wanting nothing more than to hide her face against him.

"I'm heavy, Cord," she protested.

His arms tightened and he laughed, a curiously light-hearted sound. "About as heavy as a young calf, and I wrestle them all the time. Though to tell the truth, I'd rather cart you around any day of the week."

Around her, the neighbors she'd never met, the towns-people she'd barely become acquainted with and the men whose welfare she'd been a part of for such a short time watched as she was carried in the arms of the man she'd married. Laughing at Cord's antics, they included her in their merriment.

He'd given her this, this sense of belonging, not only to him, but to this place. He'd given her a home, and for the first time since she'd looked back from the covered wagon at the big house in Pennsylvania, she felt secure.

"Thank you, Cord, for taking on the three of us," she said, a lump in her throat allowing only a whisper of sound to emerge.

"I think I should be thanking you, Rachel. You've taken hold here and made this place into a home for me. I didn't know how bad I needed a wife till you came along. I can't tell you how glad I am that I found you." He paused to swing her around in a slow circle, halfway across the yard.

She clung tighter. "You didn't marry me just because Mrs. Bryant..."

He shook his head, and his laugh rang out. "Hell, no! I already had it in mind, Rachel. You're a good cook, and awful nice to look at. And that's just for starts. Hell, Sam's been hopin' for this ever since you got here. He figures he's out of the kitchen for good."

There were worse reasons to be married, she decided. Whether or not Cord was teasing her, it was for sure she was needed here. Maybe she had a lot to thank Wilhelmina Bryant for. Cord was pleased as punch, his gaze admiring, grinning to beat the band.

Ahead of them, Lorena waited at the back door, Jay at her side. Behind them, the guests followed as Cord carried her past the buggies and wagons parked beneath the trees.

"You okay?" He lifted a brow. At her nod, he grinned at her, eyes sparkling, teeth gleaming. "It's a happy day, sweetheart. Enjoy it. Look, even Wilhelmina is smiling."

From the porch the dinner bell was ringing, Jay pulling with joyful abandon at the rope. "Lorena says come and get it!" he shouted at the top of his lungs.

And they did.

Rachel's wedding dress lay over the back of a chair, the skirt spread wide, buttons mated with buttonholes, tissue paper stuffed in the puffed sleeves. Made of silk organza, it was the most beautiful dress she'd ever owned, bar none.

Lorena and her mother had spent hours making it, taking over the dining room for the task. She made her way onto the bed, crawling up to lean against the headboard, propping a pillow behind her, the better to admire the bridal dress. Even from here, it looked like something from a fairy tale.

She sighed as she considered that thought. Life on a ranch was a far cry from a story in a book, she feared.

The bed beneath her was large, the biggest in the house, its mattress the very one Cord's mother had slept upon. Here she had known her husband's touch, had borne her sons and finally drawn her last breath.

In this room Marietta and Harvey McPherson had conducted a marriage. Empty for six years, only now had it been opened up and aired out, prepared for Cord and his bride. Rachel had sensed a certain reluctance in Cord as he told her of his decision to move their belongings into this room. So seldom did he speak of his father, she wondered at it.

Now his footsteps in the hallway alerted her to his presence and she drew in a quick breath, watching the doorknob as she waited for his entrance. A knock announced him and then the handle turned and he opened the door a crack.

"Rachel? Can I come in?"

"Yes, certainly." She snatched up a pillow from his side of the bed and held it tightly across her chest, wrapping her arms around it. In the doing, her legs straightened and the hem of her nightgown crept up, exposing her legs almost to the knees.

Her gaze met that of the man entering the room and she reached to tug at the shirttail hem of her gown. He smiled, his eyes shifting to her efforts as he closed the door behind himself.

"I've seen feet before, Rachel. Yours don't scare me one bit." His fingers were busy undoing the buttons of his shirt as he spoke, and he tugged it free. His trousers sagged against his hips, the top buttons undone, and she caught a glimpse of cream-colored underwear beneath the gray worsted material of his best pair of pants.

"I've had this nightgown for a couple of years, Cord. It shrank, and it's too short."

"Guess that's a matter of opinion," he said, his gaze slanting again to her rounded calves and narrow feet.

Sitting on the chair, he lifted one foot to rest on the other knee, and tugged at his boot. His grunt of effort did the trick and the boot released its suction on his foot. He lifted the other foot to repeat the process.

"Maybe we need to buy you a new gown next time we go into town."

"From Conrad?" Her cheeks grew pink as she considered the idea of such a thing. "Maybe I could just get some material and make a new one," Rachel said, trying to look anywhere but at the man who was undressing in front of her.

"That'd work, I guess," he said agreeably, freeing himself of the white shirt he'd worn all day. "But when you're going to find time to do much sewing is beyond me."

His chest was exposed, the dark hair a curling cover for muscles and flesh, and she lowered her gaze to the bed, her mouth suddenly dry.

The coverlet she'd carefully folded at the foot of the big bed caught her eye. "The quilt is lovely, Cord. Did your mother make it?"

"Probably. She used to have the quilting frames set up in the parlor in the wintertime. She'd sit in there in the evenings." His shirt was deposited on the chair behind him, and he paused, his hands stilling at the waist of his trousers.

"Rachel, do you want me to turn out the light before I get out of the rest of my clothes?"

"All of them?" She reached to pull the sheet up over herself, her gaze intent on the action.

"Rachel, we're married. I don't sleep in my clothes when I'm alone. I'm sure as hell not going to keep them on when I've got my wife in bed waiting for me."

"I think you'd better turn out the light, Cord." Scooting down in the bed, she placed his pillow back on the other side of the bed and, beneath the sheet, edged her nightgown down around her body.

Cord stepped to the dresser, turning down the wick on the kerosene lamp before he blew it out. The flame died, leaving him dependent on the moonlight coming through the windows to make his way to bed.

"You got room for me in there, Rae?" The bed dipped as his big body covered the middle of the mattress. He turned to his side, reaching for her, and Rachel found herself gathered against him, his arms enclosing her.

"You sure feel good, honey." His murmur of satisfaction breathed against her forehead as he formed her soft curves to the hard length of his body. Beneath her toes, she felt the hardness of his shins, cushioned by a softly curling layer of hair.

Against her belly his manhood stirred, and she shifted away, but his arms allowed her little room to maneuver.

His body was solid, firm against her, and his scent was tinged with a musky aroma that blended with his shaving soap. Burrowing her nose against his throat, she inhaled the essence of him, her eyes closing.

Without conscious thought, her lips pressed against the vulnerable flesh beneath his jaw and she nuzzled there. He shivered and his chuckle vibrated against her mouth.

"Sweetheart, do that some more, why don't you?" His whisper coaxed her and he tilted his head a bit to peer at her in the pale moon glow that flooded the room from the window. "You might want to work your way up, kinda next to my ear and across my face."

She stilled. "I don't want you to think I'm being too forward."

He squeezed her, a gentle tightening of his arms. "Not on your life, honey. You can be just as forward as you want. If you like kissing me, we're gonna get along just fine."

"You smell good," she whispered, her mouth brushing against the beginning of his morning beard.

His groan was muffled as he turned his head and captured her mouth. "Not near as good as you do, Rae. I can still smell the honeysuckle in your hair." His lips brushed against hers as he spoke and he turned her to her back, leaning over her on one elbow.

"Rachel, do you know what goes on in the marriage bed?" Hope laced his words and she peered at him in the near darkness.

"My mother told me..." How could she speak the words her mother had so haltingly uttered? She felt her cheeks burn as she explained a woman's place in her husband's bed.

"She said I must submit to my husband and do my duty as a wife."

His sigh was accompanied by a slow shake of his head and he bent to place a soft kiss against her forehead. "I don't want you to submit to me, Rachel. I'm not going to force you to do anything you don't want to."

"It all sounded pretty painful, the way she..."

His lips moved down the length of her nose to brush across her mouth as she spoke. "I guess it usually hurts the first time, honey. But there's some pleasure that goes along with it." His hand moved to the front of her nightgown and his fingers made short work of the buttons.

She looked down at what he did, watched as he opened wide the bodice of her gown, his hands dark against her pale skin. And then she gasped as he enclosed her breast within his long fingers, squeezing it gently, as if he measured its firm weight.

"Damn, you're a lot of woman, Rae," he muttered, bending to press his open mouth against her flesh. She felt the tip of his tongue, barely touching her skin, and then his hand moved and his mouth captured the crest, forming it with his teeth and tongue.

She drew in a breath, stunned at the shivering delight of his caress. "Cord, my mother didn't tell me about this."

He released his hold, chuckling as he nuzzled her, rubbing his cheek against her and moving to the other breast. "I'm glad, honey. I'd rather have you find it out this way." His fingers were gentle as he cupped her, his mouth careful as he suckled at the tender flesh.

She was lost in the magic, her hands seeking purchase in his hair, her hips moving against the bed as his mouth and hands brought pleasure to her awakening body.

He murmured small phrases against her skin, spreading an array of kisses against her plush curves as he wooed her to his will.

She heard the words, soft, coaxing her to comply, and then he lifted her, and she was aware of her gown falling to the floor beside the bed. His hands were firm but gentle, his fingers clever, enticing her to move against their coaxing touches.

Her hands rose to spread across the width of his shoulders. Beneath her fingertips his skin lay taut over the muscles of his arms, like satin covering steel.

And then her hands brushed lower, across the width of his back, and she felt the scarred flesh. Her breath caught in her throat as she sensed for a moment the pain of that scarring and she clasped him tighter to herself, as if her arms could give ease to the memory he bore.

"Rachel…" It was a groan of need, so great he could only express it in the calling of her name, and she responded, opening to him, her body rising to accept his.

He was gentle, taking her with care, then straining above her in the darkness, his manhood seeking the hot depths within her woman's flesh.

She cried out softly, shifting beneath him, her breath taken by the sensation of fullness, the quick, sharp tearing of her maidenhead. Scarcely had the sound of her distress left her throat, barely had she smothered the whisper of his name, before he held himself still, pulsing within her.

"Rachel? I'm sorry, honey. I'm sorry." Like a blanket of male flesh and bones, he covered her, his hands clasping her face. Bending to shower kisses against her cheeks and forehead, he shivered, the tension of his body telling her of the barely restrained force of his need, and she gripped him more tightly in her arms.

He'd possessed her, yet there had been no submission, only a sharing of herself with the man who had chosen her as his bride. A sense of pride filled her, replacing the almost forgotten pain of his taking, and she moved against him.

"It's all right, Cord. It just hurt for a bit." Her lips opened to him, returning his kisses, her tongue meeting and tangling with his. He groaned his pleasure, his body clenching, rising and falling again as he moved against her.

"Lift to me, honey," he coaxed. "There, like that." His hands were gentle but firm, moving the length of her body. He touched her knowingly, caressing her, bringing tingling warmth to her willing flesh, his fingers agile as he led her to the knowledge of her own desire.

He captured her cries of delight in his mouth, muffling the sounds with murmurs of praise, luring her within reach of a pleasure so intense she could only gasp his name.

And then she was there, her entire being singing with the enchantment. Her fingers clenched against his skin, her body rose to his and she was flung beyond the boundaries of her existence, aware only of the ecstasy of his touch, the presence of his manhood within her and the total consuming power of his possession.

"Was it like your mama said it would be?" Cord lay in his marriage bed, his satisfaction apparent in the tone of this voice. Rachel's head lay on his shoulder, her arm resting on his chest, her fingers combing the dense curls there. She murmured a denial against his skin.

"Better or worse?" he persisted, relishing her weariness, well pleased with the woman he held.

Her fingers tangled in the curls and tugged smartly. "A little better. Maybe."

"Ouch! That's taking advantage, Mrs. McPherson." His hand grasped hers and he drew it to his mouth, suckling her index finger. "You better watch out. I just might…"

She moved her head and her mouth touched him, taking the flat male nipple between her lips. Her teeth threatened his vulnerable flesh and a chuckle was born, deep within her throat.

"Are we playin' here, honey? Or is this for real?" If she only knew how difficult it had been to consider himself well off after the loving. He'd stifled the urge to coax her into a second blending of their bodies, knowing how tender she must be, how wearying the events of the day had been.

"Am I being too forward again?" Her mouth released him and she peered at his face in the dim light of the moon coming through the window. She moved against him, her breasts a soft weight on his chest.

"I thought you were too tired for any more lovin' tonight," he said, subduing his body's immediate reaction to her movements.

"Only if you're planning on a big breakfast," she said after a moment's consideration. "I just might put the pillow over my head when the rooster crows."

His fingers slid up from the nape of her neck, threading through the heavy weight of dark hair, to draw her face down, until their lips almost touched. "I suspect there's enough leftover cake and pie to do me. We'll make a pot of coffee and let it be every man for himself."

She laughed, a silvery sound that pleased him. She'd been more than he had ever expected, more willing than he'd any right to hope for. Taking a virgin was new territory for him. Not that he'd been a ladies' man, but he'd made his share of conquests over the years.

Yet the joy he'd found with the woman he held filled him with delight. She was warm and loving, eager to please, her slender form offering more pleasure than he'd dreamed of.

And she was his.

"Lorena said she'd cook breakfast in the morning," Rachel whispered. "It'll probably take me an hour to get the nerve to go downstairs anyway."

"Why?" He tugged at her curls, marveling at the way they clung to his callused fingers.

"I'm afraid the men will look at me...and I'm going

to blush. They're going to know what we've done to-night.''

"They care about you, Rachel. They're not gonna do anything to embarrass you.''

She sighed, a wistful sound. "All right.''

He waited for a few moments. "All right, what?''

"All right, we can…you know…do that again. If you want to.''

He laughed aloud and her hand flew to his mouth, muffling the sound. "Hush, Cord! Everyone will hear you.''

He shook his head and moved her hand with ease. "Then they'll know for sure I'm happy, won't they?'' His body rolled against her and atop her with a single movement. He wiggled a space for himself between her legs, allowing her to feel the burgeoning thrust of his arousal.

His groan of pleasure was deep, and he smothered it against her throat, inhaling the fresh scent of her skin.

Damn, she was sweet.

Chapter Eleven

"I don't want that woman standing over me!" Jake's booming ultimatum resounded down the wide hallway.

"Then take care of yourself, Jake. I suspect you could do a lot more of it if you wanted to. You're lucky Rena's willing, 'cause it's for sure I haven't got the time to spend in here every day." Cord's answer was firm, promising no retreat.

"She's all you've got, Jake. Sam's about had enough of you. He told me you can pretty well do for yourself, if you want to. Anyway, he says takin' care of you is a woman's job, and he's busy with keepin' an eye on Rachel's brothers and working in the barn."

"How about Rachel?" Jake's glance beneath lowering brows was swift, his mouth drawn into a knowing semblance of a smile.

"You're not having Rachel at your beck and call." There was no room for argument here, Cord decided. "Rena has agreed to look after your needs, and part of that includes helpin' you wash up. You're making a fuss over nothing."

"Nothing?" Jake's jaw set stubbornly and he moved his chair to the window, pulling aside the curtain to look out. "You're only half owner here, Cord. I say we put an ad in one of the big city papers, see if we can find a male attendant who'd be willing to come here and do for me."

"What's wrong with Rena?" The question was casually spoken, but Cord felt the tightening of his muscles as he prepared for the battle that was to come.

"Nothing in particular," Jake answered, swinging the chair around to face his brother. "She'll make a good rancher's wife…if she ever gives up here and trots on back home where she belongs."

Cord's mouth twitched, but he subdued the smile. "She seems to think there's a place for her here."

"I don't want her."

"No? I'd say just the opposite."

Jake's eyes flashed a warning. "Don't be trying to second-guess me, brother. My days of yearning for a bit of fluff are long over."

"Lorena Claypool is no bit of fluff, not by a long shot."

Jake's rebuttal was a growl of admonition. "Then don't push her at me as if she were."

"I'm no one's 'bit of fluff,'" Lorena said from the doorway. "Good morning, Cord."

Cord's head dipped in a nod. "Sorry you heard all that, Rena. Jake's a bit ornery this morning. He says he's not gonna wash up with you around."

"It's a pity all that hot water will go to waste then," she said cheerfully.

"I'll do my own washing up," Jake said, his gaze a dark weapon as he glared at the woman who watched him with serene eyes.

Lorena lifted the pail she'd carried from the kitchen. "Fine. Just pretend I'm a man from the big city, totin' your water to you, then," she said with a grin, pouring warm water into Jake's china basin. She reached beneath the low commode, pulling out a clean towel and washing rag.

The rolling chair nudged her legs as she dampened the cloth and soaped it thoroughly. "I won't be long here. If I start with your back, you can finish while I get your breakfast, Jake." She turned to look at him, locked in place by the presence of his footrest. "Take off your shirt."

"Damned if I will!" he roared. "You're not making a whipped puppy out of me, Lorena Claypool."

Her eyes scanned him, the broad shoulders, the muscled biceps straining at his shirtsleeves, the proud head and the strong line of his jaw.

"You sure don't look much like any kind of puppy to me, Jake McPherson," she said quietly. "I'd say more like a man ready to have a knock-down-drag-out fight."

"A man? Half a man, maybe," he growled.

"Why don't you let me be the judge of that. Take off your shirt."

It was a challenge, issued for the second time, and he reached for her, dragging her against his chair, his arms holding the strength of any two men as he subdued her.

Disheveled and wide-eyed, she was deposited on his lap, and he held her there with his wide palms clutching her waist.

"Now, since you're so all-fired determined to see a man's naked chest, just be my guest," Jake growled, his nostrils flaring with the effort he'd expended.

Lorena brushed a lock of hair from her face, looking more pleased than upset by the turn of events. She glanced over her shoulder at Cord, lounging in the doorway, barely able to contain his laughter.

"Jake's about to take a bath, Cord. You might want to leave now."

Even as she spoke, her fingers set to work, undoing the buttons that ran down the front of the shirt in question.

He'd started this nonsense, pulling her onto his lap and now he couldn't think how to call a halt.

"You think you're so almighty smart, Lorena." Jake's fingers tightened their hold on her as he fought for a semblance of dignity. The fool woman was about to strip him out of his clothing, and he was sitting here like a dolt, allowing it.

Enjoying it, as a matter of fact. And at that thought, he shot her a glance of warning. She was rapt, absorbed in what she did, her cheeks pink from the exertion of the physical encounter. Perhaps from more than that.

"You're not wearing an undershirt," she said, slanting him a look of surprise.

"It's too damn hot." His growled rebuttal made her smile.

Sliding her hands beneath the garment he wore, she forced the soft fabric down his arms, until he either had to let loose of her middle and slide from the sleeves or be held captive by the blamed things.

He dropped his hands, and within seconds he was bare to the waist, inches from a slender, more than fetching woman, who was eyeing him with admiration.

"I only planned on washing your back, Jake, but since I'm here, I might as well do the front, too," she said amiably. Reaching to the commode, she snatched up the soapy cloth and set to with a will.

He shivered. "Your warm water is cold."

"Your fault, not mine," she reminded him, reaching over his shoulder to scrub at the nape of his neck.

"I've been washing my own chest for years. Get off my lap, Rena." A ripple of sensation up his spine could not be blamed solely on cool water, but more likely on the woman balanced across the stumps of his legs.

"Help me," she said, lifting her hands to offer him full view of her waist.

The lure of her feminine curves was almost more than he could resist. Clinging to her breasts, her soft muslin dress outlined their fullness in faithful measure. His mouth went dry as he allowed his thoughts to consider their size and shape, and then he shook his head.

His hands gripped her, lifting her to her feet at his side, holding her until she found her balance.

Without a moment's pause, she leaned over him, taking up the cloth she'd left draped around his neck. "I'll warm this up."

In moments, she was scrubbing at his back and Jake leaned forward, allowing her access. She rinsed, then rinsed again. The towel was rough against his flesh, and he flexed his shoulders.

"Wait a minute. Don't lean back yet," she said. "I've got some lotion I want to put on your skin."

"I'm not interested in smelling like a flower garden."

She drew the small bottle from her pocket. "You won't. I made it up from oil and glycerine." Her hands were strong, warm against his flesh, and he inhaled sharply as she moved them firmly down the length of his back.

The pleasure of her touch had been locked away, forbidden to his mind for years, and now, for the second time in a matter of weeks, he was filled with myriad visions behind his closed eyelids.

Just so had she rubbed the soreness from his muscles after a day spent in the corral, breaking horses for sale to the government. Just so had her hands sped warmth and relief to his shoulders after hours of bending over his desk, making painstaking entries into the ledger book.

Just so had her hands spent their strength against the width of his back as she responded to the force of his passion, her mouth answering his with a desire he'd been sorely tempted to take advantage of, those long-ago days.

And now there was no barrier of fabric between hand and skin. Now she leaned against his shoulder and he felt the weight of her breast pressing his upper arm.

"That's enough!" He straightened quickly and she squealed a protest, snatching her hands from him just before they would have been squeezed against the caned back of his chair.

"All right, you can finish up your arms and chest." She soaped the cloth and handed it to him. "After breakfast, you can get your pants off and do your legs."

"Not with you around."

She turned to the door, as if his quiet protest had been unheard. "I'll bring your breakfast in just a few minutes."

"Get me out a shirt."

Silently, she did as he asked, dropping it in his lap, and then he heard the door close behind her.

His hands moved more slowly, washing his arms. He rinsed with care, cursing himself beneath his breath. She'd dug beneath his defenses, routed out his weakness and exposed his needy soul.

He'd vowed a long time ago to live without the warmth of a woman in his life, once he'd had a good look at what was left of his legs. And now Lorena Claypool seemed determined to sear him with her heat. Heat that threatened to melt the icy barrier he'd constructed around his heart.

"I hear tell there's a move afoot to bring civilization to Green Rapids." Conrad Carson spoke to the man before him, but his words carried the length of the emporium, reaching Rachel as she entered the door.

"How's that?" the rancher asked, drawing his purse from his back pocket.

Conrad's pencil was busy as he added the figures he'd scribbled on a piece of brown paper. "Somebody seems to think our town needs a theater, an opera house, I heard tell." He straightened. "That'll be six dollars even, Beau. You can put it on your bill, if you want to."

The rancher shook his head. "I'd rather pay up front, cash money, Conrad."

"I'll help you carry out the rest of your groceries," Conrad offered, hoisting a box to his shoulder. He turned and his gaze met Rachel's. She'd come halfway down the wide aisle in the center of his store and halted, lest she eavesdrop any more than she already had.

"I'll be with you in a few minutes, Mrs. McPherson." Conrad nodded politely at her, a faint flush riding his cheekbones. His eyes had veered from contact with her, and he made his way down another aisle, as if anxious to complete his task.

The rancher turned to look at her, his eyes admiring. He swept his hat from his head and nodded. "Mrs. McPherson? I heard old Cord tied the knot. I'm one of your neighbors. Beau Jackson. I live out past you a few miles."

"How do you do?" She was blushing. Sure as the world, she could feel the heat creeping up her face.

Would the day never come when she'd get used to the looks of speculation?

Church on Sunday had been one after another of well-meaning folks singling her out. Coy glances from the younger women, sidelong looks from the male part of the congregation and beaming smiles of approval from the older ladies had sufficed only to make the service seem endless.

Rachel sighed, bracing for more of the same from this stranger, but he surprised her. With a smile, he settled his hat firmly on his head and picked up the keg of nails he'd just purchased. "Good day, ma'am." Beyond him, Conrad was holding the door open for his exit, and Rachel waited as the storekeeper made his way in her direction.

"You needing groceries?" he asked, fussing with an assortment of buttons in a jar.

"Yes. I have a list, Con…Mr. Carson." Her blush deepened as she dithered over his name.

He looked up, his smile strained. "We need to decide what we're going to do with the friendship we had, Rachel."

"Did you spread rumors about me after the dance?" she asked quietly. "Wilhelmina Bryant came out to the ranch and said I was the subject of a lot of talk around town."

His cheeks bloomed with color. "I told a couple of the men that I'd asked you to allow me courting privileges. The talk was already hot and heavy, with you staying out at Cord's place." He looked at her directly. "You set the place on its ear, Rachel, with that pretty dress you wore, and what with dancing every dance."

"I didn't do anything wrong!" she protested.

He shook his head. "I know you didn't, but a pretty

girl is always food for gossip in a small town. Especially one who's living in the situation you were in.''

"I thought you might have been angry with me, Conrad. I was afraid you might have started rumors.''

"No." He had the grace to look shamefaced. "Some of the boys spiked the punch and I drank a few too many glasses. I was bragging a little about calling on you, telling them I was planning on marrying you.''

He looked directly into her eyes. "I meant every word, Rachel. I would have married you in a heartbeat.''

"Thank you," she said, her woman's heart pleased by his confession. "Let's be friends, Conrad. I didn't mean to hurt you in any way. It all worked out for the best, for me and Cord, I mean. I just hated it that people were talking.''

He shrugged. "People always talk. It's what they do best, I guess.''

"What did I overhear about an opera house in Green Rapids? Is that for sure? Or more rumor?''

"They tell me that three men came in from New York City the other day. They're trying to set up a string of theaters between St. Louis and the edge of civilization, so to speak. There's to be a troupe of players making the rounds among them, with folks from hereabouts providing entertainment during the lull between professional performances.''

"Is there any talent around here?''

"I don't know for sure, but folks are sure talkin' it up.'' He looked toward the door. "Is Cord in town with you?''

"Yes, he's gone to the blacksmith.'' She dug into her bag for the grocery list she'd scribbled on the way to town. "I'll give you my list.'' It almost covered the back of an envelope, and she began from the top. "I need coffee and sugar, a pail of lard, any fresh vegetables you've got...." She paused. "Oh, my…" They'd hit a bump while she was writing the next item, and she couldn't make it out.

"Looks like cinnamon to me," said the whisper in her ear.

She spun about. Cord was there, almost behind her, one hip resting against the walnut counter. "I didn't hear you come in," she said, one hand at her throat.

"That's 'cause you were all involved with Conrad."

"We were talking about a new venture in town."

Conrad had busied himself, dipping his scoop into a bin against the wall, measuring coffee in a cloth bag. "How many pounds you want, Rachel?" he asked.

"Ten. And a twenty-pound bucket of lard." She looked up at Cord. "Are you finished at the blacksmith shop already?"

He nodded. "I just had to pick up some nails for Sam and a set of smaller shoes for Jay's new horse."

Conrad hoisted the bucket of lard atop the counter and placed the bag of coffee beans beside it. "I've got fresh green beans, Rachel, and some tomatoes. Peas are about done for."

"I canned up enough peas," she told him. "The men aren't real fond of them, anyway. Give me all the green beans you can spare and a peck of tomatoes. When they come in real good, I'll take four or five bushel."

Cord snatched her list from her hand and handed it to the man behind the counter. "Tell you what, Conrad. Why don't you just go ahead and fill her list and stick everything in the back of the wagon, while I take my wife down to the hotel for a cup of tea."

Rachel's cheeks flushed with pleasure, and her smile was thanks in itself, Cord decided, escorting her out the door. That scamp, Conrad, had spent long enough making calf eyes at her anyway.

"What brought this on?" Rachel asked, stepping briskly beside him down the wooden sidewalk.

He covered her hand with his, holding it in place on his forearm as they walked. "I figured Conrad had your company long enough. Besides, I wanted to show off my bride."

She made a sound of aggravation in her throat, looking down at the dusty boards beneath her feet. "Conrad and I made friends, Cord. We can't live in the same town and be looking the other way when we meet, just because I turned him down. He's a nice man."

"Well, that nice man needs to find himself a girl of his own. This one's taken." His words sounded possessive even to his own ear, and he emphasized them with a firm hand against her back as they entered the hotel lobby.

Rachel looked around the big dining room apprehensively. "It looks pretty full."

A buxom waitress approached and smiled a greeting, then led them to a table before the front window. Cord seated Rachel with a flourish. "There you go, Mrs. McPherson."

He turned to the waitress, who was eyeing him with admiration. "We'd like some coffee and a big piece of black walnut cake."

"Both of you?" Her pencil poised over her pad, she looked at Rachel.

Rachel's nod was absentminded. "Yes, cake's fine."

Cord bent across the table. "It's only the best black walnut cake in the state."

"Well, I'll be sure to give my opinion when I taste it. Mine isn't too bad."

He looked pained. "How would I know?"

She glanced around from beneath her lashes. "People are looking, Cord."

"They're smiling at us, Rachel. This is your first trip to town since the wedding. Everyone's curious. By next week, we'll be old news."

"Oh!" She straightened in her chair. "I almost forgot, speaking of news."

"Somebody else getting married?" he asked, smiling at her abrupt announcement.

She shook her head impatiently. "No, of course not. It's just that Conrad was talking to a neighbor of yours about a new venture some people from New York are working on." She leaned back in her chair and smiled with open delight. "It seems that they are considering Green Rapids for one of the opera houses or theaters they're building."

"Here?" His tone was incredulous.

"Why not?" She eyed him cautiously, taken aback by his disbelief. And then as if recovering her aplomb, she tilted her chin. "I'd think it would add a lot to the town, bring people in from all around. I'll warrant you'd find new businesses opening in no time at all."

"Like what?"

She considered. "Maybe a new dress shop. Perhaps another hotel. Certainly a parlor for ice cream and—"

"Folks make their own ice cream at home."

She looked at him, fluttering her lashes in a broad attempt at flirtation. "You wouldn't take your bride for ice cream if such a place opened up on Main Street?"

"Damn, Rachel, I'd carry you to St. Louis on my back if you coaxed me like that."

"Cord! Don't be so…"

"Sweetheart, I find it hard not to be so…" He lifted

an eyebrow and grinned. "In fact, just looking at you gives me all sorts of ideas."

"Well, save it until you get home, at least," she retorted, her mouth pursing.

"See there? Now you've got your lips all scrunched up, and I'd swear you were just beggin' me to lean across the table and—"

"Your cake, sir?" The waitress was there, tray in hand, her amusement obvious as she smiled at Cord. With a flourish, she placed his cake before him, then served Rachel.

"Will you be wanting anything else?" she asked, her lips twitching as if she was subduing laughter.

Rachel's gaze was focused on the cake before her and she shook her head. "No, thank you."

"I've got everything I need, ma'am," Cord responded, ignoring the cake, gazing instead with hungry eyes at his wife.

"It was good cake, Cord." From behind the screen in the corner of their bedroom, Rachel donned her new nightgown.

"Best in the state," he said agreeably. Sitting erect, his back propped against the headboard, he awaited her appearance. "You about done back there, Rae?"

"This gown doesn't have much to it," she said, emerging as she cast a glance over her shoulder at the mirror behind her.

"That's why I bought it." He lifted his arms, meshing his fingers behind his head. "I sure do have good taste, honey."

Her fingers plucked pins from her hair as she released the heavy weight from atop her head. It fell in a coil down her back and she shook her head, sending it flying as the strands were released from captivity. Hairbrush in her hand, she bent over to bring order to the wavy length.

"Come here and let me do that," Cord said, his lids heavy as he watched her movements.

She straightened, brush in hand, her hair a tousled frame for her face. She was golden from the sun, a flush like that of a ripe peach staining her cheeks. Her eyes sparkled with humor, blue as the columbine in the meadow.

"That's too good an offer to refuse." She sauntered. There was no other word to describe the motion of her hips, he decided. In less than six paces she had brought him to arousal, her form almost visible beneath the gauzy nightgown.

"You're teasing me, Mrs. McPherson," he murmured. And then as she stood beside the bed, he widened his legs, making room, his hand reaching for her, lifting her.

Her fingers were warm within his palm as she knelt at the edge of the mattress, easing her way to sit on her heels in the place he offered. He released her, and her fingers brushed reluctantly against his callused skin, as if she delayed the loss of his touch.

With precise movements, his hands reached again, his palms spreading over her thighs, just above her knees. "I'll brush your hair later," he told her, willing to promise the moon if need be.

Beneath his work-roughened skin she was soft, yet firm to the touch, and his fingers curved to fit the bend of her knees. They slid back and forth, like ten clever entities, ever rising, causing the filmy gown to slide upward with each movement.

And then he'd attained his goal. His fingertips were

beneath the delicate fabric, sliding around to the back of her thighs and he drew her upward to kneel before him.

She inhaled sharply, her eyes narrowing as she allowed the intimacy, and as if she'd drawn in enough air to suffice for a time, she ceased to breathe. His hands moved higher, barely skimming the lush curves of her bottom, fingers pressing against the tender skin.

And then he caught his breath, his eyes narrowing as he savored the delicate flesh, brushing callused fingertips where only his touch had trespassed. Her head fell back, her breath exhaling audibly, and she trembled, swaying before him.

"Come to me." His whisper was taut, as filled with demand as was the arousal he made no attempt to hide from her. He was naked beneath the sheet, exposed and vulnerable, and she knelt before him, as beguiling and as delicately made as a vestal virgin in the temples of old.

Temptation, formed in the flesh and blood of a woman, but no longer virgin flesh, no longer bound by the bonds of innocence. She looked down at him and her lips parted, pink and damp, her nostrils flaring with each breath she took, her eyes shimmering with the fire of remembered ecstasy.

Her gaze traveled from his, her mouth trembling as she pulled aside the sheet, looking fully upon his manhood. She smiled, a knowing, intimate caress of her eyes that brought new life to the already burgeoning member.

"Come to me." Urgency threaded the words, and he tugged gently on her hand.

"Yes…" It was consent to his need, and yet there was in her no degree of subservience, no trace of submission to a greater will than her own. She bent forward, her hands resting upon his shoulders as she met his lips in a kiss that sealed her response.

"Yes." She repeated the word and it was more than permission to do as he pleased. More than a promise to fulfill his need. Submissive to his hands upon her legs, she let him lift her, fitting her astride. She felt the sheer fabric of her gown tugged from between their bodies, and lifted her arms high to permit its removal. And then shivered as he penetrated the depths of her womanhood.

"Rachel! Rachel!" Like a chanted refrain, he spoke her name, his head back, his eyes closed, teeth clenched against the pleasure she brought him.

She rose on her knees and he gripped her tightly, his fingers pressing without caution against her hips. With indelicate haste, he urged her to enclose him once more in her depths and she allowed it, her small bubble of laughter echoing in the throbbing of his heartbeat.

Again she lifted herself from him, slowly, leaving him bereft as his yearning body strained upward. And again, he pressed her to contain his manhood.

"Rachel!" It was a groan of need, his heart pumping his life's blood in a frantic pace.

"I love you." Almost, he failed to hear the words, and he stilled.

"I love you," she repeated, the whispered vow unmistakable, as she took the full portion of his male self into her depths. Once more her vow escaped on a sigh.

"I love you."

Chapter Twelve

"That dust rag isn't doin' much good just layin' there next to you."

Spoken in a low growl, the words brought a smile to Rachel's lips. She ducked her head as she played the final notes of the song she'd been humming all morning. Reverently, her hands closed the lid of the piano and she picked up the cloth from the seat beside her.

"Who put you in charge of the household servants?" she asked, working at the thin layer of dust on the music rack.

"I hired the cook and the wash lady, and seems to me you look a whole lot like both of them."

There was in Cord's voice a teasing lilt she'd seldom heard and her hands stilled in their task. His presence warm against her back, Rachel leaned her head against his shirtfront.

"I wish..." She laughed softly and closed her eyes. "No, I don't either."

"Now how can I make your wishes come true if I don't even know what they are?" he asked, his hands clasping her shoulders.

"I was going to wish for more time to play the piano,

but then I decided that if I could play it any time I wanted to, it wouldn't give me that pleasure to look forward to.''

He bent low over her, his face against the side of her throat, his mouth pressing damp kisses against the soft skin. ''Maybe I ought to hire somebody else to live in and give you and Rena a hand with the heavy work. We should be able to swing the expense.''

''Should I be more careful what I spend at the emporium, Cord? I try not to waste any money.'' The vision of four new dresses she and Lorena had made in the past week loomed in her mind. ''You've spent a lot on me and the boys.''

''You haven't taken a paycheck from me since we got married, Rachel. I had to figure out something to do with the money.''

''Oh, you…'' She turned on the bench and smiled up at him. ''You know I couldn't take wages for doing a wife's work.''

He rocked back on his heels. ''Seems to me you were better off just working here as household help. At least you had some change to rattle around in that little old purse of yours.''

She slid from the piano bench and stood. ''You've given me more than I ever hoped to have, Cord. I have a home and a family all around me, and I can put down roots here for me and my children.''

He tilted his head, his brow quirking a bit. ''Children? Is there something you need to tell me?''

She shook her head. ''No, of course not. I've just been thinking about the future a little. About having a family. Your daddy must have planned on a whole slew of young'uns when he had this house built. There are enough bedrooms upstairs for a half dozen or so, if we double them up a bit.''

His grip tightened, then slid the length of her arms to lock his fingers with hers. "You really mean that, don't you? You're willing to fill those bedrooms with my sons and daughters?"

She nodded, meeting his gaze, wondering at the emotion that drew his mouth into a firm line. His jaw clenched and his eyes narrowed as he tugged her against him. His hands released her fingers and his arms surrounded her.

"Rachel!" He called her name in a whispered growl that pierced her, a sound that brought tears to her eyes. He held her fiercely, his head bent to her, and she tilted her chin upward, seeking to meet his gaze.

"Cord? Did you think I wouldn't want to have your children? Are you surprised that I..."

His mouth halted the words she spoke, and his groan was one of fulfillment as he lifted her in his arms, forming her to the muscular length of his body. His lips took what she offered, nibbling at the softness of her mouth, his tongue edging its way in a delicate foray past the edges of her teeth.

It was a gentle invasion, and she wrapped her arms around his neck, clinging to his greater strength. His arms gripped her firmly, one beneath her bottom, the other across her back. A flush of desire warmed her, his scent feeding the flame of her need, and she inhaled the musky, male aura of the man she loved.

"Cord?" It was a question without form, only the calling of his name, the essence of her need alive in the speaking of that lone syllable.

He shuddered and his arms released their hold, allowing her to slide the length of him, his hands holding her firmly as she caught her balance. "I'm sorry, Rachel. I didn't mean to get so carried away. Maybe the idea of you carrying my baby..." He grinned, a crooked twist of his mouth. "Damn, the parlor's no place for this!"

His eyes scanned her face and he drew in a deep breath, his nostrils flaring with the effort. His voice was husky, his lips barely moving as he spoke. "You don't hold anything back, do you, honey?"

"Should I?" Her blush was fading, but the brilliance of her eyes and the shudder she could not control gave evidence of her desire for the man she'd married.

He shook his head. "No. I like you just the way you are, Rae. Honest as the day is long."

Her heart thumped more slowly, and her delight was dimmed by the words he spoke. He liked her. He liked her! He thought she was honest. And obviously, the love that had bloomed and grown to fullness within her heart was not matched by the emotion he was willing to bestow upon her.

"Cord..." She stepped back from him, her glance flitting to the open door. "I've got a pile of work to do this morning."

He grimaced. "And I'm keeping you from it."

It was an effort to smile, but she did. It was hard to look pleasant as she eased from his touch, but she managed. And when his fleeting kiss brushed against her mouth, she was the first to draw back from the caress.

"Get on outside," she said brightly, turning toward the mantel. "I've got to finish up in here before I put dinner on the table."

"I smelled sauerkraut when I came in."

She nodded. "I found some jars on the pantry shelf. I'm cooking it with a piece of pork."

"With new potatoes?" he asked hopefully.

She waved the dust cloth at him. "Go on, now. You'll

have plenty to eat.'' She looked at him and laughed aloud at his mock pleading, his grin coaxing her humor.

He backed toward the door and his gaze swept her from top to bottom. ''Hiring you was the best move I've ever made, ma'am.'' He was gone then, stepping quickly into the hallway, his boots noisy against the uncarpeted floor.

She finished quickly with her dusting, aware of the need for haste. Jake's room was no longer hers to worry about, Lorena having taken on the task. The double doors of the library were closed, and Rachel paused as she glanced that way.

Her playing the piano had brought about the sliding together of those tall doors, that was obvious. They'd been wide open when she began work in the parlor. If only...

There had to be a way. Somehow, in order to put his life together, Jake had to regain the joy he'd once found in music. Rachel shook her head. If only...

''We're gonna go up to the line shack with Sam, Rachel!''

Henry's joyful claim resounded from the kitchen walls, and his sister turned from the ironing board she'd set up on the backs of two chairs.

''Who's we?'' Her iron held in midair, she lifted her brows, awaiting his reply.

''Me and Jay, and a couple of others. Sam said we could ride pretty good and he'd take care of us, Rae.''

The excitement overflowed from the boy as he stood first on one foot, then the other. ''We need to take a blanket along and a clean shirt, Sam says.''

The screen door opened with a bang, and her younger

brother stepped across the sill. "Did you hear, Rae? Did you know we're gonna sleep—"

"I heard." She placed the iron back on the stove, picking up its mate. Licking her finger, she touched its surface, listening to the sizzle with a smile. A few swift passes over the ironing board took her attention and then she put the iron aside as she lifted the shirt.

"Is it all right?" Henry's voice quavered as he spoke.

For the past months they'd been within call or reach. Somehow, allowing the overnight trip was more difficult than it ought to be. She turned to the boy, forcing a smile to her lips.

"Yes, of course it's all right. I'm sure Sam will look after you both." She watched as the two children grinned their delight then fought for space as they shot back through the kitchen doorway onto the porch.

"We can go, Sam!" Jay shouted as he jumped to the ground, his legs pumping as his feet carried him toward the barn.

Henry turned back abruptly, the top step beneath his new boots. "Thanks, Rachel. We'll be good."

"I know you will," she managed. As if they were her own children, she released the strings that bound her to them. And they were, in reality, hers. Her responsibility, her only kin in this new life they were forming.

"Sam says we'll ride out after supper. He said to fix up a sack of bacon and coffee and beans and..." His youthful forehead wrinkled as the boy sought to remember the list he'd been entrusted with. "I think he said bread too, Rae."

"I'm sure he did," she answered, her mind busy with the supplies needed for such a venture. "Tell Sam I'll work on it as soon as I finish the ironing."

Supper was to be side pork and corn bread, along with

a kettle of green beans from the garden. They were the first pickings from the lush rows she'd tended with care. A burlap bag of sweet corn, fresh from the Claypools' place, had been dropped off early in the morning. Lorena had peeled for almost an hour, filling the biggest kettle and storing the rest in the pantry for the next day's dinner.

Within the hour the ironing board was stowed behind the pantry door. The pile of freshly folded shirts awaited their owners as Cord came in from the barn. With unerring aim, he came around the table, reaching his goal, his arms encircling Rachel's waist.

"The boys told you?"

She nodded. "I've got a box of things packed for their breakfast and enough for dinner, I think."

"Sam'll take care of them," he assured her.

"I know."

"You're worried already, aren't you?" He turned her in his arms, tipping her face upward with the palm of his hand.

"I can't help it, Cord. They're my responsibility."

"Mine, too," he reminded her. "And Sam will guard them with his life. Buck and Jamie are riding along. They're going to be mending fences and checking for strays we might have missed in the branding."

She shook her head impatiently. "I know they'll be fine. It's just hard for me…"

He tilted his head to one side. "Wanna hear something that'll please you?"

Her lips formed a pout. "You think I'm fussing for nothing, don't you?"

He watched her silently, and his gaze narrowed a bit as he focused on her mouth. "I think I'm gonna have to kiss that sour little look right off you in a minute."

"I'm not sour!" Her chin firmed as she shot him a warning glance. "What are you going to tell me?"

"I heard something from Cecil Hampton at the bank." He rocked on his heels and grinned widely. "Seems they're going to be breaking ground for a new building in town. The biggest Green Rapids has ever seen, in fact."

"The theater?" Her eyes widened as she caught a glimpse of his excitement.

"The very same." His smile was satisfied now. "Told you you'd be pleased."

"Who's to do the work?"

"They're sending in an architect fellow from New York to lay out the plans and another man to supervise things. They expect the townsfolk to supply half the labor."

"Like a barn raising?"

He nodded. "Sorta like that, only on a bigger scale. The fancy stuff inside will be shipped in from New York in a month or so, once the building is up."

"It's really going to happen!" Her whisper was hushed, her brow unfurrowed, as a smile of delight brightened her face. "Oh, Cord! Won't it be wonderful to have music and plays and everything, right here?"

"Not for a while, Rachel," he cautioned her. "It's going to take some time to get things rolling, I'm sure."

She shook her head impatiently. "I know! But, just think. By the fall, maybe. Or at least by Christmastime, we'll…"

"Uh, Mr. Hampton wants to talk to you, Rachel." Cord's words halted her excitement.

"Whatever for?" she asked.

He had the grace to look apologetic. "I told him you were pretty talented on the piano."

She shook her head. "You didn't! I'm just mediocre, Cord. Passable, maybe. My teacher back home said I had a nice touch, but I certainly don't have a tremendous amount of talent."

"Jake thinks you're good." As if that were the last word to be said on the subject, Cord folded his arms across his chest.

"He said that?"

Cord nodded.

"What does Mr. Hampton want with me?" Rachel pulled out a chair and sat down at the table.

"He said they'll be needing someone to help with practice, before the troupe of actors and performers comes into town. They want some locals with talent to put on performances, maybe do some short plays and such."

"I wish—" Rachel covered her mouth, her fingertips resting against her lips. She looked up at Cord, once more caught up in the misery that Jake McPherson lived with daily.

"What, Rae?" Cord sat across from her and reached for her other hand. "What do you wish, honey?"

"'If wishes were horses, then beggars would ride,'" she returned with barely concealed sadness.

"Jake?" he asked quietly.

She nodded. "I've said so many 'if onlys' about him, Cord. If only this and if only that, and it hasn't changed a thing. He closes the library door whenever I play the piano."

"He's come a long way. You don't know what he was like before you got here."

She laughed, a joyless sound. "I know what he was like the day after I arrived, though, and that was pretty much as bad as I ever want him to be." She considered their hands, clasped tightly in the middle of the table. "Do you think he and Lorena will ever…''

"I don't know. Maybe." He laughed aloud.

"Sounds about as certain as my opinion," she said, her mouth relaxing in a smile.

Supper was over and done with and the riders had headed out, Jay and Henry waving with enthusiasm. Rachel watched from the porch until the small caravan disappeared from sight, then drew a deep breath and turned toward the kitchen.

"I've got the dishes done up, Rachel. Why don't you just sit on the swing and rest for a while?" Lorena stood in the doorway, wiping her hands on a kitchen towel.

"How'd you talk Jake into coming to the table tonight?" Rachel asked. "He hasn't come out of that room for almost a week."

Lorena looked over her shoulder, then pushed the screen door open, stepping closer to where Rachel leaned against a porch pillar. "He just decided all on his own. It was right after you played this afternoon. He closed the door, just like he always does, but you can hear the music anyway, you know."

"Maybe I shouldn't play anymore, not if it's going to upset him that much."

"What he said was that you could use a little help with your timing and maybe he'd give you—" Lorena broke off, looking stricken. "I don't mean to offend you."

Rachel straightened, her mind spinning with the possibilities Lorena had presented. She waved her hand in a dismissive motion. "No, no… I'm not offended. Not at all. I was just thinking that if Jake was willing to help me, maybe he'd be willing to lend a hand in town when the theater is built.''

"What on earth are you talking about?" Lorena asked.

Rachel whirled from the railing, pacing to the end of the long porch and back. "Wait till I tell you, Rena. Cord just heard about it in town, from Cecil Hampton at the bank.''

"Need some help getting ready for bed, Jake?" Lorena stood in the doorway, her golden hair looking like a silken veil about her shoulders.

He'd have been willing to bet a five-dollar gold piece that she'd brushed it and left it loose for his benefit, Jake thought, turning his chair from the temptation she offered. "I can manage," he muttered, his fingers clenching as he resisted the urge to take her up on the offer.

The doors slid shut, a last rattle and then a soft click as they latched together. He drew in a breath, his eyes closing as he treasured, for just a moment, the image of golden hair and rounded curves. Lorena Claypool was edging her way back into his life, and he'd be damned if he let her take over.

"I'll just turn down the covers for you, Jake," she said quietly from behind him, and his eyelids snapped open, even as his chair spun, allowing him to face the intruder. She was bent over his bed, intent on sneaking around, even after he'd told her to leave.

"I can pull that sheet back myself," he growled. "When are you going to understand that I don't need a nursemaid, Lorena?"

She looked at him over her shoulder, and for just a moment he caught a flash of a hurt so deep, so ingrained, it almost brought him down. And then it was gone, and a patient, good-humored smile covered the glimpse of sadness he'd seen there.

"I have to earn my keep, Jake," she said cheerfully. Her hands plumped his pillows, and then she bent to place them just so, piling two on the side of the bed he slept on. She folded the sheet at the foot, leaving him room to swing from his chair to the mattress.

"You planning on undressing me, too?" he asked. "You haven't had a good look up close at the cripple, Rena. Is that what you're hangin' around for?"

She shook her head, the natural glow of her complexion fading at his words. "I'll do anything you need to have done, Jake. That's what I'm here for."

"Really?" He stopped the snail-like progress he'd made and leaned back. Bracing himself on one arm, he lifted his left leg, the material that had been tucked beneath falling to dangle loosely. Then he shifted and extended his right leg, making apparent the absence of flesh and bone just below the knee.

"You can help me undress, Lorena. Come on over here and undo my trousers. I'll get in bed and you can strip me naked, get a good look at the results of the surgeon's skill."

"Jake…" It was a whispered plea, uttered from lips gone white. As if her own limbs had lost their power to hold her erect, she sat down on the edge of the mattress, her hands limp in her lap.

"What?" His heart was pumping at a rapid pace and he moved the chair closer, moving his right leg up and down, the loose pant leg waving in an obscene dance.

"Don't you want to see what the war did to the great Jake McPherson? That man who was going to take you to Europe on his first tour of the Continent. Who was going to play on the concert stage in London…"

"Jake!" The sound of his name was a cry for mercy, and she fell from the side of the bed to kneel next to his chair. "Don't do this to yourself! Don't do this to me." She gripped his arm, bending to place her cheek where her fingers clenched against his flesh.

"Ah, damn!" His curse was a reproach of his own cruelty, and Jake shook his head as guilt enclosed him with dark tentacles. "Rena..." He covered her fingers with his right hand and bent low to brush his face against her head.

Her hair held the scent of sunshine and lilac soap, and he inhaled its essence, as if his lungs hungered for the sweetness she offered. "Rena."

She trembled, and his arm moved to enclose her shoulders. "Rena!" With an intensity that spoke of his deep regret, he whispered her name again and she lifted her face from its hiding place.

"Back up, Jake. I'll leave. Give me room, please."

"No." His hand touched her head, his fingers burrowing beneath the waves to cup the nape of her neck. "Look at me, Rena." As if he'd drawn the words from some deep well of agony, he groaned them aloud.

He gripped the heavy tresses and with a gradual tightening of his hand, tilted her head. She relaxed in his hold, allowing him the sight of her closed eyes, tears seeping from beneath heavy lids.

He bent, almost doubled over in the chair, his mouth touching the pale flesh of her cheek, taking the tears she shed between his lips, brushing her face with his, as if he would take her grief for his own.

"Jake, let me up. Let me leave. I won't bother you again. I promise." The words spilled from her lips, the tears flowed, and still he sought to halt the cascade of sorrow.

"Please, Rena. Come here. Let me sit near you." He tugged at her, his other hand tight around her shoulders, an awkward position that threw him off balance. "Damn, I can't do it, Rena. I can't lift you this way. I'm a miserable excuse for a man! You need someone who can…"

"Stop, please." Her eyes opened as he spoke and she shook her head, her entreaty halting his bitter words. Her whisper was so low, he strained to hear it. "I don't need anything or anyone but you, Jake McPherson. Why can't you understand that?" She blinked, forcing back the tears and swallowing as though she would gather her composure about her like a cloak.

"I'm not good enough for you, Rena. I can't earn a living or take care of you. I'm half a man, stuck in a chair for the rest of my life."

"How do you know what you can do?" The words gritted between her teeth, her voice trembling with the effort. "You're willing to stay in this room and call it quits, instead of…?"

She shook her head. "I don't know why I love you, Jake. I wish I didn't. I truly wish I could walk away and forget you and never look back."

"It'd probably be the smartest thing you ever did," he muttered darkly, his hand lifting to brush golden wisps of hair from her tearstained cheek.

Her jaw clenched against the fresh tears she refused to shed, and her whisper was bleak in the stillness of the room.

"Are you going to let me? Are you going to watch me walk away, Jake McPherson?"

Chapter Thirteen

"Not on your life." Jake's jaw hardened, his teeth clenching so tightly, he felt they would surely crack from the strain. What he was about to ask of this woman was more than he had a right to demand. And yet, without her full knowledge of the ruination of his body, their lives were at a standstill.

If she lacked the strength to face his scars, and the terrible sight of his butchered flesh, he would lose her. In a final rending of his heart, he would turn his back on the joy he might have found with Lorena Claypool.

Backing the chair from the bed, he looked at her, his gaze intent, as though he would stamp her image indelibly upon the pages of his mind. Should she be unable to accept his injuries, he would send her away. No shame, no recriminations, only the knowledge remaining that once, in a faraway time, this woman had loved him with all that she was, pledging herself to his keeping.

"Give me room to swing into bed." His instructions were terse, and he watched as she obeyed. Rising to her feet, she stepped back, her hands clenched tightly, her eyes upon him as he swung from the chair to sit upright against his pillows.

"Now, come here and sit beside me. Watch me, Rena." His voice was gruff. "I want you to see what you're asking for, talking about spending your days and nights with me." Quickly his hands undid the buttons of his trousers, lifting himself with an awkward movement to slide them from his lower body.

The underwear, he left in place. It covered his thighs partway, and he winced as he caught sight of what he exposed as the trousers were pushed from him. With a quick twist of his wrist, he cast them to the floor and dared a look at the silent woman who sat beside him.

She met his gaze, pale and obviously shaken by his words and actions, but unmoving. "Do you think I'll run, Jake? Do you think I've come this far, just to cover my head and cry for what might have been?"

He shook his head. "No, I guess not. I suspect I should have known as much."

She leaned forward, her eyes touching only the lines of his face, and he permitted the scrutiny as she brushed his skin with her fingertips. Her mouth was soft, her lips pink once more, as if she allowed the blood to flow by some unheard command within herself. Her cheeks no longer held the pallor of hopeless despair, but bloomed with the flush of hope.

"I love you, Jake. No matter what has happened to your legs, the rest of you is still worth more than any other man in the world in my book."

He drew in a breath, overwhelmed by the vehemence in her voice, the crystal-clear meaning of her words. "Look at me. Now! Look at my legs! Then tell me again how much I'm worth."

She nodded and her eyelids lowered, even as her head tilted, allowing her gaze to move the length of his torso. With no trace of hesitation, she slid to kneel beside the bed, and her hands lifted to rest against the firm muscles of his thigh.

Through the knit fabric of his underwear, her touch was warm, caressing, and he shivered as his body responded to the stimulus of a woman's slender fingers where only his own had strayed over the past years. It was his left leg she touched, the one that had not even a knee to boast of. Her fingers edged beneath the hem of his short drawers and she nudged the fabric upward, exposing the scarred, tortured remains of his limb.

She bent low, as if only a close scrutiny would expose the minute details to her gaze, and he allowed his head to fall back against the high headboard, unable to watch as she ran her fingers over his damaged flesh.

And then, as if in a dream, her mouth touched him. There, where the ugliness of war had left its mark, she lent her healing touch, her mouth warm and damp against the marred skin. She turned her head, her cheek against his thigh, and he opened his eyes, looking down at the woman who loved him.

She leaned to touch the other leg, where his knee bent, pressing the short stump against the sheet. Her hand slid the length of his calf, a matter of inches, and she cradled her fingers around the scarred remainder.

"Does it hurt when I touch it?" she asked haltingly, lifting her gaze to his. Her eyes were filled with an indefinable sorrow, a sadness so deep it defied the presence of tears.

He shook his head, unable to speak, aware of the arousal he could no longer ignore. Hurt? He couldn't tell where her touch was affecting him most. Perhaps not even the physical touch of her hands, but the pain that radiated from her eyes to blend with the ache in his heart.

And yet his manhood ignored the dictates of his mind, rising against his body with each movement of her hands, each breath she spent against his wounded legs.

She bent once more to his ruined flesh, and her lips spread an array of silent caresses, her mouth open as she bathed and suckled the wounds he had hidden from the view of others for so long.

"I love you, Jake McPherson," she whispered, the words a fierce litany as she claimed him, her possession a renewal of the private, secret vows she'd made all those long years ago.

"Rena!" It was a strangled gasp as he acknowledged the raging of a tumescence he could not ignore.

She smiled then, turning her head to glance up at him, even as her hands moved up the ridged muscles of his thighs, easing beneath the knit garment he wore, to lay claim to the aching need he could not conceal. She held him, her fingers pressing the length of his manhood, his urgency hovering on the verge of eruption.

His lips drew back over his teeth as her hand moved on his turgid flesh and he moaned, a sound of blended agony and ecstasy.

"I love you, Jake McPherson," she whispered again, her hand clenching tighter as he shifted beneath her touch.

"Rena!" It was a warning cry, one she ignored, even as she offered him the gift of release. A gift he accepted with a muffled groan, a murmured whisper of her name.

Breakfast was a simple affair, with only Shamus and Moses coming in from the bunkhouse to sit at the long table. Cord looked toward the hall doorway as he took his seat.

"Where's Rena this morning? Did Jake get his breakfast yet?'' His fork lifted two pancakes from the platter as he spoke, and he slathered them with butter before he poured a dollop of syrup on top.

"I saw her earlier. I'll check on them in a few minutes." Rachel scooted sideways into the chair beside him, her look guarded. Her head shook at his offer of bacon. "Thanks, but I'm going to just have some coffee and a slice of toast." She busied herself with jam, her mouth pursed, her forehead wrinkled, as if she considered some great problem to be solved.

"Rachel?" His query was soft, his look inquiring as Cord paused in his eating to watch her. "Is something wrong?"

"I've been thinking about the boys ever since I got up, Cord. I keep wondering if they're all right." She broke off a piece of toast and shredded it between her fingers, then lifted a jam-smeared fingertip to her mouth.

His sigh was subdued. "Sweetheart? They'll be fine. I promise you, Sam will be with them every minute."

"I know. I just have this feeling." She leaned closer. "Cord, Lorena looks different this morning, kind of glowing and happy."

He sat up straighter, his eyes narrowing as he considered her descriptive phrases. "You don't think…" He shook his head. "Naw, that couldn't be." Another forkful of pancakes were chewed as he considered the idea.

"Where did she spend the night?" he asked in a whisper, his glance at the two men sitting at the far end of the table guarded.

Rachel looked stunned for a moment and then indignant as his meaning penetrated. "Where do you think? In her room, of course!"

"Are you sure?"

She nodded. "I heard her door close, early."

Cord nodded. "Yeah. But was she comin' or goin'?"

Rachel rose swiftly, gathering her cup and plate. "I won't even try to answer that." Her cheeks were flushed and her hands trembled. "Lorena Claypool is a lady, Cord."

It was obviously going to be her final word on the subject, and Cord found no reason to dispute her opinion. Even ladies found enjoyment with a man, especially when the lady in question was so clearly in love with the man involved.

"We're goin' to turn those yearlings out to pasture this morning, boss," Shamus said, hat in place, as he headed out the door.

"I'll be out in a few minutes," Cord answered, snatching at his coffee cup to drain its contents.

Rachel turned from the sink. "Cord... you don't really think..." Her eyes were wide with unspoken wonderings, and he felt a smile stretch his lips.

"Jake's not one to take advantage of a woman, Rachel. If they spent time together, it was probably just getting things straight between them. They had a lot of catching up to do." That part of the reunion might have been spent with their bodies in close proximity was a possibility he could not dismiss, but leaving Rachel with some semblance of purity in her imaginings might be for the best.

She nodded. "You're probably right. I just don't want Lorena to be hurt."

He stepped to her, taking her in a gentle embrace. His kiss was soft against her forehead. "Quit fretting, honey. Jake's a good man, and Rena's the best thing that's come his way in a long time." His hands gripped her shoulders and he shook her with an indulgent movement, his grin widening at her fretful look. "And don't worry about the boys, Rachel. They'll be home for supper, and they'll be bursting with all sorts of tales to tell.''

"Boss, that young'un was gone when we got up at daybreak. His blanket was in a tumble and he was nowhere to be seen.'' Jamie Callahan held his hat, twisting it in his hands. "I feel awful bad, boss, but poor old Sam is about pullin' his hair out. He's out there searchin' the woods beyond the line shack, and Buck's holdin' the fort where we were camped. In case Jay shows up, we didn't want him to think we'd gone off and left him.''

Cord's string of curses were enough to send the young cowhand stepping backward. "I'm sure as hell sorry, boss,'' he muttered, his gaze wary as he listened to words he'd never heard from Cord McPherson's mouth.

"Damn, damn, damn! I've got to tell Rachel!'' Cord pulled his hat from his head and threw it from him, sailing it across the yard.

From the porch, Rachel called his name, her voice shrill. "Cord! What's wrong?'' She jumped to the ground, ignoring the steps, and ran toward him, holding her dress high.

She seized his hands and tugged at him. "Cord, answer me! What's wrong?''

"Rachel, listen to me!'' He freed himself from her grip, holding both of her hands in one of his. His other palm wrapped the nape of her neck and he leaned toward her.

"Jay's gone missing from the camp, probably wandered off to explore before daybreak. At any rate, Sam's looking for him and I'm heading up there right now to lend a hand.''

"I'm going along,'' she said, her voice deathly quiet, her jaw clenched.

"No. You stay here. I can ride faster alone, honey. I'll be back before you know it, and you can scold him all you want."

"If I have to walk, I'm going, Cord."

He drew back, scanning her features. His sigh was deep and he nodded. "I'll have Moses saddle you a horse."

She turned to run back to the house. "I'll only be a minute." The words were gasped in one breath as she gained the porch and shouted at him.

"Moses! Saddle up the black mare for Rachel. She's riding with me." In the depths of the barn, Cord snatched a length of rope from a hook, then gathered up a blanket and a box of bandages and salves from the tack room.

Barely had he led the two horses from the wide barn door when Rachel ran from the house, a bundle in her hands. "I brought along dry clothes for Jay, in case he's wet or dirty," she gasped. She was visibly trembling and Cord reached for her.

"You don't have to go, Rae. It's going to be a hard ride and..."

Her chin lifted and she glared at him, determination alive in her gaze. "I'm going. That's all there is to it."

His shrug signified defeat and he tied the bundle in place behind her saddle. "Mount up, honey." He lifted her into the saddle, smoothing her wide skirt beneath her, tugging it down to cover her legs.

She went ahead, the small mare obeying Rachel's command, and Cord waved a hand at Moses as he followed her from the barnyard.

Buck Austin waited at the small campsite near the northernmost boundary of the McPherson ranch. He met them astride his horse, his frown telling Cord that Jay was still missing.

"Sam's gone back out. Took Henry with him. The boy said he'd know where to look, and Sam didn't have the heart to leave him behind." Buck nodded to Rachel. "We never heard him leave, Miss Rachel. He must'a snuck off before daybreak for some reason or another."

"Did anybody see any tracks?" she asked, bringing her mare to a halt.

"Sam followed what he could, but once he got into the woods up yonder, you couldn't tell much."

"I'll need a gun." Rachel looked at Cord.

"We'll ride together," he told her.

She shook her head. "We can cover more ground separately, and when I find him, I'll fire twice."

His smile could not be suppressed. "*When* you find him?"

Her nod was emphatic. "I'll find him, Cord. Don't you doubt it for a minute."

He dismounted, pulling his rifle from behind his saddle, and sliding it into the scabbard behind hers. He looked up at her, his hand tugging at her stirrup, then gripping the pommel. "Don't get too far into the woods, Rachel. If you get lost, don't be too proud to fire that gun for help."

"Which direction are you going?" she asked.

"I'll ride a half mile or less to the west, then head north, so I'm riding parallel to you. Call out for Jay every hundred feet or so. The woods muffles the sound, so you'll have to listen hard."

"All right." She loosened the reins and turned the mare, cantering quickly away.

"She rides pretty good, Boss," Buck said.

"Better than I thought," Cord answered. "Stick close,

Buck. If I find Sam, I'll send him back and you take a ride due west of here, toward the other line shack.''

Buck nodded glumly, turning his mount back to the campsite.

It was a whimper, so low she held her breath and closed her eyes, to be sure of what she heard. It came again, almost a sob, and Rachel was sliding from the saddle before the sound had faded into the silence. She turned in a half circle, her gaze sweeping the undergrowth around her.

Sunshine scattered in a random pattern, the trees overhead sparse as they reached leafy branches to the sky. She was only a hundred yards or so into the woods, but it might as well have been a mile, so hushed were the sounds about her.

A bird squawked overhead and she looked up quickly. A squirrel chattered on a limb to her right and then, as if it joined the chorus, she heard again the stifled sound of a human voice.

"Jay?" Her tone was quiet. She spoke his name, then listened. "Jay?" she repeated.

"Rae? Is that you, Rae?" From a thicket beyond where she stood, his voice piped her name and Rachel dropped the reins of her mare to run pell-mell through the rustling leaves. Oak trees towered in this glen and beneath one of them stood the form of her brother, dirty and bedraggled, his face tearstained.

She knelt before him and held him to her bosom. His skinny arms wrapped around her neck and he hung on for dear life, whispering her name.

"I was scared, Rae, but I knew you'd come to find me. I was hopin' it wouldn't be Cord, cuz he'll probably be mad as hell, won't he?"

She ignored the cuss word he spoke so solemnly, willing to forgive any lapse for the moment. The feel of his slender body beneath her hands was proof of his wellbeing and she set him away from her to scan his face.

"Why did you wander off that way, Jay?" She watched as his eyes squinted and his mouth trembled, and then he shrugged, as if his reasons were too complicated to explain.

"Jay?" she prompted. "I'm not angry. We were all worried about you."

"I heard this calf makin' a fuss and nobody else but me was awake, and it was still dark out. So I thought I could maybe find him and bring him back and Sam would say I was sure enough a big help." He ran out of breath and his shoulders slumped beneath her hands.

"Did you find the calf?"

He nodded. "It was in the woods and I had to go a ways followin' him. Then I wasn't sure how to find my way back out. But I talked to him, Rae, and he quit bawlin' right off." Pride tinged his voice as he told his tale. Then his shoulders lifted in a shrug as he continued. "So I laid down by him and he was already sleepin' and I just musta gone to sleep too."

He looked around him and his eyes wore a wounded look. "I think he left without me knowin' it, Rae. And then when I woke up, I didn't know how to find my way back."

She stood, relief a shining presence within her. "I'll have to shoot off Cord's rifle and let him know where you are," she told the boy.

"He's gonna be mad, ain't he?" Jay's lower lip trembled as he watched his sister tilt the barrel of the gun upward.

"I wouldn't be surprised."

* * *

The tools were gathered and packed up, the horses fed and watered and the boys mounted, ready to ride. "We'll finish up the line fence, far as the swamp, and then head for the barn," Sam told Cord.

"That'll work. Rachel and I will check things out to the east a ways and meet you back home by supper-time."

"Aren't the boys going back now?" Rachel asked from behind him.

"No, they can go on and help finish the job," Cord said, waving Sam on his way.

"I'd just as soon take Jay home, Cord. He's been through a lot and he needs a bath and a good meal."

"He'll eat with the men down the line. Sam gave him a piece of bread to chew on while they ride."

"Cord! He's just a little boy and he was lost for half the morning." Rachel looked past him to where the riders were strung out along the fence line, Jay riding behind Sam.

"He's fine, Rae. Don't baby him."

Her hands flew to fist against his chest. "Don't you tell me how to take care of my brother. He's still just a little boy, not much more than a baby, and if I hadn't listened to you he wouldn't have gotten lost in the first place."

His big hands captured hers easily and he tugged her against him. "Listen! He left the camp without telling anyone, and I was mighty tempted to give him a good whack on his seat for that stunt. If I hadn't thought he'd learned his lesson, being lost like he was, I'd have lit into him. As it is, I'll warrant Sam is readin' him the riot act right now."

"Don't you dare hit my brother, ever!" She tugged

at his grip on her and stamped her foot in frustration as he allowed her no room to escape.

"You're all upset over nothing, Rachel. I didn't hit the boy. I wouldn't hurt him anyway. A whack across his bottom might save him some real pain later on if he's tempted to pull this kind of stunt again."

"I'll keep him where I can watch him after this," she said tightly. "I want to go home now." Her mouth set in a mutinous line and she jerked from his grasp.

"We'll go home in a while," Cord told her. "Get on your horse and we'll ride to the east. I want to check out the valley where you stayed. It's got a nice meadow and the cows like it there. I don't want to miss any, as long as we're out this far."

"I'm going back," she repeated. "You can ride by yourself. I'm going to be home when the boys get there." She turned to her mare and pulled up her dress, toeing the stirrup for purchase. Reaching for the pommel, she was an easy mark, and Cord slid his hands around her middle, snatching her back down.

He held her against himself, her feet kicking. "Might as well simmer down, honey. You're not going anywhere without me. It was bad enough I let you ride off after the boy by yourself."

"I found him, didn't I?" she shouted defiantly, dangling in his grip.

"Yeah, you did." His words gave her credit, but his voice trembled on the brink of laughter.

He bent and nuzzled at her throat, his mouth tasting the salty flavor of her skin. "Don't fuss at me, Rachel. Just do as I ask you, please."

She shivered, as if his mouth had touched a nerve. "Don't be trying to make up to me, Cord. I'm really upset with you."

He lowered her until her feet touched the ground and then turned her in his grasp. "Well, if you're gonna be mad, I'll just have to make you glad, won't I?"

"Not much chance of that." Her lips formed a pout and she glared at him.

He leaned to her, swinging her up in his arms, and his strides were long as he headed across the clearing to where a tall oak tree shaded the grass beneath.

"What are you doing?" she shrieked, stumbling as he lowered her to the ground.

Without giving her a chance to gain her balance, he dropped to his knees, taking her with him. She was struggling, rearing back, and he rolled with her, his hands surrounding her head, lest she bump it on the ground.

"Hush." It was a whisper, spoken against her lips, and he repeated it as she opened her mouth to speak. "Don't say a word, Rachel. Just listen for a minute."

He rested his forearms on the grass, cradling her head, lifting his weight from her breasts. His legs spread to either side of hers and she wiggled only once, as if to test her limits.

Above them the birds sang, taking wing as they flew the boundaries of their territory. The breeze caught the scent of meadow grass and wafted it to where they lay, the freshness of summer bathing them in its aura.

A blue jay shrilled a warning, and Cord laughed softly. "Somebody's comin' too close to his nest," he surmised in a low tone.

"Well, somebody's liable to come wandering by this nest, too," Rachel warned him tartly, her cheeks flushed from the exertion of their tussle.

"Nope," he said, denying her words. "We're as alone as we'll ever be, sweetheart."

"Cord?" It was a question, and a warning, and he grinned as he heard it.

"I just want to spend a few minutes with you out here where no one can intrude. You don't have to think about cookin' supper or making butter or anything else. Just for an hour or so, all right?"

As if she heard the unspoken need of the man who held her captive, Rachel relaxed within his hold. "You sure nobody will be nearby?"

He nodded. "Sure as the sun's shining in the sky, Rae."

Her hands wiggled against his weight and he lifted, allowing her room to free them from between their bodies. She twined her arms around his neck and tugged gently. "I don't want to take off my clothes, Cord." Her gaze was wary and he smiled at the modesty of his bride.

"Not all of them, sweetheart. Maybe we can just rearrange things a little."

The ground beneath them was hard, but Cord's arm was a pillow beneath her head. Rachel's gaze skimmed the tree branches overhead, peering to where sunlight sparkled between the leaves.

"It's so peaceful here." As if she hesitated to disturb the silence, her whisper was barely discernible.

Cord's grunt of agreement pleased her and she turned her head, her mouth touching the edge of his jawline.

"I know you wouldn't hurt Jay, Cord. I was wrong to get angry with you."

He made a sound in his throat, as if he acknowledged her words. Her lips pressed a kiss against his throat then, and she murmured a wordless, questioning sound, as if she sought his pardon.

He turned to her, his arms circling her waist, holding

her firmly. "I'd cut off my arm before I'd do anything to hurt you or your brothers, Rae."

"I know that. I was just upset over Jay wandering off that way and finding him the way I did. He looked so forlorn." She sighed and wiggled against him. "He felt badly because the calf deserted him, you know."

Cord chuckled. "Darn fool animal. If he hadn't wandered off from his mother…" His laughter rang out. "You know, I really owe a debt of appreciation to that little fella." He levered up onto his elbow and traced her brows and the line of her cheek with his index finger.

"We managed to have an hour all to ourselves, Mrs. McPherson. No listening for sounds from the other parts of the house."

"I forgot to listen, in case anybody did find us here, Cord." She laughed and nipped at his finger. "I don't know how you managed to…you know."

"How I managed to get you out of your clothes without you catchin' on to what I was doin', you mean?"

She felt the flush rise to cover her cheeks. "You make me forget everything else but you sometimes." She turned her face against his chest. "I love you, Cord."

His fingers slid through her hair, cupping her head as he bent low over her. He turned her with care, rolling her to her back, rising over her. "Rachel, you're the most important thing that's ever happened to me. My heart hurts when I look at you. It makes me feel warm inside when your hand touches mine, or when you smile at me across the room. I guess I don't know what love is supposed to feel like, but if wanting to be with you and needing you has anything to do with it, then I suspect that's what's going on. I just know… I know that my arms ache to hold you sometimes."

He bent his head, hiding his face against her breast.

"It's like the light goes out when you walk out the door. As if my house was dark inside before you came."

She closed her eyes against the elation washing over her, her heart leaping within her breast. "Cord!" She circled him with her arms, holding him with the force of her passion, wanting to be contained by his flesh, as though she could not be close enough to satisfy the longing in her heart.

"Can we come back here again?" she asked after a moment.

He nodded. "Whenever you like, sweet."

His mood made her brave and her question had a casual tone. "Can I ask you something, Cord?"

"Sure." The word was slurred, his head heavy against her, as if he hovered on the edge of dozing off.

Her hands rubbed against his back, feeling the ridged scars through his shirt. "How did these happen? Who did this to you?"

Chapter Fourteen

"My father called me a coward, Rachel." Cord's words were bleak and without blame, as if he concluded that the opinion of his father had been just and fair.

Not so Rachel. Her heart lurched at the pronouncement, her face flushing with an emotion she barely understood, only that the man she loved with her whole heart had been maligned.

And by his closest kin, the man who had sired him.

"Then your father was blind or foolish, Cord. No one who had made it his business to know you well would ever consider you a coward."

She pushed him from her, her anger lending her strength, and he moved to lie beside her.

His mouth twitching, he turned his head to view her from beneath lowered lids. "You didn't tell me you had such a temper, Mrs. McPherson. You've managed to scold me roundly, twice today already."

She cast him a look ripe with scorn. "I didn't scold you. I merely expressed my opinion."

He sat up, lifting one knee, his scarcity of clothing no deterrent to the bold look of him. Her gaze swept the length of his muscled frame, draped only by an unbuttoned shirt. He would stand up well against the statues in the museum in Philadelphia, she decided.

Those cold, marble effigies that held no power to beguile her feminine heart.

As did Cord McPherson.

"Ordinarily I would consider any opinion you offer to be valid, Rachel," he said quietly, his smile fading in the somber face of her gravity. "But in this case, you weren't there. My father was. He heard me choose to stay at home rather than fight the battle against the men in gray. He listened when I decried the conflict and the reasons men choose to wage their wars. And disagreed with me."

"He called you a coward because of your convictions?"

Cord nodded. "I had to do what I felt was right, Rae. So I stayed on the ranch, breeding, raising and training horses. I sold beef to the army and provided the men in blue with some dandy horseflesh. We made enough money to keep body and soul together, but if I hadn't stayed at home, this ranch would have been sold for taxes."

"And he still thought you were a coward?"

"He died, Rachel. He accused me, he dealt out his punishment for shaming him, and he collapsed at my feet.

"The doctor called it a fit of apoplexy. Whatever it was, he lived only a week and drew his last breath cursing the day I was born."

"Your punishment?" She'd picked out the phrase, heard it resound in her mind, and was deaf to the tone of regret in Cord's voice.

"Your punishment?" Softly, she repeated the words, her lips trembling as she moved to kneel before him.

He met her gaze, his eyes dark with a pain she'd seen there before. When he spoke of Jake he'd worn the same look.

She repeated the words, her voice a whisper. "He punished you?" She closed her eyes. "He whipped you? And you allowed it?"

"I didn't fight him, Rae. He was my father. He knocked me down, caught me unawares. I took the brunt of his hatred. I think he wished me dead that day. He'd been miserable since my mother died. Jake had joined the Union army, and my father cursed me."

He clenched his jaw tightly, and she watched as the skin stretched over the grim line that bespoke his pain. "He'd have brought the roof down on my head if he'd been here the day Jake came home. I'd have been doubly cursed."

"You weren't responsible for your brother's wounds, Cord. Don't take that blame on yourself."

He shrugged. "Maybe my own scars make it easier for me to look at him."

"Who tended your back, Cord?"

"Shamus. He was the only one who knew. Until now." His smile was bitter. "You didn't see Jake when they brought him to me, Rae. He sat in the back of a wagon, his bandaged stumps in place of the two good legs he left with, and I…"

He shook his head. "I'm glad my mother never saw it. My father, either, for that matter."

Rachel leaned to him, balanced on her knees, reaching for his shoulders to stay erect. Her hands clenched the wide, muscled width and she dug in her nails. Like an oak tree, he was solid and stalwart, and strong enough to allow her the anger she expended on him.

"I never want to hear you revile yourself again, Cord

McPherson! You're a good man, honest and upright. Having the strength to live by your convictions doesn't make you a coward.''

She caught a breath and her voice trembled. "Hiding your head and pampering your brother does."

His brow lifted as she spoke. "Pampering?"

"Yes! You were all set to smack Jay for running off, weren't you? You expect him to accept responsibility, and yet..." Her tone took on new strength. "You've allowed Jake to live in that dark room, hiding from the world for more than three years. Surely in that length of time, he should have come to grips with his injuries. He may be bitter and ornery the rest of his life, but coddling him while he turns into a hermit hasn't helped a thing."

"You think I coddle him." His eyes narrowed as he repeated the accusing phrase.

"Probably more than I coddle Jay. And he's only a little boy, while Jake is a man, full-grown. What would you call it?" She released him from her hold and leaned back on her heels.

"That's different."

"Really? Then you tell me?" she said, her challenge alive between them.

What would he call it? Cord's mind reflected for a moment on the brother he loved, and yet... At the same time he felt...what? Resentment, maybe?

He glared at Rachel, aiming his anger for a moment at the woman who'd dared to speak to him so roundly. She was about half his weight, dripping wet, and totally vulnerable out here in the far reaches of the ranch.

And yet she'd had the guts to accuse him. That impudent little mouth of hers had spit out words he'd never thought to hear from anyone. Certainly not from the woman who claimed to love him.

Damn! Even half-mad at her, he found himself wanting her beneath him on the ground. He reached for her, suddenly needing to assure himself of the validity of her words. His hands gripped her, with a touch far from gentle, drawing her across the grass that separated them.

Losing her balance, she fell against him, her hands reaching to steady herself. He turned her, neatly and quickly, sliding her into the shelter of his big body, her bottom perched on his folded leg.

"Now tell me again how I've pampered my brother," he said, his fingers curving beneath her chin and along the firm line of her jaw.

As long as she was going to give him holy hell he could at least have the pleasure of feeling that plump fanny against him. He watched her soft pink lips open, willing to hear her out.

"You've allowed him to do absolutely nothing to help you, Cord," she began, her tone even as if she guarded each word. "Rena told me that Jake did the accounts before he went away to New York. She said he's got a mind like a steel trap. He can add and subtract in his head and have the totals down before anyone else could manage to get them written on a piece of paper."

She drew in a deep breath, and he readied himself for another barrage.

"Your brother needs some responsibility for the ranch, Cord. You said his name is on the deed, but all he does to contribute is to sit in that chair and raise havoc to let you know he's there. And you let him get away with it."

He shifted beneath the pressure of her weight against him, torn between the accusations she flung at him and the effect the proximity of her body was having on his.

She wiggled again and his hands gripped her waist,

lifting her and settling her once more a few inches from his groin.

Rachel's mouth opened, then shut, her cheeks pink, perhaps from the force of her scolding words, he decided. And then she turned her head to look fully into his face.

"You can just stop that funny business, Cord McPherson. Rubbing your…your *thing* against me isn't going to change how I feel about this!"

"Sweetheart, that 'thing' of mine doesn't seem to care whether you're mad at me or not." A surge of desire for the woman he held washed over him, the need for her almost beyond his ability to control.

Rachel cocked her head, as if she had only now become aware of his inattention to her words. "Cord? Why are you looking at me like that?"

He felt a smile curl his lips. Jake and his problems could go hang for now. Rachel's opinions were probably worth his full consideration. And if she had hit the nail on the head with all her carrying on about Jake, he'd be the first to admit it.

But not right now.

"Cord!" Her warning cry was spent against his mouth as he twisted in the grass, turning her to her back and coming down over her. "You haven't listened to a word I've said."

"Oh, yes, I have, and I promise I'll do something about it. But right now I'm going to shut that sassy little mouth of yours, and enjoy doing it."

It was a kiss of passion, a caress that bypassed the tender foreplay he'd previously favored. Her mouth was invaded by his, the barrier of lips and teeth overwhelmed by the force of his desire. He allowed her no quarter, his hands noting the curves of her body as a territory he had every intention of claiming as his own.

And yet there was in his handling of her delicate flesh a gentleness she could not deny, a forbearance signifying the great care he took that she might find pleasure in his touch.

His hands swept away the clothing that hid her from him. His fingertips spread wide over the softness of her breasts, then edged lower to curve with possessive greed against the fullness of her hips, pressing her against the surging need he would not deny.

She inhaled deep breaths of air, his scent filling her, a musky, delightful aroma that spoke to her of sweetness and satisfaction, of male need and the craving of his flesh for her own.

Her anger had prepared her, her emotions peaking readily as Cord rolled with her upon the grass. Each word he spoke, each gruff word of command, filled her with anticipation.

Moving with her, he lifted her, his mouth offering adulation to the curves and hollows of her flesh.

And then he was there, the driving force of his very being seeking out the wellspring of her womanhood. He merged their bodies, a groan of triumph and satisfaction erupting from him, even as she whispered his name in a gesture of submission to his greater strength.

He was ever the victor, and she allowed it.

He was the aggressor, and she reveled in it.

He was the giver of pleasure, and she accepted it, filled to overflowing with a supreme knowledge that without her, his joy would be incomplete.

That no other woman fulfilled his needs as could the one he had taken as his wife.

She was swept into a maelstrom of delight, a world

of sensation that precluded all else. He was above her, beneath her, his arms enclosing her, his very breath filling her as he entangled them into a pulsing entity.

They were one flesh. Man and woman beneath the summer sky, their bodies brushed by the sunshine and shadow of the leaves overhead.

A cry of triumph burst from her and she gripped him, her legs strong and firm, her arms muscled from the hours of physical labor she embraced.

An ecstasy beyond her understanding filled her to overflowing and she sobbed aloud, tears flowing in a flood tide that wet her face and his, their frenzied bodies clinging together in a fierce celebration of their love.

Cord's mouth brushed at the dampness and he smiled, a satisfied upturning of his lips that brought a like expression to her own. Rasping and rough against her hearing, his words acclaimed her.

"There's never been another woman like you, Rachel McPherson."

It was homage spoken with deep emotion, and she accepted it, knowing it was dealt her as her due. In this time and place, they had formed a new bond, reaching beyond the meeting of their bodies to a melding of souls.

Cord McPherson had made her his own on their wedding night. Today, he had given her a deeper glimpse into his heart, and in the doing had offered up his very self into her care.

For this, she would be ever grateful.

A trip to town took on new significance, once the theater construction began. Teams of workers gave their time, working during the evenings when their own chores were completed. Saturdays found the surrounding community surging into the town square, bursting the boundaries of townsfolk and farmers, blending the whole into a work force that defied description.

The women were the driving force, many of them hungry for this new touch of civilization, of culture brought to the level of small-town living.

Some had come from bigger cities than Green Rapids. Some had known the joy of sharing music and drama.

Others just came to town for the camaraderie of community spirit that drove men to sit astride beams high over the ground, to blend the hammering of their tools with those of others.

Whatever the reasons, the theater was being built. No doubt, Rachel decided privately, the investors from New York were delighted that their building was costing them not much more than the materials they sent to the site.

The train station had been a beehive of activity since the beginning. Twice a week, the afternoon train was met by a string of wagons. The crates and boxes, their outsides stamped with names of faraway places, kept the children enthralled.

"Look here, Rae! There's stuff clear from New York City in here," Jay chirped, standing tiptoe in his attempt to see the top of a tall box.

Rachel nodded at him, watching from the shade of the station, cooling herself lazily with a cardboard fan. Cord's last stop was to be at the barber shop.

He'd talked Rachel into trimming the back of his hair twice, but she'd persuaded him that the town barber needed to make a stab at cleaning up her efforts. His dark hair hung straight, resting against his collar, and no amount of clipping on her part was able to even it out.

She blew a stray curl from her forehead, fanning from a new direction, wishing she'd left off her petticoat this morning. A thought that would surely have caused her mother to scold her endlessly, had she but known.

She smiled, a bittersweet thorn pricking her memory, and then thought of Cord. One glimpse of him would be enough to lift her spirits, she decided.

And it was. From beyond the corner of the railroad station she caught sight of him, one hand lifted in a wave, as he headed her way.

"You about ready to head for home, Rachel?" he called from the other end of the platform.

Her breath caught in her throat as she watched him, his slim-hipped stride lending an air of arrogance to the tall rancher. His hat was tilted at an angle, his face shaded beneath the brim. He lifted a hand in greeting to several men as he passed them, but his eyes were trained on his wife.

As if he were aware of her unspoken curiosity, he swept the hat from his head and grinned. His hair gleamed darkly in the sunshine and it had been shorn considerably. Later, her hands could conduct their own survey, she decided.

Her gaze lowered, drawn by the masculine width of his shoulders. His shirt was snug over his chest, sleeves rolled up partway to disclose muscular forearms.

A wide belt held his denim trousers tautly above his hips, and in his boots he towered over the scattered groups of watching townsfolk and the sweating workers who loaded the wagons.

No matter what the Bible said, pride in this case could not possibly be a sin, for mixed as it was with love, Rachel embraced the emotion wholeheartedly.

Cord McPhcrson belonged to her, and her possessive heart beat faster at his approach.

His eyes warmed as he watched her and his mouth

turned up at one corner. She sent him a silent plea, just a twist of her lips, a half smile. Her hand gestured at her brothers, who were scampering about with half a dozen town boys.

"Jay and Henry are having a good time, Cord."

He nodded agreement, ambling over to where she stood, then leaned against the building next to her, one foot flat against the siding. His fingers slid into his shirt pocket, drawing forth a slim cigar and he lifted his brow in her direction. "Do you mind?"

She shook her head. "My father used to smoke cigars, usually after dinner at night."

He held the brown cylinder between finger and thumb, as if he measured the length with his eye. "Conrad gave it to me." A match sparked as he struck it against the sole of his boot and his eyes squinted at her through the puff of smoke as he lit the tobacco.

She waved the fan more vigorously and her nose wrinkled. "I'd just as soon you smoked it here, Cord. I don't really like the smell in a house."

He moved it to the far corner of his mouth and spoke around it. "Well, that's one thing we agree on then." The thumb of his left hand was caught in his side pocket, and with his other hand he reached for her.

"You find everything you needed at Conrad's, Rae?" he asked, holding her hand within his palm. It was a casually possessive gesture and she smiled, aware of his need to own her in public.

Cord McPherson wasn't above setting his brand on his belongings, and she suspected that he considered her as just that. Maybe more prized than his horse, certainly a step or two above the herds of cattle he raised. That thought nudged her sense of humor and she chuckled, a soft sound beneath her breath.

"What's got you tickled?" he asked, leaning to look down into her face. He squeezed her hand and lifted it, drawing her closer.

She shook her head. "Nothing, just a foolish idea."

"You're havin' a good time, watchin' the fixings for the new building come to town, aren't you?" he asked, blowing the smoke from his cigar upward.

"Mrs. Hampton says it's probably the most excitement Green Rapids has ever seen, Cord. She said her husband told her it's guaranteed to bring new money into town."

Cord grinned widely. "And old Cecil's no doubt rubbin' his hands together, waitin' for a chance to get his hands on it. I'll bet he's the reason there's some fella ready to start building a men's clothing store, down past the hotel."

"When did you hear that?"

"You'd be surprised at all the gossip in the barber shop these days," he said, slanting a look at her. "They're even talkin' about Lorena living at the ranch."

"Nothing bad, I hope?" Rachel frowned at the idea of Lorena being the object of conversation.

Cord grinned. "Naw. Nobody seems to consider that Jake might still have feelings for her. Guess the general idea is that he's lost more than the use of his legs."

Rachel felt a hot flush creep up her cheeks. "That's no way to talk, Cord. Lorena's a lady."

The cigar flared briefly as he drew on it, and he clamped it between his teeth. His eyes glittered teasingly as he watched her. "Yeah, but don't forget, Jake's a man. He and Rena were gonna get married a few years back. I doubt he's forgotten how things were between them."

"I don't want Lorena hurt just because she's staying with us," Rachel said firmly.

"I'd say she's willing to take that chance." Cord's fingers plucked the cigar from his mouth and he eyed it cautiously. "Can't figure out why Cecil Hampton sets so much store by these things. Conrad says he orders them by the box."

Rachel's mouth twitched with amusement. "You don't think you'll be placing an order any time soon?"

He shook his head, dropping the cigar to the ground and grinding it beneath his boot. "Can't say I much enjoy the flavor. I'll settle for a piece of apple pie any day of the week."

"Rae! Can we stay a while longer?" Jay had raced to her side, moisture beading his upper lip, his hair damp with sweat. He caught his breath, rocking on his heels.

"Everybody's gonna follow the wagon to the new building and watch 'em unload. Can me and Henry go, too?"

She looked at Cord for approval and was pleased at his indulgence. "I don't see why not," he drawled. "Your sister and I can probably find something to do for a little while. We'll come by and pick you up in a half hour or so."

"I'm surprised the whole town's not watching the wagons today," Rachel told him. "They're supposed to be bringing in the stage fittings, I heard. Everyone's champing at the bit to get the curtains hung."

"I heard tell the piano's coming next week," he said, lifting an eyebrow as he glanced in her direction again. "I s'pose you'll want to be here when it arrives."

She sighed, a reluctant sound. "We can't be trotting to town every time the train goes by."

He squeezed her hand. "I was thinkin' maybe we

could load Jake up in the wagon and bring him along. You think he'd go for the idea?" As casual as his words seemed, she sensed a deep, underlying hope within each syllable.

"Well..." Her pause was long as she mentally crossed her fingers. "I was thinking. Maybe when they send a man to tune it, I could talk Jake into being there. I'd really like for both of us to be there for that, if they'll let us in."

"They hafta have a special fella to tune the thing?" Cord's frown doubted the notion.

"Hauling it all the way from New York, it'll be out of tune for sure." She chewed at her lip for a moment and then turned her head, meeting Cord's gaze. "I was thinking that maybe, as long as the tuner was here, we could ask him to come out to the ranch and work on the one in the parlor. It's been a long time since it was set to rights, Cord. The top two octaves and most of the bottom one are way off."

He shrugged. "Sounds pretty good to me."

"Well, if it costs a lot, I could pay the fee," she said, her cheeks warming with the boldness of her request.

"If you want it tuned, we'll see to it," he told her.

"I mean it, Cord. I wouldn't mind paying the fee."

He shot her an impatient glance. "I pay for whatever you need, Rachel. You just keep your money tied up in a hankie in your drawer. You might need it for something important someday."

She thought of the meager hoard she'd gained by working for him before their wedding. He'd only allowed her to spend a small amount at the store. The rest she'd squirreled away, a nest egg for the future.

"You seem to buy me everything I need, Cord. Even things I could do without, sometimes."

"When you run my bank account dry I'll let you know, ma'am." He leaned closer, his glance darting from one side of the platform to the other as he bent over her.

"So far, you've been worth the investment," he whispered. His head dipped and he snatched a kiss, his mouth full against her lips.

It was quick, but potent. A meeting and melding of their flesh that brought high color to her cheeks once more. His eyes flashed with humor, tinged by a dark flavor of desire as he straightened, moving to stand before her.

"No one's watching, honey. I checked first." He brushed at her cheek, a gentle caress that only served to heighten her blush.

"You're a rascal, Cord McPherson," she told him sharply, casting her own glances past him. "You'll make me the talk of the town."

He shook his head and turned, offering his arm. "Naw, you did that the night of the dance. I'd warrant they were takin' bets down at the barber shop, tryin' to figure how long it would take for me to get a ring on your finger."

"Cord!" She was agape at his words.

He shrugged. "True as the good book, honey. Conrad did me a favor with his braggin' about you and him gettin' married. It just pushed things along a little, and I ended up with the prize."

He tugged her along the dusty road, heading for the emporium where his wagon waited. His smile teased her and his hand held hers with a possessive grip. She stepped quicker, matching her pace to his, aware of watching eyes and envious glances.

"Are we leaving now?"

He nodded. "We'll give the boys a few more minutes and then head for home. Unless there's someone over at the theater building we can talk to about the piano tuning."

"I doubt anyone will know anything until the instrument gets here," she told him, peering toward the other end of town where the rough lumber structure towered over the other buildings.

"They're havin' a paintin' bee come Saturday," Cord said. "Everybody and his brother is comin' to town. I heard tell the New York people bought three steers from Howie Peters to roast out beyond the theater. They're sendin' a chef from St. Louis and eight bushel of potatoes to bake in the coals."

Rachel grabbed his arm in both hands and stood stock-still on the wooden sidewalk. "That's the best news yet, and you waited till now to tell me?"

He grinned. "I knew we'd be coming. Wasn't any big thing, I figured. All the women are s'posed to bring a covered dish or pie or something."

Rachel felt like dancing in the street. A picnic for the whole countryside, right in the middle of town.

"Cord? Do you think…"

His hand was gentle as he spread his fingers over her lips, and he shook his head, as if he read her mind. "Don't count on it, sweetheart. He's not about to let the whole county see him in that chair."

A bubble of frustration built within her, and Rachel's mouth tightened lest it burst forth in a spurt of anger.

Maybe it was about time everyone quit mollycoddling Jake.

Chapter Fifteen

"I don't see why you think I need to be included in your picnic plans, Rachel." Jake's jaw was set, his eyes hard with restrained anger as he faced the young woman in the doorway.

The wheels of his chair were spun with abrupt movements of his agile hands as he neared her. "Just leave me alone, and go about your party planning."

To her credit, Rachel held her position, aware that Jake's maneuvering would not endanger her one mite. He could sashay that chair all over the place, but not for one second did she fear he would bruise her with its wheels or frame.

"Cord wants the whole family to attend. It's the biggest thing that's ever happened to Green Rapids, Jake. The theater is already causing folks to rally round, getting involved with the building of it. Everyone's excited about the cast of the first production coming to town next month."

"Everyone does not include me, Rachel." He turned from her, his words ringing with a finality she could not dispute.

And yet she must give it one more try. "Jay and Henry want you to come along," she said quietly.

He turned his head to glare at her over his shoulder. "Don't turn your brothers loose on me. I'm not fond of children, and there's no point in drawing them into this discussion."

"Did you ever think that they might be fond of you?"

"They barely know me." His hand lifted in a gesture of dismissal. "Forget it, Rachel."

"I told you he wouldn't go." The words were a barely audible whisper from the hallway, but Jake's shoulders hunched as his sensitive hearing came into play.

"I don't think he likes us." It was a solemn statement, one that would brook no discussion, and even in the youthful tones of a child, it held a sadness that was unmistakable.

Rachel winced at the dejected tone of Jay's voice. She turned to where the two boys waited in the hall, unseen from the library. Her mouth opened to speak, her mind searching for words that would heal the hurt of rejection.

"Wait...hold on." Behind her, Jake's harshly spoken command silenced her and she bit at her lip, awaiting his approach.

The wheels on his chair turned slowly as he neared the doorway. "Jay...Henry...come here for a moment." His hand lifted, bidding them near, and after a quick look at their sister, they obeyed.

"Yessir?" Henry's response was quick. Beside him, Jay watched hopefully.

"Why do you want me to go on this picnic with you?" His hands rigid on the wheels, Jake leaned forward in his chair.

"Rachel said you were our uncle now, and we never had an uncle before." Jay's thin voice spoke with solemn fervor. "We didn't have no family when we came here, Mr. Jake. Now we got you and Cord and even Rena."

"He don't have to go if he don't want to, Jay," Henry put in, his arm circling his younger brother's shoulder in a protective gesture.

Jake's gaze flickered over the older boy, but his attention focused on Jay. "If you want me to be your uncle, you'd better learn how to say the words, young man. Try it on for size, why don't you. Uncle Jake."

Rachel cleared her throat. "I didn't mean to infringe when I told the boys…"

The imperious wave of his hand halted her explanation. "It's a shirttail relationship, but it'll do."

"Will you really be our uncle…Uncle Jake?" Jay asked.

"I've never been an uncle before. I'm not sure I know how," Jake said gruffly.

He was a good man. Beneath the bluster and the frowns, Jake McPherson had a kind heart, and never was Rachel more pleased to see evidence of it than right this minute.

"You just hafta do stuff with the family, I guess," Henry said, breaking his silence.

"Like going on a picnic." Less a question than a statement of fact, Jake's voice intoned the words.

"Yeah." Henry uttered the word of agreement and then met Jake's gaze with a sober look. "I told Rachel you probably wouldn't go."

"This was Rachel's idea?" Jake asked, slanting a look in her direction.

"No, it was mine," Jay piped up. "It's gonna be fun—and I told Rae you don't ever have any fun—and I wanted you to go along."

"Oh, I have fun every once in a while," Jake told them agreeably. "Just getting your sister riled up provides me with a lot of enjoyment."

"She gets mad at us when we do that," Henry said.

"Yeah, me too." Jake's smile was rare and its effect on the two boys was immediate.

Dissolving in giggles, Jay punched Henry on the arm. "He was just funnin' us. He really wants to go along, Henry. He was just gettin' at Rachel, makin' her mad."

"Jake?" She spoke his name, the warning implicit.

"I'll go along." His glance in her direction held an element of pain. That being viewed by the whole community would be difficult for him was an understatement, she knew. Yet, to please two small boys, he was willing to face curious eyes and expose himself to their scrutiny.

The wagon bed was full to overflowing. Jake's chair, surrounded by picnic baskets and a low bench for Lorena to perch on took up the front half of the bed. The back portion was piled with planks to make up tables for serving food, and a washtub filled with watermelons sent along by Mr. Claypool, his wagon already being overloaded.

Cord and Rachel sat on the seat, his new shirt still bearing pressing marks from the iron she'd wielded early this morning. "I don't want you painting in this shirt," she told him for the second time.

"I brought along an old one." His smile was warm as he leaned closer to whisper in her ear. "I don't know how you did it, honey."

She reached up to brush a lock of hair from his forehead, her fingers lingering to thread through the heavy strands. "I didn't. The boys did."

A huge maple tree spread its branches widely just beyond the area where the painters assembled to receive their directions. There, beneath the shade that would remain constant throughout the day, Rachel spread quilts and deposited their belongings.

Jake's chair was rolled to sit next to the enormous trunk and he shifted himself to the ground, where Lorena had arranged a thick padding of quilts for him to sit on. He leaned back against the tree trunk, his chair moved aside.

It was a vantage point for the whole proceedings and he held court there throughout the day. Townsfolk approached, at first with a diffident air, then as the parade of well-wishers continued, they became more friendly.

Those who had been at Cord's wedding passed the time of day recalling that event. Others came by to be introduced, or to renew old acquaintance, some recalling the days of Jake's youth in the town of Green Rapids.

The new theater was the topic of conversation, the men working on the high walls with scaffolding and paintbrushes. By late afternoon, the job was done. Rising tall at one end of town, the building gleamed in the sunlight with a double coat of white paint. An air of camaraderie embraced the workers and their families. Among them, three men from New York City supervised the enormous task of feeding the crowd. With jovial goodwill, they wholeheartedly joined in the celebration.

The piano had arrived on Friday, and just before sundown it was rolled on a makeshift platform to the door of the building to be seen by the assembled townsfolk.

"We have a young lady here who I understand is quite a gifted musician," Cecil Hampton bellowed from his post next to the instrument. Shielding his eyes from the rays of the setting sun, he searched the crowd before him. And then he waved vigorously, catching sight of Rachel beneath the tree.

"Mrs. McPherson! Come on over here and give us a small rendition. Just so's we can see if this here piano is fit for our fine building." His wide smile belied the words he spoke, one hand caressing the gleaming surface of the instrument.

"Me?" Rachel almost choked on the word, her eyes meeting Cord's with a frantic plea in their depths.

He urged her with a firm hand on her back. "Go on, honey. Play that song I like so well. The one we waltzed to that night at the dance…Blue something or other."

"'The Blue Danube,' he means," Jake said with a trace of humor. Seated once more in his chair, he shook his head, as if mortified by his brother's ignorance, and Cord responded with a quick swat against Jake's shoulder.

Jake nodded at Rachel. "Go on, sister-in-law. I heard you playing it just the other day."

"In front of all these people?" She was flushed with excitement, trembling with the fear of performing before so many eyes.

"For me?" Cord asked quietly, his hands holding her in a grip that granted her the strength of his confidence in her.

She played, and played well. The enthusiastic crowd surrounded her and she responded to their encouragement. The waltz was followed by another, then a voice called for a tender, romantic ballad. It was one she was familiar with and she chorded it nicely.

The darkness surrounded them before the men pushed the piano back inside the building, torches lighting their way to the doorway. Buggies and wagons rolled down the main street and headed in four directions from town, their occupants weary but filled with good food and memories of the day.

"You all right?" Cord asked quietly as Rachel snuggled next to him on the wide seat of the wagon.

"Did you know they were going to ask me to play?" she asked, peering up at him in the starlight.

"Cecil asked me if I thought you would."

Her sigh was one of happiness. "It was fun, wasn't it? Not just the music, but the whole day."

"Thank you, Rae." His mouth touched her ear as he said the words. "I never thought I'd see such a thing come to pass."

"Jake?" she asked, the single word barely uttered.

He nodded.

The piano tuner was a blind man. Past middle age, accompanied by a male companion, he was not an imposing figure. Rachel stood at the back of the theater, the scent of fresh paint in her nostrils, and watched as the stooped frame of David Solomon crossed the stage.

The young man with him guided him toward the new piano, bending to speak in low tones as they walked from the wings. His voice carried to where Rachel watched from the shadows, and she smiled with benign pride at his remarks.

"Looks pretty spiffy, Mr. Solomon. Walls are all painted already and the curtain's hung."

"I have a nose to smell with," the older man said, his voice sharp with impatience. "Tell me something I don't know."

They reached the piano and any reticence the piano tuner had heretofore displayed disappeared, once his hands touched the wooden surface of the upright model.

He eased his way to the keyboard, lifting the lid with reverent hands, then positioning the bench.

As if he knew his presence was no longer required, the younger man stepped back, searching the stage with a sweeping glance. A chair, far to the left, caught his eye and he stepped quickly to move it closer to the piano.

"Go on! Take care of the hotel and the bags," David Solomon told him with an impatient wave of his hand. "I have work to do."

Rachel smiled in private amusement at the imperious directions. The piano tuner back home had been such a man, a gifted pianist in his own right, but without the funds for a career. To her childish notions, he had been fit for the concert stage. She'd been abashed at her father's opinion of the man's talent. Second-rate, he'd said.

David Solomon's long fingers spread to cover three octaves and a little more, the tones almost liquid in their purity. And then he moved up the keyboard and Rachel heard the disparity in sound. The trip from New York City, no matter how delicately the crate had been handled, had disturbed the stretch of the strings.

Rachel moved from the back wall, her feet silent on the carpet runner that had been laid only yesterday on the center aisle of the theater. Smaller than those she'd attended in the city, yet splendid when seen through the eyes of Green Rapids, the structure held seating for more than two hundred.

She'd reached the center of the building when David Solomon lifted his head, tilting it to one side. His hands hovered over the keyboard and he turned on the piano bench toward where Rachel stood, frozen in place.

"Who's there?" His voice was curt. "Horace? I thought I sent you to see to things."

Rachel moved forward, no longer attempting to muffle her steps. "Mr. Solomon? It's not Horace. My name is Rachel McPherson."

"I asked that this building be empty," he said abruptly. "What do you want, young woman?"

She walked quickly to where a set of steps gave access to the stage at the far left, holding her skirts high to climb. "I didn't mean to disturb you, sir," she said, her words wispy as she caught her breath.

His sigh was one of patience stretched to its limit. "I have work to do here, and you have disturbed me already."

His small bag of tools lay beside him on the bench and he placed a protective hand on the black leather satchel as she neared.

"I only wanted to watch and listen as you worked," Rachel said quickly. And then her innate honesty compelled her to continue. "Actually, I also wanted to beg a favor of you."

His brow furrowed and his heavily lidded eyes opened a bit. "I can do nothing for you, young lady. I have other places to travel to when I leave here, eight pianos to tune in the next three weeks."

"I…rather, my family, has a piano that needs your skills, sir." She spoke humbly, aware that she might not gain access to another man of David Solomon's talent for more years than she wanted to count.

"I imagine that most every piano west of St. Louis could use my skills," he said abruptly. "I have no time to spend on your parlor upright."

"It's a Steinway."

His head lifted and he tensed visibly. "You play?" He waited for her reply.

"Not as well as its owner," she said quietly. "Or as well as he could play it, were he able, I should say."

He waved her away, an imperious movement of his veined hand. "I will talk to you later."

Rachel released her breath, a sigh of relief. Stepping to the lone chair on the stage, she settled herself in to wait.

The name of Jacob McPherson apparently rang a bell in the mind of David Solomon. "He was promising, a talented man."

Faint praise, perhaps, but when Rachel asked her favor, it was granted without hesitation.

"Is it Jake he wants to meet, or the piano he wants to tune?" Cord asked as he lifted Rachel from the buggy.

"I don't know. And to tell the truth, I don't care," she answered, climbing the steps to the porch. "He's coming here in the morning to tune the piano, and if Jake isn't at least polite, I'll be furious."

Buck Austin headed for the barn, leading the sleek mare. Cord watched as his latest acquisition, the shiny black buggy he'd purchased only last week, rolled away.

"I don't think you even paid attention to the new buggy," he told Rachel, following her into the kitchen. "All I heard was David Solomon's name all the way home."

"Not true. I noticed my skirt didn't get snagged when I slid across the seat," she said, casting him a sidelong glance.

"You didn't bounce around either," he pointed out.

She turned to him, a placating smile curving her lips.

"I noticed, Cord. I didn't even need a bonnet to keep the sun off, and the padding on the seat was most comfortable."

"I bought it for you," he said, slipping his arms around her waist.

She lifted an eyebrow in doubt. "You bought it so that we could attend the theater in style. Although I don't know what you'll do when everyone wants to go at once. There's only room for three people in that seat."

"It affords a bit of privacy, though," he pointed out.

"I noticed your arm around me," she admitted, reaching to stroke her palm down the firm line of his jaw.

"There's leftovers in the oven," Lorena said from the doorway. "Didn't mean to eavesdrop, but I thought you might be hungry, and we didn't wait supper for you."

"We were late. Rachel waited to talk to the piano tuner at the theater, and I sent Jamie on home with the wagon." Cord released his hold on Rachel and bent to open the oven door. "Smells pretty good in there."

"I'll get out some plates," Lorena volunteered. "We had johnnycake and a kettle of beans with ham and new potatoes."

"I'm too excited to eat," Rachel declared, and then denied her claim as she inhaled the aroma from the stove. "Well, maybe I could manage just a little."

"Jake all right?" Cord asked quietly. That Rachel counted heavily on his brother's good behavior in the morning was a fact. His spirits had been somewhat lighter of late, but Jake might very well resent the intrusion of a stranger in the house.

"He came out for supper. Said I didn't need to be carrying trays back and forth when he could very well make it to the table." Lorena's eyes were lit with a glow akin to happiness, Cord decided as she announced her news.

"Just for tonight or every day?" he asked dubiously.

She shrugged. "Sounded like he meant every day, to me."

"Mr. David Solomon will be here in the morning," Rachel told her. "He's come to town to tune the piano at the theater, and I've asked him to work on Jake's."

Lorena was silent for a moment as she considered the news. "I'll tell him, if you like."

Cord shook his head. "No, I'll go in when we've finished eating and give him the news."

"I don't want some fly-by-night fella touching that piano." His mouth set in a firm line, Jake faced his brother from his chair.

Cord shook his head. "He's far from that." He hesitated, and Jake eyed him watchfully.

"Rachel said the man thought he recognized your name."

Jake's frown denied the idea. "I doubt that."

Cord shrugged, as if accepting his theory. "Well, I only know what she said."

Jake's mouth twitched as if he barely stifled the urge to know more.

"Rachel said the man heard you play in New York. He'd like to meet you."

"I can't imagine why." Jake's words were tinged with sarcasm.

Rachel spoke from the doorway. "I can't either, now that I think about it. A more disagreeable man than you, I can't conceive of."

"I don't need everyone on my back," he said after a moment. "Cord gave me what-for this morning. Rena made me ashamed of myself before supper, and now the both of you come in here asking me to be a good boy tomorrow.''

Rachel's eyes narrowed as her gaze moved between the brothers. "You had a fuss this morning?"

Jake considered her. "I suspect you had more to do with it than you'll admit, Miss Rachel."

"What happened?"

"He told me I was a lazy dolt, in no uncertain terms." She turned to her husband. "You said that?"

"Among other things. I told him to tend to the account books, on a daily basis."

Rachel's mouth twitched. "And did you agree?" she asked Jake.

Jake looked sulky, his brows drawing together. "I can't see that I have much choice. Cord was about as sore at me as he's ever been in his life."

"I suppose he'd be understanding if you can't handle the chore," Rachel said smoothly, as if Cord were not present. "Should I talk to him?"

Jake's head jerked up quickly. "I suspect you've already done that, ma'am. He said you accused him of letting me malinger in my room."

She looked thoughtfully at him. "I may have suggested the idea."

"I'm surprised it wasn't his idea for me to take my meals at the table. How did the pair of you manage to let me think of that by myself?"

Cord grinned at his sarcasm. "Now, here I thought you took pity on Lorena, carrying all those heavy trays down the hallway."

A sheepish smile tilted his lips. "That was part of it. She was cooking and bustling around the kitchen while you were in town, and I didn't have the gall to ask for a tray. I said I'd decided it was time to join the family for meals.''

Rachel closed her eyes, fighting the sudden rush of tears that followed his words. He'd come so far, so soon.

''Rachel?'' His chair rolled closer to where she stood. ''What's wrong?''

She blinked back the moisture. ''Nothing, actually. I suppose I feel like I'm imposing to ask you for more than you've already conceded today.''

His sigh was grumpy. ''Go ahead. Ask away.''

''Come into the parlor in the morning when Mr. Solomon arrives. Just be polite and shake his hand. He's a wonderful man, Jake, skilled and talented.''

''Most tuners have a certain amount of talent.''

Cord's voice provided a further nudge. ''He's staying over an extra day, Jake, just to come here.''

He glowered, his glare moving first to one, then the other. ''You're putting on the pressure, Cord. I don't like being the object of anyone's pity. Here's the poor, legless pianist. Come out and take a look.''

''I can promise you he won't look at you with pity,'' Rachel told him quietly.

''Really.'' Jake's tone doubted her word.

''Really. He won't be able to see you, Jake. He's blind.''

His ear attuned to the upper registers of the keyboard, David Solomon appeared unaware of the wheelchair in the wide doorway of the parlor. He struck a note, then stood, leaning forward over the strings to make the adjustment, repeating the process several times before he was satisfied.

It was a tedious job, Jake had decided years ago, but the rapt expression on the man's face belied that assumption. Slender fingers touched the notes of a chord, then spanned octaves, his head tilted to listen to the sound.

Shaking his head, he bent to his task once more, then spoke, his words abrupt. "Why don't you come closer, instead of watching from over there in the doorway?" he asked, holding a pair of pliers aloft.

"I didn't want to disturb you." Jake rolled his chair across the room slowly. "Mr. Solomon?"

His fingers sought the small tool bag, and David Solomon replaced his pliers within. "Yes. I assume you are Jacob McPherson."

Jake nodded. "Yes, I am," he added quickly, his gaze taking in the half-closed, deep-set eyes of the piano tuner.

"I heard you perform in New York City, at a recital, while you were studying there." The older man swung around on the piano bench and held out his hand, palm up. "Let me have your hand."

Jake rolled closer and leaned forward a bit, placing his fingers against the older man's palm.

They rested there for a moment and then both of the veined, aged hands enclosed the more youthful, graceful one. David Solomon touched the fingers, the knuckles, ran his own sensitive fingertips over the full length of Jake's hand. Then released it.

"The other, please," he said quietly.

Within his chest, Jake's heart beat a stronger cadence than before, his breathing deepened and he felt a strange vitality sweep beneath his skin to penetrate his inner self.

He placed his left hand where the right had been, watched as it was handled with the same intense scrutiny by the aged hands of the master tuner. And then it was released and Jake rested it against his thigh.

"You no longer play?"

"No."

"Why?" He tilted his head questioningly. "Because you are in an invalid's chair?"

"Enough of a reason, I would think, Mr. Solomon." A flush of combined anger and embarrassment rose to heat Jake's face. The urge to turn and roll from this room, from the abrasive presence of this man, was almost more than he could resist.

"Are your hands damaged in any way that I could not perceive?"

"No." Abrupt and chill, the word put an end to the interrogation, as far as Jake was concerned.

"Wait, don't go."

Before wheels could be put into motion, the words halted him. Jake paused, fingers poised to spin the chair about.

"All of us bear wounds of one kind or another, Mr. McPherson. Yours and mine are more obvious than those of others, perhaps." Mr. Solomon drew forth a wrench from his bag of tools and leaned over the exposed strings to apply it to the appropriate place.

"I have no legs, no feet. Hence, I cannot use the pedals, sir." Jake's voice rumbled from his chest, and the pain of his words resounded in the room.

"Have you lost your knees, too?" He sat upright and touched the uppermost keys, playing a downward scale slowly, then reached the octave, playing each end alternately.

Jake waited until David Solomon had made his next adjustment before he answered. "I have my right knee."

"How fortunate for you." Sitting erect once more, his fingers played a short passage, imbuing the notes with a strangely tender resonance. "Without eyes, I must rely entirely upon my memory. At least you are able to learn new music."

"Which amounts to tinkling sounds without the pedals. Without being able to sustain the—" He stopped abruptly. "You know what I'm saying, Mr. Solomon."

"Yes, I do." He nodded his understanding. "But with a right knee, you should be able to press a pedal put in place beneath the keyboard. Fastened to a steel bar, then wired to the loud pedal. You'd lose the soft control, but then..." He shifted his shoulders, and his smile was radiant.

"I think you could live with the use of one pedal, Mr. McPherson. I think you could make music to stir the soul."

Jake's snort of disbelief was loud. "A pedal beneath the keyboard? Where have you ever seen such a thing?"

"I've never seen it, I have to admit. But I know it can be done."

Jake blushed anew. "I spoke too quickly. I apologize. Of course, you haven't seen it."

"A matter of speaking," said the tuner. "I took no offense."

"How could it be done?" A faint lilt of hope touched his speech, and Jake wished for its retrieval. There was no sense in wishing for what might never happen.

"Surely you have a blacksmith in town?"

"Yes, certainly."

David Solomon spread his hands, a gesture of finality. "There you have it. Ask him to come here and take the measure of what you need. Better yet, I'll go back to town and talk to him. Between us, we should be able to sort out the situation."

"You'd do that for me?"

"No, not just for you. For the music you have in you.

For the lives of others you may yet reach with your talent.''

"I'll never be on the stage again," Jake said bitterly. "There is no room in this world for a man who must carry his own custom-made piano with him."

"Then make this part of the world a better place. Make your own world brighter. Allow your music to feed your soul, Jacob McPherson."

Chapter Sixteen

The train whistle sounded in the evening air, blown on the prevailing wind from the west. The station platform held only four people, two satchels and a covered basket.

"I hope you'll enjoy the bread and jam Lorena packed for you," Rachel said, her heart overflowing with a gratitude she could not find words to express.

"Bread and jam? I opened the lid, Miss Rachel," David Solomon said with a gentle smile. "I smelled ham and fresh melon and my fingers found a tin of cookies."

"We wanted you to have home-cooked food until you reach your next stop."

"No one has ever treated us so well, I must admit," the younger member of the duo said.

"You've done more for us, for my brother, than I can ever say," Cord told David Solomon, his hand clasping that of the master tuner.

A brilliant smile touched the face of the blind man. "I only hope Jacob will find his way back to the world of music. He has an abundance of talent, but a soul that is starving for sustenance."

"Did he try the pedal?" Cord asked.

David Solomon shook his head. "Not while I was

there. Your Mr. Hunsucker said he would be willing to come back out to make adjustments if the apparatus did not work out as planned."

He bent his head for a moment. "I suspect Jacob wanted to be alone when he worked the knee pedal for the first time. If he cannot operate it, his disappointment will possibly be more than he is willing to allow another to see."

The train whistle blew again, a lonesome sound in the early-morning air. The two men were facing a long day's ride to their next stop. With a mighty clanging of its bell and a flourish of steam and cinders, the engine passed them by and the passenger car pulled up alongside.

Horace placed his arm under his companion's hand and together the two men boarded, the train hardly stopping before it picked up speed once more.

Rachel lifted her hand to wave and then found her fingers pressing instead against her mouth as a sob erupted from her throat.

"Tears, honey?" Cord asked, his hand rising to brush away the moisture that trickled down her cheek.

"That man worked a miracle for Jake." She fished in her pocket for her hankie and blew into it. "I think his life will be much different from now on."

"Only if he makes it so," Cord answered. "He's the one who has to make changes. Like you told me, neither of us can be responsible for Jake's happiness, Rachel. And the good Lord knows you've done more than enough already."

Her glance was swift, but she caught the element of anger he could not hide. "I wasn't aware I'd taken on that task."

"Seems to me like you have," he stated firmly.

She huffed out a breath and opened her mouth, only to close it again, her lips squeezing tightly together.

Well, so much for that, he thought with a surge of irritation as she lifted her chin defiantly. A flicker of unease gave him pause, and he turned her from the edge of the platform toward where the new buggy waited.

Surely she knew how much time she'd spent with Jake. She wasn't taking any pains to conceal her presence as she stopped by to pass the time of day with him. It was obvious enough to him that there was a bond between his wife and his brother.

A bond that had even infringed at times on his own needs. The ugly specter of jealousy had been an unwelcome visitor on more than one occasion of late, Cord admitted to himself. Could Rachel be so blind that she did not know how often Jake's name intruded?

The buggy cut a wide circle as it left the station, and Cord waved at Conrad Carson, who was sweeping the sidewalk in front of his store. Another fine example of Rachel's influence on the men in this town. Even now the man was probably gazing after the buggy with envious eyes.

Cord snapped the reins sharply over the back of his mare and she swung into a showy trot, her tail swishing as though she would draw eyes to her performance. John Hunsucker pumped the bellows in the doorway of his blacksmith shop, lifting one hand in greeting as the buggy passed.

It was not totally his imagination that John had spent considerable time speaking with Rachel yesterday. She'd offered him coffee and served it while he drew up a diagram of the apparatus he would build for the piano.

Then, upon his return several hours later, the burly blacksmith had asked her help as he put together and adjusted the metal adaptation to the pedal. Cord had watched for a few moments from the parlor doorway as those enormous shoulders had fit carefully beneath the keyboard, Rachel bending to hand him his tools.

Even the old gentleman, David Solomon, had been subject to her charm, accepting the cup of tea she prepared for him with a courtly bow. And holding court was about what she'd done, there in the parlor with three men.

Although, in good conscience, he could not include Jake in that particular scene, since he'd retired to the library while the blacksmith worked his miracle. Tense and almost rude in his behavior, Jake still sulked within the walls of his sanctuary this morning.

He'd managed to speak kindly to the piano tuner as the elderly man left yesterday. In fact their moments together had been touching as Jake sat on the porch with the gentleman. Cord had watched from the barn door, feeling a stranger in his own home, what with all the commotion over the Steinway in the parlor.

He sighed, aware suddenly that he was halfway back to the ranch and hadn't paid attention to one yard of the distance they'd traveled over the past little while. Beside him, Rachel was silent, looking off across the fields to where the river ran through a verdant meadow.

"What are your plans for today?" he asked, shifting in the seat to turn in her direction.

She shot him a look of mixed surprise and elegant reserve. Her chin lifted a bit and she shrugged. "I'm not sure. I have the last of the tomatoes to put up and Lorena will have washwater ready. There should be enough to keep me busy."

She was in a snit, sure enough, Cord thought glumly. Not one word had passed between them on the trip home, and she was probably stewing over what he'd told her at the railway station. We can't be responsible for Jake's happiness....

Damn! It was the truth. She'd put herself on the line for his brother, trotting around like his personal representative, hauling David Solomon out to the house and dealing with the blacksmith as she had. Between Rachel making the arrangements and all the rest of it, two days had been spent getting the damn piano set up for Jake to play...and then he'd gone and hibernated in the library instead of trying out the thing.

Cord leaned forward, his elbows on his knees, the reins threaded through his fingers. For the first time in their short marriage, he felt a separation from Rachel, as though their thoughts were on two different paths.

"I suppose Lorena will have started dinner already."

She turned her head aside. "I would imagine so."

"I'll carry the washwater out to the tub for you before I head for the barn."

"Lorena and I can probably manage it by ourselves."

He sighed deeply. "I always carry your washwater, Rachel." An undertone of impatience edged his voice.

"I can manage," she told him shortly.

He sat erect and snapped the reins, urging the horse into a lope. The buggy lurched and Rachel bounced on the seat. One hand swept to adjust the tilt of her bonnet and she muttered beneath her breath. The words were unclear, but her expression told him that he might be better off not catching the gist of what she'd said.

Cord pulled up into the yard with a flourish, the mare rearing a bit as he drew her to a halt. With a courtly gesture, he swept his hat from his head.

"I've delivered you safe and sound. Since you don't need me for anything, I'll be on my way to the barn."

Rachel's head swung about as if it were on a swivel, her eyes wide with an astonishment he could only relish. Served her right. For the first time in their marriage, he had her on the run. She was speechless and stunned.

She could still move though. He watched as she climbed down from the buggy, her legs stretching to reach the step and then the ground. Wasn't much to her, seen from this angle, only the lush lines of her breasts as she drew in a deep breath.

Her bonnet was awry and she tore it from her head, leaving it to dangle from one finger. He watched as her eyes blinked and her tongue moistened her lips, and then one hand lifted to brush at her hair.

A pang of guilt stabbed him. He should have helped her down. But she'd refrained from seeking his help, and now, unless he missed his guess, she was even madder than she'd been ten minutes ago.

Perhaps he'd pushed her too far. But damn it all, she had time and sweet talk and warmth for every man Jack in the county! She could just tend to herself for a while, without him waiting on her.

The washboard gave her the outlet she needed, Rachel decided, scrubbing for all she was worth. Lorena had offered to work at the first tubful, but Rachel had shaken her head and bent to the task with a vengeance.

The sound of the dasher's regular rhythm inside the churn caught her ear, and she glanced at the porch where Lorena had set to work making butter. A frown creased her forehead and Rachel knew a moment of guilt.

She'd bustled into the house, changed her clothes and scurried around gathering the wash without saying a word. Lorena had had Buck give her a hand with the boiler, and by the time Rachel returned to the kitchen, the water was steaming in the washtub out back.

Now the braided length of Lorena's golden hair swayed over her shoulder with the movement of her arms as she bent to her task. Rachel leaned back from the washboard.

"When you get tired of churning, I'll switch with you." As an olive branch, it wasn't much, but it was the best she could offer right now, she decided.

Lorena's blue eyes widened, and the thumping came to a halt. "I thought you were mad at me."

Rachel shook her head. "No, not you."

A grin twisted the corner of Rena's mouth. "Not Cord, surely?"

"Let me know when you want to switch," Rachel said with a half smile, her anger already dissipating. She'd sure scrubbed the bejabbers out of Cord's white drawers and everyday shirts. Not a smidgen of soil remained on his Sunday shirt either. A good, healthy fit of anger was worth something, she decided, wringing the water out of his clothes.

She fished around in the washtub, coming up with a blue and white shirt of Jake's. It hardly needed to be washed, as seldom as he soiled or stained anything. Her movements slower, she swished it in the water and held it up for inspection. The underarms probably needed a scrubbing, but not much else.

"I'll do Jake's things." Lorena stood by her side and Rachel looked up in surprise.

"I don't mind." A lock of hair fell across Rachel's forehead and dangled over her right eye. She blew at it, an ineffective solution. One sudsy hand rose to brush it aside, and she felt the residue of soap she'd left on her face.

Lorena smiled broadly. "I do. I've dreamed for years of doing Jake McPherson's laundry and now I've got the chance. Move over. The butter's almost ready. You can finish it up."

Rachel gave up her place willingly. Washing a few whites had never worn her out so quickly before. They floated now in the clear rinse water she'd brought out, soap bubbles popping as they rose to the surface.

"Dinner's about done, Rachel. By the time you finish working the butter, it'll be time to drop dumplings on top of the stew." Lorena cast an eye at the sky. "I dare say it's pretty near eleven o'clock."

"You're probably right. I'll hurry." Rachel climbed the steps and lifted the churn, carrying it inside the kitchen. She turned just inside the door and looked toward the barn.

Inside, standing in the shadow of the big doorway, Cord watched, hands on his hips, hat tilted forward. Across the wide expanse of the yard, their eyes meshed and she was struck with a sense of loss.

He was angry at her and she wasn't really certain why. He'd made a remark about taking on the responsibility for Jake's happiness and then fallen into a gloomy silence.

If she didn't know better, she'd think he was jealous of the time she spent with his brother, little enough as it was. Seemed like she catered to men every living hour of the day, she thought, her gaze unwavering as she studied her husband.

Oh well, if he didn't like it, he could just lump it. She had a pile of work to do before the day was over.

The easy routine they'd established early in their marriage was marred by a silence that could have been cut only with words of contrition. And from the looks of things, Cord was fresh out of apologies.

Rachel sniffed, stepping behind the screen in the corner of the bedroom to undress. It was cramped quarters, but she'd be jiggered if she was going to shed her clothing in front of Cord tonight.

She stripped quickly, pulling an old cotton gown over her head. A quick wash in the basin was sufficient, she decided, stepping from behind the screen, hairbrush in hand.

He'd undressed and climbed into bed already and she barely glanced his way as she settled in the rocking chair to brush out her snarls. She bent almost double, allowing her long hair to fall forward. Then, catching it up to braid it quickly, she fastened the end, circling it with wisps of loose hair from her brush.

The remaining strands of hair were removed to the hair receiver on the dresser, and there were no more excuses to keep her from joining Cord. She turned to the bed, only to find herself facing her husband's back. He'd rolled over toward his side of the bed, and she was struck with a sense of loss she found difficult to contain.

At least she was climbing into a clean bed. The sheets were cool and she relished the scent of them, fresh from the clothesline. It had been a long day and her muscles ached, arms and legs both. Reaching to catch at the billowing sheets and pillowcases, not to mention the lines of shirts and smallclothes, had been tedious. Between them, she and Lorena had folded two big baskets of clothes, sprinkling some down to iron on the morrow.

She stretched, her toes seeking the foot of the bed, with no success. It was good, this languid weariness, making her ready to sleep. Especially since Cord gave every appearance of having arrived at that state already.

Her head turned in his direction. He was unmoving, but she'd have bet her bottom dollar he was wide-awake.

"You ready to tell me why you were so hotheaded today?" she asked pleasantly.

He snorted and shifted, his shoulder hunching beneath the sheet.

"I take it that's an answer of some sort," she persisted, suddenly enjoying her first experience with taunting an angry man.

"Don't push it, Rachel." His voice was gruff and just a bit testy, she thought.

"Well, don't tempt me, Cord McPherson, or I just might." The urge to plant her foot in the small of his back and send him over the side of the bed was almost irresistible. She turned to her side to consider the idea from another angle.

"One more word and I'm liable to lose my temper, Rachel. I mean it. You've pushed me far enough. Just turn out the lamp."

From another man it might have been cause for alarm, but the thought of Cord doing her any harm was beyond believing, and Rachel grinned, her last shred of pique vanishing.

She lifted her legs, drawing her knees up. Then, placing her feet squarely against his bottom, she pushed, lending all her strength to the effort.

He yelped, a quickly muffled sound, as he caught himself midway to the floor. One hand slapped the bare wooden boards and he levered himself back up, rolling over in a single furious movement.

His eyes were narrowed slits, his nostrils flaring and his mouth a firm line as he lunged for her. Hands grasping and fingers gripping her wherever they could, it was to his credit that he didn't exert any great amount of pressure.

One palm had managed to grasp her upper arm, fingers wrapping it firmly, the other hand snagged against her gown, his widespread palm enclosing her breast. He looked down at what he held, then quickly up at her. Their eyes clashed in a gaze rife with surprise, and he growled a muffled curse.

In an automatic response to the hand that cradled the softness of her bosom, she gasped, shrinking back from his touch.

"Don't!" Gruffly, he uttered the single word, and she obeyed, catching a deep breath, aware of the pressure of each fingertip that rested against her. His grip on her arm tightened and he drew her closer, until the shadows between them became a blending of their bodies.

"Don't you know I wouldn't hurt you?" The words were harsh, but the hands that held her were gentle and Rachel leaned to him.

"I know that. You startled me."

"Really? And what do you think it did to me to be pushed from my bed?"

"I couldn't resist. You were so angry and ornery…I just couldn't help it."

"I was trying to leave you alone."

"Oh? Why would you want to do that?"

"Damn it, Rachel! I've been sore at you all day and if I were to come at you tonight, I'm afraid I might be rough."

"I'm still not sure why you were angry, Cord, but I doubt your hands would ever cause me pain."

"I've never seen a woman so confounded…" He pressed his lips together and glared at her. "You had those men eating out of your hand in the parlor."

She wrenched from his hold and he let her go. With a rustle of sheets and a mumbled oath, she managed to sit up beside him. "What are you talking about?" The words were a harsh whisper, and she forced them out on shallow bursts of breath.

"John Hunsucker and that piano tuner and Jake. They kept givin' you sheep's eyes...."

"That piano tuner is blind! He couldn't look at me if he wanted to. You are out of your mind, Cord McPherson!"

"He kissed your hand!" His roar was enough to wake the dead and Rachel slapped her hand across his mouth. Sort of like closing the barn door after the horse had run off, she thought ruefully.

Her whisper was pushed between barely parted lips. "He didn't kiss my hand. He bowed over it, a very courtly gesture, I thought. I gave him a cup of tea. Then I handed tools to Mr. Hunsucker while he worked on the piano."

"And he laughed and preened, showing off his wide shoulders and all those muscles for your benefit."

"I don't believe you!" She forgot the need for silence. "You were jealous of a blind man and the blacksmith, not to mention your own brother, who merely tolerates me most of the time."

"I'm not jealous. I simply want you to behave yourself around other men. Even old Conrad was tryin' to peek inside the buggy to get a gander at you when we went by the store."

She picked up her pillow and slammed it down on his head. "He was sweeping the walk, and barely took a second to nod at you."

His words were muffled by the pillow and she held it firmly against his face. That he could have freed himself readily was beside the point. She'd managed to silence his accusations, and that was enough to keep her on the attack.

"You have no reason to be jealous of me, Cord McPherson. I've never been unfaithful to you in any way."

Her voice caught as she uttered the words and her hands loosened their grip as she turned away from him. The pillow was pushed aside and he reached for her, his hair falling over his forehead, his eyes filled with a passionate intensity she could not fail to recognize.

"Don't you try to make love to me when you're angry. I won't have it!" she said in a husky whisper, even as he pushed her back against the mattress.

"Ah...that's where you're wrong, Mrs. McPherson. You will have it."

"No, I don't want you to..." Her protest was stilled by the touch of his mouth against hers, his lips nibbling against her flesh, even as he swept his hands the length of her body to rest against her hips.

"You don't want me to what?" Flesh brushed against flesh as he spoke, and then he coaxed her mouth to open, his tongue a gentle weapon, easing its way beyond the barrier of her teeth to draw her own into a duel in which neither would be loser.

She felt the familiar shivers of desire, the flash fire of need his caresses evoked, and her flesh tingled with anticipation. That this man could entice her, beguiling her so readily, was a mystery she stood no chance of solving.

But it was so, and her eager heart embraced the fact of it. His touch was ever welcome, even in this moment, when she'd but a minute past assured him that she was not willing. Her mouth opened wider to welcome his intimate caress, and she pressed against his firmness, acknowledging the male strength of the man she loved.

He released her mouth, his lips suckling for a moment on her lower lip, pulling it with a gentle rhythm between his teeth. "Damn! You've got me pokin' at you with a fence post, girl," he growled against her throat.

She'd noticed, and the words he spoke only served to bring a low laugh from her.

"Still mad, Cord?" she asked in a whisper.

"Ah, hell! You know better than that. I wouldn't hurt you, Rae." His teeth caught at the bodice of her gown. "I might bite a little, though."

She wiggled against him. "Maybe I'd better get those buttons out of the way."

His male strength pressed against her, and the urgency of his arousal was firm against her thigh. With a guttural sound of impatience, his hands met where buttons joined and in a single movement, he tore them asunder.

"You ruined my gown!" she said in a whisper of amazement.

"I'll buy you a new one," he told her gruffly. "Two of them, in fact. Although you don't need any, as far as I'm concerned."

His hands were swift, his fingers clever, as he divested her of the torn garment, lifting her, shifting her to suit his purpose. He'd hidden nothing beneath the sheet but his own male flesh, and now there was only the sensation of soft, woman's skin and the hard muscles of her mate forming a unity that defied understanding.

She gloried in his possession, bending to his need. Her heartbeat increased with every stroke of his hand, every touch of his mouth against her skin. He lifted her, his hands strong beneath her. He coaxed her, whispering enticements against her ear. His fingers lured her ever nearer the point of fulfillment her body had learned to crave, and then in a single, forceful thrust, he took her with him to a place where only the two of them had ever been.

To a joining so far removed from what had gone before that her cries of completion rose sweetly on the night air, unhindered by his mouth to hush the sound. His head thrown back in his own ecstasy, he called her name, a dark, frantic sound that clutched at her heart.

Her arms tightened their grip on him, fingers grasping for purchase as she held tightly to the taut flesh of his backside. Tears slid from her eyes as she watched him, gazing on the man who had claimed her with unbridled passion.

He opened his eyes and they blazed with pure emotion, finding her and focusing on her face. "You're crying."

She shook her head. "Not from pain or sorrow, Cord."

"What, then?"

"Sometimes I love you so much, it just rises up in me like the tide, and then overflows in tears."

His palms held her face, his fingers lacing through her hair.

From one lower lid, then the other, a single drop fell to roll down his face.

She lifted one hand to touch a teardrop as it trembled on the edge of his jaw, then reached to wipe away the other. Her smile was fragile, quivering on her lips as she brushed her fingers over his mouth.

And then, beneath the touch of her fingertips, his mouth opened and he uttered the words she waited to hear.

"I love you, Rachel. As God is my witness, I love you as I've never thought to love a woman. You're my heart's desire, all I've ever wanted in a wife."

His voice lowered to a whisper, and his eyes held hers as he repeated once more the joyous revelation she'd craved so long.

"I love you, sweetheart."

Chapter Seventeen

The sun was barely up when the first notes reached Rachel's ears. Muffled by the walls between, they were not enough to waken her, but loud enough to disturb the silence of early morning, bringing her to that half state of sleep and awareness.

She opened her eyes, listening to the faint sound of the piano in the parlor below. One note struck with a delicate touch, sustained, and then blended in with another, then a third, forming a chord.

Sliding to the edge of the bed, her feet touched the floor. Rachel rose and stepped to her dresser, opening the drawer to search out clean underwear for the day.

A muffled footstep alerted her to Cord's approach and she looked up into the mirror on the wall. Behind her, his tall figure stood in the shadows of early morning, his hair in disarray, his big body surging with the strength of youth and male arrogance.

She watched as he approached, until her paler flesh was silhouetted against his darker form. Until he stood with his chest touching her shoulders, the furry texture of his body brushing with intimate knowledge against her own smoother skin.

"I love you," he whispered, and she closed her eyes, the better to hear the tenderness that lurked in the deep tones of his voice. That this strong, stalwart man was hers, that his love for her had been spoken aloud, that she was safe, secure in that love, was almost more than her heart could contain.

She tilted her head, allowing his mouth to venture closer to her own, and her words were a husky whisper that echoed his own. "I love you, Cord."

He smiled, a lazy movement of his lips, meeting her gaze in the mirror. "You're awake early."

She nodded. "I heard the piano."

He stilled, his lips unmoving, his body tensed, as if his whole being listened for a sound.

Again the single note vibrated in the silence, its tone sustained as it was joined by another, then a third. The pressure on the pedal relaxed, and the blended trio of notes was silenced.

Rachel released her breath, only now aware that she had held it within her lungs as the faint notes shimmered in the morning air. "Jake." His name was borne on a wispy exhalation.

She turned to Cord, sliding her arms around his neck. "He's at the piano, Cord. He's using the pedal." She leaned her forehead against his chest, her ears attuned to the next sounds that would surely follow.

Cord's arms tightened around her and they swayed together in the first rays of the rising sun. Beyond the window, across the pasture where horses grazed and yearlings stood beneath tall maple trees, the horizon grew brighter, drawing the sun into the morning sky.

"Has he eaten?" Rachel stood outside the parlor doors, where Lorena kept watch. Opened barely a crack, they offered a glimpse of the man who sat on the piano bench.

He was in the midst of a simple melody, his fingers moving slowly as he improvised, playing a song unfamiliar to Rachel. "He's composing as he goes along, isn't he?" she whispered.

Lorena nodded. "I think so. He's run through about everything he knew by heart already."

Since sunrise, Jake had been at the keyboard. During breakfast the men had listened, exchanged glances across the table, their faces lit with a wonder that warmed Rachel's heart. They probably didn't recognize the music his fingers formed, she decided, but their appreciation was no less keen, their approval no less valid.

"Should we disturb him? He needs breakfast." Rachel peeked through the narrow opening as she spoke.

Even as her words were uttered, Jake's hands ceased to play, his fingers lifting from the keys, then falling in his lap. "Come in, Rena...Rachel. Don't stand out there whispering."

The doors gave way easily and Lorena led the way. She stood behind him, her hands hovering then lowering to his wide shoulders, fingers flexing as she caressed the muscles, easing the ache they must feel after such continuous strain.

"Congratulations, Miss Rachel," he said, his voice quietly sarcastic. "You've managed to place me where I thought never to be."

She was stung by his tone, her eagerness tainted by his obvious ill will. "Is that all bad?"

Lorena's hands squeezed tightly against his shoulders, as if she would warn him to watch his tongue.

It had no effect.

"Nothing is ever all bad," he answered. "Neither is

anything ever all good. Giving me the means to play this cursed instrument was a fine gesture on your part.'' He glanced at her over his shoulder, his cheek grazing Lorena's wrist in the passing.

"Why do I feel as though I'm waiting for the rest of the sentence?'' Rachel asked sharply, her good mood laid aside.

He bowed his head, a gesture that lacked submission, given his arrogance. "I'm sure I'll be a source of entertainment to all the ranch hands and even to the ladies of the household,'' he said lightly. "And when I've gained back all my competence, I might even play for the parson on a Sunday afternoon.''

"I only wanted to return to you the joy of music, Jake. I never intended to begin arranging your schedule for a tour of Europe.'' She spun from him, long strides taking her from the room, and behind her she heard Lorena's gasp of dismay.

In the kitchen, the bread was rising nicely on the top of the warming oven and Rachel's eyes lit on the rounded mass. Leaning forward over the range, she lifted the pan to the tabletop, whisking away the dish towel that covered it. A bowl of flour awaited the task and she cast a handful over the wooden breadboard, white puffs sifting to the floor as she added a second helping after the first.

The dough was turned out with a swift touch and she began the pummeling that would tame it and eventually turn it to light, tasty fare for the household. For now, the battered dough simply became the object of her anger.

"Don't beat the poor stuff to death.'' From the doorway, Cord watched, and she ignored his good-natured gibe.

"Rachel?'' He stepped closer, as if he sensed that all

was not as it seemed. "What's wrong?" His tone turned dark, dangerous as he neared her. "What's happened, Rae?"

She felt the fire rise in her cheeks as she allowed her gaze to rise from the glutinous mass she handled. "Your brother is an ass."

He was not altogether successful in hiding his grin. "I've known that for years."

"No, I mean, he's really an arrogant, idiotic ass!"

He nodded his agreement. Then, leaning back on his heels, he ventured to vent his curiosity. "What's he done now?"

She shook her head. "I've got bread to take care of. Go ask him."

Somehow, he'd gotten into the midst of a mess here, Cord decided, his footsteps lagging as he trod the hallway toward the library. From within, Lorena's clear tones were being overridden by Jake's caustic remarks.

"I didn't ask for interference in my life. I don't know why I should be grateful for a chance to play my pretty little pieces for the benefit of—"

"Damn you, Jake McPherson! You are the most ungrateful, inconsiderate man I've ever had the poor judgment to make acquaintance with."

"And how many men have you known, Miss Claypool?" he returned quickly.

She huffed her disdain. "That's neither here nor there. The point is, you hurt Rachel's feelings and all she intended was for your life to become better."

"Thus far, I haven't noticed much improvement."

"Well, for one thing, you've managed to stir yourself beyond this room. For another, you've played the piano and played well."

"And you are qualified to be a critic, I suppose?" he gibed with sarcastic skill.

"I only know what I like, and after all, that's all any critic manages to base his review upon, isn't it?"

"There is such a thing as skill and training and varying degrees of talent," Jake reminded her smoothly.

"Do you have any of those?" she asked him.

The room was silent, and Cord leaned against the wall beside the library door, hoping for a continuation of the warfare within. So much easier for the two of them to hash things out in his hearing, telling him what he wanted to know without the task of questioning the miserable specimen of manhood his brother had become.

"I had all of them...once." Jake's words were tinged with bitterness.

"You've hurt Rachel terribly," Lorena said after a moment.

"Offer her my apology, will you?" The words were stiff and formal, and yet within them hovered a note of sincerity.

"You can offer your own apologies, Jake McPherson. You didn't mind causing the pain. Now you can just get yourself out there and start the healing."

"Don't ask me to do that, Rena."

"I love you," she said with quiet despair, "but, sometimes I don't like you at all."

Light spread a path from the doorway, as the draperies within the room were pulled apart. A great commotion was taking place inside the library and Cord smiled as he listened to Lorena's banging and clattering.

"Are you planning on tearing up the whole room?" Jake's voice came from nearby and Cord backed off a few steps.

"I'm cleaning up your mess for the last time, and then I'm heading for home."

"You're leaving me?"

A loud thump, sounding suspiciously as though she'd pitched a stack of books on the floor, assailed Cord's hearing.

"Yes, I'm leaving. I'm tired of watching you pout. I'm sick of your selfishness. And most of all, I'm disappointed in you."

"Then leave, if you feel that way. I got along before you got here. I suspect I'll manage after you're gone." The words lacked force, spoken beneath his breath, and Cord lowered his head as he reluctantly absorbed his brother's pain.

He turned, his footsteps silent as he retraced his path to the kitchen.

The bread pans were full, lined up like metal soldiers atop the warming oven, and Rachel's hands snapped open a dish towel as he watched from the doorway. The checked fabric drifted over the pans and she stepped back, an air of satisfaction alive in her face.

"You thrive on this, don't you?" he asked quietly.

She glanced at him, her features more relaxed now. "Kneading bread is good for me, Cord. I manage to come back to the fundamentals when I..." She tilted her head, eyeing him carefully.

"You look like you've been through a war of your own," she said.

He nodded. "Kinda. Listened in on one, really."

"Lorena?"

"Yeah. She says she's leaving."

"I hope not for my benefit. I don't need her to stick up for me."

"Well, she is anyway." He reached her in two long

strides. "No, not really. She's mad at him all on her own. Called him selfish and a couple of other things I can't remember."

"Give him a day or two," Rachel said easily.

His arms slid around her waist and he drew her into a loose embrace. "You're not mad at him?"

She shook her head. "Sounds like Lorena's mad enough for both of us." Her smile was quick. "He's got a musician's temperament, Cord, and he's feeling the length of his tether." She looked up at him and he was struck once more by the gentle beauty of the woman he'd married.

"You sure get over bein' mad in a hurry, Rae." And thank God for that! His lips twitched as he considered the benefit to himself of that particular quality of hers. She didn't hold a grudge for long, this small creature he held in his arms.

"I'm thinking his tether may be longer than he knows, Cord," she said slowly. "If he's willing to make concessions."

"He's not much for that sort of thing."

She smiled, as if she knew a secret. "He may have to do some changing."

"I'm leaving." The words left no room for doubt. Lorena's bag was bulging, her face was flushed and her eyes glittered with traces of an emotion Rachel could only guess at.

Whether anger or hurt drove her, the golden-haired woman had reached her limits, and the loser in this game would be the man in the library. Probably even now he was nursing his aggravation in front of the window, shoulders hunched and hair all awry, as if he'd lost his hairbrush and wasn't interested in finding it again.

"Don't leave on my account," Rachel told her firmly.

"That's part of it," Lorena admitted. "On the other hand, I can't face watching him go downhill for the rest of his life. He's not even making an attempt, Rachel."

"You're wrong," Rachel replied. "He did make an attempt. He played that piano for hours, until his arms and fingers probably ached beyond belief. And then he decided it was all for naught, that he'd never be able to go beyond that parlor or past the walls of this house."

Lorena sat down in a chair at the table. "You're a better woman than I am," she announced. "And I'm the one who loves him."

"I do too," Rachel admitted. "I love him for his talent, for his bravery in going to battle when he knew he was risking more than his life. I love him for finding the courage to tackle the piano this morning, and I love him because he's still sitting upright in that chair and not pounding the floor with his fists."

"I thought he might, for a few minutes there," Lorena said softly.

"He'll come back from this."

Lorena's glance was doubtful. "You really think so?"

"I'm going to see to it."

Lorena eyed the bulging satchel she'd plopped near the screen door. "It'll be a chore to unpack that thing. Everything's in it all every which way."

"We'd like to make you an offer, Mrs. McPherson. Could you come over to the theater when you've finished your business here?" The dapper gentleman faced her on the wide sidewalk in front of Conrad's store, and Rachel was stunned.

"An offer to do what?" she asked, although she was almost certain of his words before he uttered them. If the banker's word could be depended upon, she would be asked to assist in rehearsals before the actual musicians arrived on the scene, whenever theater groups or vocalists came to perform.

"It has to do with having someone here to take charge during the times when no representative of our corporation is present. Sort of an on-hand manager."

She nodded. "I see." Lifting one hand in a vague gesture, she groped for a coherent thought. Food, supplies…her list. She'd do first things first.

"I'll be the better part of an hour," she said finally, surprised at the confident tone of her voice.

Mr. Baldridge tipped his hat, stepping back to open the door of Conrad's store for her entry. "I look forward to speaking with you," he told her.

Rachel stepped through the doorway into the comforting scents of leather and starched bolts of cotton fabric. The pungent smell of wax greeted her as she approached the counter, a reminder of Conrad's diligence this morning. The counter gleamed. The wooden showcases, a blend of glass and walnut, gave evidence of loving care, and Rachel was aware once more of the man she had spurned in favor of Cord McPherson.

He'd have been a fine husband, she was forced to admit. But when all was said and done, he didn't hold a candle to the rancher she'd married. And then she looked up to find Conrad facing her across the counter. His brows were lifted, his mouth pursed, and he leaned toward her, couching his question with an air of gaining her confidence.

"What does the gentleman from New York want with the wife of a rancher? If you'll pardon my curiosity," he added as a hasty afterthought.

"I'm not sure," Rachel answered. "I'll find out soon enough, I suppose. I'm to meet him when I leave here."

"I heard the piano tuner spent the best part of the day at your place a couple of days ago." He took the list from her hand and perused it, scanning it quickly. "Heard tell that John Hunsucker did some work for you, too."

"I'd think Green Rapids had more to do than speculate over the goings-on at the McPherson ranch."

He shrugged, turning to the shelf to begin filling her grocery order. "Not much. Since the day Jake came to town for the picnic, he's been the subject of half the gossip in the barber shop, and most all the speculating in this place."

"Are you aware of his enormous talent, Conrad?" Rachel leaned against the counter, conscious of several women who spoke in soft tones on the other side of the room.

He turned to her. "Everyone who knows the family knows that he was heading for the concert stage when he chose to join the Union army. We all watched that big piano come off the train the month after he went to New York to study. His pa wanted it ready for him when he came back, so he'd have an instrument to practice on."

"It must have cost an awful lot of money," Rachel said, aware of the amount her own father had spent on her small upright back home in Pennsylvania.

"The old man could afford it," Conrad said simply. "Too bad it never got played. By the time they brought Jake home from the war, his piano-playing days were over, what with losing his legs."

She couldn't resist. "He played it yesterday. All morning in fact."

"Miz Bryant said he'd never be able to make decent music without being able to use the pedals."

"He managed," Rachel told him. "Between David Solomon and John Hunsucker, they fixed things so he could play."

"Do tell!" His eyes lit with delight, and Conrad shook his head, as if amazed at the news.

"What's so exciting, Conrad? Good morning, Mrs. McPherson." From behind her, Rachel heard a voice that rang a bell within her memory, and she turned to greet its owner.

"Mr. Jackson! How nice to see you," she said courteously.

"You ever met Rachel's brother-in-law?" Conrad asked the rancher.

"Saw him at the picnic. A war hero, I assume." His tone was neutral, Rachel decided, as if he held his thoughts in abeyance.

"A man wounded by the surgeon's knife," she answered.

"A bitter blow, I'm sure," Beau Jackson said with a nod.

Conrad spoke softly, as if he hesitated to deny her story. "Now, Miss Rachel, I heard tell he got frostbitten when he spent the night with his legs hanging down in the river, all covered with ice and snow. Someone said it was morning before he was found and it was a miracle he lived through it."

She nodded, agreeing with his telling of the tale. "That's what I heard too, Conrad. The head wound that felled him was a mere scratch, just enough to knock him unconscious for a time. The men around him were all dead. Cord said Jake huddled between two of them in the early-morning hours, trying to stay alive until he was found.''

"Nasty business," Beau said. "War should be banned from the face of the earth, in my opinion."

"I must leave," Rachel said, turning back to Conrad, feeling suddenly that she had betrayed family confidences in the past few moments. "I'll run by and meet with Mr. Baldridge. Perhaps he'll be available a few minutes early."

She walked down the sidewalk, a sense of belonging permeating her as nods and smiles greeted her progress. Conrad would load her purchases in the wagon for her. The men seated in front of the emporium would keep an eye on her supplies while she did her business at the theater. In fact, the thought of anyone pilfering another's belongings was entirely foreign to her mind. She belonged here, she was a part of this town, and the knowledge that it was so gave her great pleasure.

Cecil Hampton stood next to Mr. Baldridge, just outside the double front doors of the new theater. Rachel's feet slowed a bit as she approached them, as if she could somehow savor the anticipation for a few moments longer.

She was being sought after for her talent. For the first time in her life, she felt utterly selfish, absolutely centered upon her own satisfaction, her first chance for an exciting opportunity, with money to be earned.

Working for Cord McPherson had been a godsend. This happening was a bonus directly from the angels as far as she was concerned. Over and above the necessities of life, everyone needed a chance to use the talents they'd been given, needed the joy that came with some small bit of appreciation.

And then her heart began a slower beat, as if she must

stop and reconsider. Perhaps Jake would be better at this than she. After all, that was what she had considered for several weeks now, once the theater had become more than just a dream. And Jake needed to be needed, perhaps more than she did.

On top of that, maybe the job would be more suited to a man. She'd borne that in mind for days, that Jake might find a degree of usefulness here in this place.

Mentally, she shook her head. Why shouldn't a woman do as well as a man? Her heart yearned for the satisfaction she might gain from such an opportunity as this.

She'd have to be careful that it didn't interfere with her chores at home, that the time spent in town didn't take from her hours with her family. She brushed the thought aside, too filled with excitement to contemplate such mundane considerations right now.

"I'm purely selfish," she whispered to herself. "And for right now, this very minute, I don't even care."

"You're early, Miss Rachel," Cecil Hampton said from his post next to the door, tipping his hat in her direction.

"Come inside, won't you?" Mr. Baldridge invited, holding the door open with a flourish.

Rachel held her skirts, navigating the three steps, and entered the large building. It smelled of newly painted walls and fresh lumber. Perhaps roughly finished to the sophisticated observer, it looked like a dream come true to Rachel.

"I came as soon as I could," she told Mr. Baldridge, folding her hands before her.

"Mrs. McPherson, your husband was told a while back that we might like to have you play for rehearsals in the future. It might only be an occasional thing, unless you were willing to take on the position of an on-hand manager.''

''I wasn't sure your husband would agree to your spending that many hours here,'' Cecil Hampton put in quickly.

Rachel considered that idea. ''I can speak to him. As to the other, the working with those who need an accompanist in order to rehearse for their performances, I should be able to do that with no trouble.''

Mr. Baldridge nodded slowly. ''In the future, when the schedule fills in, as we are certain it will, a man in town will be necessary to keep order and handle things for us.''

''You expect a lot of performers to head this way?'' Rachel asked. The thought was more than she could conceive, although she welcomed it wholeheartedly.

''Yes. There are a number of theaters on this order, all on the railway line. Their schedule will allow our artists to go from one town to another, then start all over again, with a new program to offer.''

''It's doing big things for our town already,'' Cecil said proudly. ''We have interest in a new stockyard on the far west end of the town, what with the cattle drives coming this way more and more all the time. There's a mill being built down by the river and a ladies' dress shop being considered next door to the newspaper office.''

''I'll talk to Cord,'' Rachel said. Surely he would agree.

''We'll wait to hear from you.'' Mr. Baldridge lifted his hat and ushered her back to the front door, Cecil Hampton nodding as she favored him with a smile.

Her steps were light as she walked back to the emporium. To think that she might work with real professionals, playing their music as they prepared for concerts. She imagined herself at the theater piano, music spread across the rack, a hushed crowd sitting on the edge of their seats.

Before the play began, she would play music that put the audience in the mood for the performance. During intervals, she would fill in the time until the curtain should be pulled aside for the next portion of the play.

She denied the urge to skip down the sidewalk, fought the delight that coaxed her to sing aloud as she made her way back to Conrad's store. Her wagon was ready to roll, the purchases tucked neatly inside the box, and Conrad watched from the doorway.

"Take care, Mrs. McPherson," he called cheerfully, careful not to use her given name, lest he cause gossip to follow her wagon home.

She waved, her smile wide, holding her happiness inside until she passed the last building marking the outskirts of Green Rapids. The schoolhouse lay just ahead, a scattering of houses on either side of the road, and she waved at several youngsters who played in the dusty yards. A dog barked at her, his tail wagging furiously as she passed, and she even waved at him.

A song burst from her lips, an aria she could not begin to do justice to, but she sang it anyway. The sound rose on the air, losing itself in the trees that shaded the road for the first mile out of town. The river ran not far from here and she cast a glance to where it glittered in the sunshine, the whole world assuming a patina of brilliance to her eye.

She was on the upside of a shallow slope, the horse clipping along at a nice trot when the wagon lurched. The horse hesitated, his gait broken, and then with a terrible shudder, the wagon tilted to one side, throwing

Rachel from the seat. She landed in the middle of the road, bonnet over her eyes, dust clogging her nose, and shaking like a leaf in a windstorm.

The left front wheel was gone and she spotted it across the road, leaning against a rock, as if it had been placed there by an unseen hand. Her food stuffs were in disarray, a bag of sugar spilling with slow precision from a small hole punctured in one corner. Rachel stood quickly, grasping the bag and halting the flow, then stood there with dust and dirt covering her from stem to stern as she debated what she would do with the sweet stuff.

A cardboard box had a vacant corner and she stuffed the sugar into it, then busied herself with arranging the rest of the food. Her bonnet was in the middle of the road, her hands were covered with dirt and her dress was enveloped in dust. She had begun to shake her skirts, managing to feel downright sorry for herself, when she heard a horse approaching at a good pace just behind her.

Atop his big gray stallion, Beau Jackson rode at a full gallop. "Miss Rachel! Are you all right?" he called out, sliding from his mount as he reached her side."

She nodded once, shifting her shoulders and moving her arms, and then, to her everlasting mortification, she burst into tears.

Chapter Eighteen

Beau Jackson's hand patted her shoulder, as if he would lend his sympathy to her plight. The yearning for Cord's wide chest upon which to shed her tears gripped her with all the agony of a toothache, and she sobbed anew.

"Miss Rachel...Mrs. McPherson... Are you sure you're not hurt?" Beau's words were hurried, his voice harsh, and she nodded her head abruptly, anxious to assure him of her well-being.

And yet, she didn't feel well at all. Her stomach churned with a terrible nausea, and her head was spinning as though she'd just jumped from a merry-go-round going full tilt.

A lurching within her signaled imminent disaster and she stumbled to the side of the road, leaning forward over a patch of weeds. The contents of her stomach erupted and she swayed as she lost every bit of dignity she'd ever possessed.

A strong arm snaked around her waist and a wide palm supported her forehead as she suffered another session of gagging and retching.

"I've got you, honey. Just relax." Beau Jackson's

soothing voice was a comfort, she had to admit, leaning heavily on his support. His hand left her forehead, returning just seconds later with a wrinkled, but thankfully clean, handkerchief.

With a deep breath, she muttered words of thanks, wishing only for the privacy of her bedroom. Throwing up was an indignity itself. Doing it with an audience was probably the most embarrassing thing she'd ever done in her life.

She wiped her mouth, blew her nose and stood erect, horribly aware of the man behind her. Finally, unable to put it off any longer, she turned to him, brushing stray wisps of hair from her face.

"I'm so sorry, Mr. Jackson. My stomach must have reacted badly to the fall I took." She looked up at him and her gaze met a crooked grin.

"No problem, ma'am," he said with merciful courtesy. "We've all chucked our cookies once or twice." His eyes narrowed as he watched her. "You dizzy, ma'am? You're still pretty pasty-looking."

Rachel shook her head, then promptly wished she hadn't. The sky and earth changed places for a few seconds, whirling with an audible buzzing in her ears, and she found herself carried in strong arms to the other side of the road.

Beau settled her on the ground and eyed her cautiously. With a brisk movement he removed his hat and began waving it with a slow tempo, wafting fresh air across her face.

Rachel groaned. "I feel so..." She drew up her legs, dipping her head to rest against them.

"Sick?" he prompted.

She shook her head. "No, just embarrassed, mostly. A little dizzy yet, but better since I..."

"Threw up?" he supplied.

Drat the man! Why couldn't he just disappear and leave her alone in her misery?

Now his hand was beneath her elbow and he was dragging her to her feet. "Miss Rachel? I think I need to get you home."

She waved her other hand distractedly at the wagon and the horse, standing dejectedly with its harnesses hanging askew. "What about Cord's horse?"

"We'll leave her here. I'll get some help and be back in no time to fix the wheel. I don't think you're in any shape to help with it, and I'm not real interested in doing it alone."

"All right," she agreed, willing to do most anything to get back to the ranch, where soap and water and a clean dress would be the first order of business.

He gathered up his horse's reins and mounted, slipping his left foot from the stirrup. "Can you reach your foot up here?" he asked, hoisting her with an arm beneath her shoulders.

It was a simple matter, and within seconds, Rachel was astride behind him, tugging her skirts to cover as much of her legs as possible. The big stallion set off at a gentle pace and Rachel placed reluctant hands at Beau Jackson's waist.

"Hang on good and tight," he told her cheerfully. "I don't want you rolling in the dirt again. You scared the bejabbers out of me the last time, when I saw you take a header off that wagon seat."

She clung a bit tighter, peering past him as she watched for the turnoff that would lead to the ranch. "It's just ahead, Mr. Jackson," she told him after a few minutes.

He nodded, glancing back at her as the horse cut the

corner. "You feeling all right back there? I was thinking maybe I shouldn't have put you up on the horse. You're not...there isn't any chance you might be..."

Rachel frowned. Whatever was the man trying to say? A little spell of dizziness was to be expected after a jolt. And she'd felt a bit queasy several times lately. Probably just a touch of stomach discontent.

"You think you might be in a family way?" The words were blurted out in a rush, as if Beau Jackson worried that it were true. He slowed his horse to a walk, waiting for her reply, and Rachel felt a blush climb slowly from her chest to cover her face with a heated glow.

"Really, Mr. Jackson..." Her voice trailed off as she considered his question. Of course she wasn't...that way. Surely any woman would recognize it if she were to be... Her brow furrowed as she considered the thought.

"I should have gone with her." Cord's grumbling had gone on for more than half an hour already, and Sam Bostwick muttered his opinion of the whole situation.

"Dang it all, Cord. You act like the girl don't know how to drive that wagon. She was holdin' the reins long before you ever met her. You can't ride a green horse when your mind's on a woman. That's a fact, son!"

Cord picked himself up from the dust of the corral and slapped his hat against his leg. He was aching in several spots already. Damn horse was about the most hardheaded cayuse he'd ever had the dubious pleasure of hanging a saddle on.

"Well, whatever you say, Sam, she's been gone long enough to get her runnin' around done, and then some." Cord gathered up the reins in his left hand and waited for his chance. The horse rolled his eyes and turned in a circle, Cord tightening his grip and closing in as they maneuvered in the middle of the corral.

He saw his moment and seized it, his foot snatching at the stirrup; and with a single, graceful movement, he attained the saddle. The horse bunched beneath him and he tightened up on the reins, his knees gripping, his thighs taut, his backside still throbbing from the last spill he'd taken.

"Wal, what the hell's that?" From the corral fence, Buck's voice caught his attention, and Cord's head swung to where the youthful cowhand was straddling the topmost rail.

Just beyond the house, where the long lane wound between a line of fencing on either side, a big horse approached, two riders taking their good old time about getting to wherever they were going.

The animal between his knees jerked sideways and Cord followed the movement with an automatic reflex, wincing as his bottom hit the saddle with a thump. Damn, he was getting the worst of this ride, he decided, and in no mood for company.

Allowing a quick glance at the approaching riders, he swallowed an oath. Rachel! The horse spun and he lost sight of her.

"Well, I'll be a suck-egg mule! What's Miss Rachel doin' riding double with Beau Jackson?" Sam's gruff drawl penetrated his concentration, and Cord cast a quick look over his shoulder.

Damn if it wasn't Rachel, her arms hugging the neighbor, and him looking like he'd just had a good laugh over something.

Cord's bottom left the saddle and he felt the reins snatched from his gloved hand. The sky turned to dirt and he landed with a thump, his head touching down first. For just a second's time, he felt the thud of ground meeting skull and then his back slammed against the hard-packed earth. With a mighty *whoosh*, he lost every bit of breath in his lungs.

"Cord!" It was a single, whispered sound, yet the echo of his name resounded over and over again in her mind.

"Hang on there, ma'am," Beau said tightly. "Don't you be falling. One of you on the ground at a time is enough, and you already had your turn."

She'd watched Cord twist his neck to see her, noted the frown he wore, and then her gaze had followed his descent to the ground, arms and legs spread wide as he hit with a thud.

Now she slid from behind Beau Jackson and fell into Buck Austin's arms. He righted her quickly and she ran to the corral. Sam and Moses were bending over Cord, Shamus kneeling at his head.

"Is he all right?" she cried, jerking at the gate, tears flowing too rapidly for her to find the latch.

Buck gripped the bridle of the horse Cord had been working with, and he led the animal to the barn, opening the gate and allowing Rachel past him.

She stumbled to where Cord lay, her hand reaching to spread wide against his chest. "He's not breathing," she cried. "Do something! Sam! Shamus!"

Shamus grunted, his hands gripping Cord's belt, lifting the big man off the ground for a moment. He dropped him back to the ground, then lifted him again. "Lost his wind," he announced, breathing heavily. "Damn, he's a big one!"

The third try produced results as Cord's mouth opened

wide and an audible gasp brought a grin to Shamus's face. "Works every time," he told his audience.

Cord coughed, gasping again and rolling to his side, sucking in great gulps of air. "Damn horse!"

Rachel knelt behind him, her eyes closed tightly. She'd thought, for just a moment there...she'd thought he was dead. An emotion unlike any she'd ever before experienced had flooded her with such devastation, such horror, she'd been struck dumb by the weight of it.

In the space of an instant, he might have been taken from her. In less time than it took to blink, he might have had the breath of life sucked from him forever, and no amount of jerking and tugging by Shamus Quinn would have brought him back.

She rose to her feet and turned from the men who gathered to help Cord to his feet. Her back straight, her eyes unblinking, she trudged toward the house, and a suddenly silent group of cowhands watched her depart.

"I don't need to be in bed," Cord grumped as he made his way into the house. "I just need my back tended. Feels like I've scraped half the skin off. Somebody get Rachel for me."

Where she'd gone in such a hurry was cause for concern, he decided. It wasn't like her to turn from an injury. He'd fully expected her to pet him and even maybe kiss his cheek. Not that he'd have stood for it with all the men looking on, but the gesture would have been appreciated.

Instead he'd had to send two men off with Beau Jackson to put the wheel back on the wagon and bring it home, while Sam and Moses gave him a hand to the house. Now everyone was debating whether or not he should be in bed, and if they didn't all leave him be and let Rachel take a look at the part of his back that was burning like fire, he was going to pitch a fit and a half.

"Rachel!" he boomed, once he got his feet inside the kitchen. "Come take a look at this, will you?" He edged onto the nearest chair and waved his hand dismissively at the two men who watched him warily.

"Cord?" She stood in the hallway, her face as pale as moonlight.

"Come here, honey. I need you to look at my back. I think I scraped it up pretty bad. Probably needs some salve on it." Not to mention the thumping in his head and the pain in one shoulder, he thought grimly.

She straightened, her lips compressing. "Yes, of course. Sit up to the table, Cord. I'll get a basin of water."

Within moments, she had him scooted next to the table and he bent his head to rest against his crossed arms, relieved that he no longer needed to hold it erect. A groan escaped him and she bent to touch her lips to his temple.

Finally, he was getting the sympathy he deserved.

"What were you doin' riding with Beau Jackson?" he asked, his voice rough, muffled against his sleeve.

"Of all the… Let me get this shirt off you," she told him. "Sit up a minute." Her hands were efficient as she loosened his buttons and stripped the shirt from his body. She dropped it to the floor and kicked it aside, moving behind him to examine his back.

"You had enough scars back here before. There wasn't any sense in adding to them," she said sharply. Her hands held a cloth and she spread it over him with care, her touch a contrast to the words she spoke.

"Lorena! Get me the supplies from the linen closet, will you?" she called, raising her voice.

A muffled reply appeared to satisfy her and she leaned to wring out the cloth in fresh water. "This is going to sting," she said quietly. "But I want to get the dirt out." Her hands were gentle, but the soap she applied to his scrapes felt like fire. He muttered beneath his breath, his curses falling against the tabletop as she worked.

"I saw you huggin' Beau Jackson's middle," he grumbled.

The woman was ignoring him, he decided, cringing as the cloth wiped carefully at his back.

"Don't blame me for making you fall off that horse," she told him after a moment.

Behind him, footsteps announced another presence and Cord jerked, attempting to sit upright.

"Cover me!" It was a low command, but no less urgent for it.

"Here, Rachel." Lorena sounded breathless, and then she caught her breath, an audible gasp. "What happened?"

Rachel placed the cloth over Cord's injuries. "Not much. Just took a couple layers of skin off. The horse went one way and he went the other. I'll take care of it."

He felt exposed, indignant at his naked state. "Damn, Rachel. Get it over with, will you? I don't want anybody else in here."

"What's going on?" Jake's chair hit the kitchen doorway with a thump. "What's all the fuss out here? Cord? You all right?" He rolled up to the table, pushing Rachel to one side with the force of his concern, his hand reaching for the covering cloth.

"I'm fine. Leave me be," Cord grunted, aware that it was too late, that his back was being exposed to everyone in sight. The shame he'd borne in the privacy of his own skin was now the object of attention in this room.

"Get out of here." It was a harsh demand, and Jake uttered it in a tone of voice that allowed no dissent.

It was to their credit that Rachel and Lorena fled the scene, their whispers fading down the hallway. Cord straightened gingerly, careful to keep his flesh from the back of the chair.

"Seen enough?" he asked dryly.

Jake turned his chair to the side, then around the table, in order to face his brother. "What happened? You didn't get those scars yesterday." His face was gaunt with reflected pain and his eyes bored dark holes in Cord's memory.

"You don't want to know, Jake. It was a long time ago and it's too late to be shedding tears for me." He managed a half grin, his lip quivering with the effort.

Damn, he'd managed to keep his secret for more than four years, and now with the advent of one snippy miss, the whole ranch was probably all agog. Some days just weren't worth getting up for, he decided glumly.

"How did the other fella look?" Jake asked, leaning back in his chair, fingers widespread on his thighs.

Cord shrugged his shoulders, wincing at the stretching of his skin. "About as good as usual," he allowed.

"Pa?" Jake uttered the single syllable and then followed it with a string of curses as Cord reluctantly nodded. "Why?" he asked gruffly.

"I didn't go to war, and you'd already joined up. He said I was a lily-liver and he was gonna whip me to see if my blood ran red or yellow."

"You let him." It was a statement.

"I didn't fight him, Jake. Miserable old coot was my father, like it or not. Maybe there was a little guilt involved, anyway. I was safe and sound, here on the ranch, and you were wearing a uniform.''

"You worked your tail off,'' Jake said quickly. "You weren't hiding out in the bushes.''

Cord nodded. "Yeah, you're right there. The boys in blue got a lot of free beef from this place.''

Jake eyed him from beneath lowered brows. "Any more secrets I should know?''

Cord considered him for a moment. "Yeah, something you should know, but I'm not keepin' it a secret.'' He pushed away from the table and shoved his hands deep into the front pockets of his denims. "If you ever hurt my wife's feelings again like you did the other day, I'll paste you one.''

Jake's grin was slow. "All right. That's plain enough.''

"Now go get Rachel. I need a little pampering.''

Jake nodded. "I'll be in the office. The accounts are almost up to date, Cord. We need to talk about a couple of ideas I have when you get the chance.''

He was gone, the chair rolling at a good clip down the hall, his strong voice calling for Rachel even before he reached the parlor doors.

"You never did answer me this afternoon.'' Cord watched from a chair as Rachel pulled the sheet down on the bed. His sore muscles had turned to aches and pains and his backside felt as if he'd been kicked by a mule.

"You knew why I was on the back of Beau Jackson's horse,'' she said, frowning at him over the width of the mattress. "The wagon wheel fell off and he brought me home.''

"I think you forgot to tell me everything, Rachel.

Beau mentioned the fact that you were tossed out of the wagon and landed in a heap in the road.''

She sighed, an exaggerated effort, and turned from her task. ''I didn't get hurt and you know it. Get in bed,'' she told him. Snatching a nightgown from her drawer, she went behind the screen in the corner of the room.

''Rae?'' He sauntered across the room, leaning to peek over the three-part barrier.

''Go away!'' she said sharply. ''I don't need you inspecting every single thing I do.''

''Tell me, Rachel.'' He rocked the screen with one hand. ''Tell me about throwing up in the weeds and getting dizzy. Did you hit your head?''

She looked around the corner, gracing him with a glance that was enough to chill his eyeballs, if he hadn't already figured out how to melt Rachel's icy glares in jig time.

''No, I didn't hit my head. I threw up in the weeds and got dizzy. What else do you want to know?'' Her head disappeared behind the screen and he fought a laugh that threatened to split his aching head, should he lose it in her direction.

''Beau Jackson suggested you might be hiding secrets, Rachel. I acted like I'd been thinking along those same lines, but it took some fancy footwork to come up with a straight face when he said...'' He paused, waiting for her to shove the screen aside and fly at him.

An ominous silence brought made him frown. ''Rae? Are you listening? He said he thought you looked like a woman who was havin' hard thoughts about being a mother.''

He peered over the top of the screen. Only the top of her head met his gaze. She'd parked her bottom on the small chair back there and was looking at her toes, as far as he could tell.

"Rachel?" He called her name in a careful tone, his heart setting up a turmoil in his chest, throbbing against his ribs to beat the band. "Honey?" It was a whisper this time, and still she curled in the chair, unmoving.

"Well, damn!" He fit his big body behind the screen, feeling like a bull ox squeezing into a mole hole. There wasn't room for the both of them back in that little dressing and undressing spot, what with the slop pail and the commode with its pitcher and basin, not to mention Rachel, all huddled on her chair.

His hand touched the top of her head, his rough skin tangling in the dark silk of her hair, and his heart melted within him. "Sweetheart? I can't pick you up without knocking this screen to kingdom come, and I can't squat down in front of you without stickin' my hind end on the slop pail." His other hand cupped her cheek and he slid it beneath her chin, tilting her head upward.

His palm was damp, and more tears were overflowing even as she looked up at him.

"Rae…baby, don't cry! Whatever I said, I'm sorry."

She shook her head. "I'm the one who's sorry, Cord. I'm so dumb I didn't even know I was going to have your baby. My mama didn't tell me how to get that way, and she didn't tell me how I'd know when I got there."

Somehow he found there was room after all to kneel before her, his arms reaching to enclose her in his embrace, his heart breaking with her pain.

"You're not dumb, Rachel. You're smarter than the whole bunch of us. Matter of fact, you're just about perfect, as far as I'm concerned."

Her mouth was pressed against his throat and she

kissed him where his pulse beat beneath his ear. "I'm far from perfect, Cord. I'm selfish."

"Now that's enough!" With a strength gained from surprise and outrage, he lifted her, clasping her against his chest and belly, her feet dangling. With a mighty shuffling of feet and moving of furniture, he carried her to the bed he'd come to think of as his own small part of heaven.

Careful to keep his weight from her, he covered her with his body, holding her hands beside her head, his gaze searching her face. "What's all this silly stuff about you being selfish?"

"Mr. Baldridge and Mr. Hampton want me to work for the theater, playing for rehearsals and filling in when their own musicians aren't there." She gulped back a sob. "For the first time in my life, I felt like someone wanted me because I was special, and—"

"Not the first time, Rachel." He bent, his mouth fitting against hers in a soft blending of their lips. "I wanted you because you were beyond being special. You are the only woman I've ever met who fit the bill for me. Your talent at the piano can't hold a candle to the music you've brought to this house without touching one single key. You fill every room with your laughter and your humming and singing and bustling about, fixing things up to look pretty."

He sighed, resting his forehead against hers. "I'm not saying this well, Rae. I appreciate your piano playing. I do. I'm proud of you. That night at the picnic, I wanted to stand up and tell everyone you belonged to me. I'm the happiest man in Kansas, knowing you're going to be beside me for the rest of my life."

"Oh, I think you said that very well," she murmured.

"I didn't know you had it in you to make a speech like that, Cord McPherson."

"Well, you'd better remember it well, because I don't know if you'll ever hear all that at one time again. And don't ever say you're stupid, you hear me? I won't have it," he told her sternly. "And if you want to play for those people down at the theater, you go right ahead. We ate cold dinners before you got here, and if we have to, we'll make do."

"I'm going to have a baby," she whispered. Her eyes lit with satisfaction, her mouth widening in a smile. "I've been thinking about it ever since before supper. Nothing so wonderful has ever happened to me before." Tears slid from her eyes and she sniffed loudly. "I think I'm going to need a hankie, Cord."

His long arm snaked to the bedside table and he snatched at one she'd left there. "Here, sweetheart. Blow."

She did, then brightened, as if she'd made a monumental decision. "I told Mr. Baldridge I'd like to work at the opera house, and I was so excited about it, Cord. And then when Beau Jackson suggested I might be in the family way, it all just flew out the window. I felt like Christmas morning had come and I was the one with all the presents."

His laugh spurred her on, his eyes crinkling as he listened to the words pour from her lips.

"I've decided something important. I don't think I want to be gallivanting off to town, Cord. Maybe it was enough that they wanted me, that they offered." Her hands pushed against his chest and he lifted himself from her.

"I think we ought to find out if Jake will do it," she

continued. "There's going to be need for someone to oversee the whole thing before long, and…"

"I wouldn't count on it, Rae. He'd have to be up in front of people, and I can't see him doing that."

"He'd have a wonderful time, telling everybody what to do. They'd have to build a ramp of some sort, so he wouldn't have to worry about the steps, but Lorena could push him…"

"Don't be arranging it already, honey," Cord warned her. "We just managed to get him being useful around here. Should have done that years ago, instead of lettin' him sit in that library like he did."

"Maybe he wasn't ready."

"Well, I was more than ready. I was about fed up with his carrying on. I just felt too damn guilty to do anything about it."

She pulled him back, urging him closer, her fingers careful where they touched. "I'm afraid I'll hurt your back. It looked pretty sore, all scraped up."

"It's just scratches, Rae. They always burn like hell, but I've been dumped by an ornery horse before, probably will be again."

Her breath caught in her throat, an audible sound. "I thought you were dead, Cord. For just a few seconds, I thought you'd stopped breathing forever."

He framed her face with his hands. "I'm sorry you were scared. It looks bad when somebody gets the breath knocked out of 'em."

"I wasn't scared, Cord. I was beyond that. I was sure my life was over, in that minute, that quickly. And I hadn't even known, but for just a few minutes, that I was going to have your baby. I've never felt so much pain, just for those few seconds."

"Well, we both know now…about the baby. I've

been thinking about it all day long, ever since Beau Jackson told me how you—''

''I don't think we need to talk about that again, Cord,'' she said, her fingers covering his lips.

''You haven't done that woman thing for quite a while, Rae, now that I think about it. How far along do you figure you are?''

''A couple of months, I guess,'' she answered. Her eyes sparkled as if a delightful thought had crossed her mind. ''I might have a girl.''

He thought a moment. He already had two boys. Henry and Jay were as much his own as any two young'uns could be. ''A girl will be all right with me.''

She drew him down, her arms circling his neck. ''Will you talk to Jake?''

''Tomorrow,'' he said.

''Does your head still hurt?'' Her fingers rubbed at the back of his neck.

''I believe if you were to kiss it, it would feel a whole lot better.''

''Your head?'' She moved her fingers. ''Back here?''

''Well…you could start with my mouth.''

''Your mouth. You want me to kiss your mouth,'' she repeated, eyeing him askance.

''Seems like a fine place to start,'' he said agreeably. ''And then?''

''And then I kiss you a little bit, and then we…''

She giggled, then chortled, a contagious sound. He hugged her tightly as his chuckle joined in, and the room rang with the sounds of their laughter.

Laughter that promised joy for all the days to come.

Epilogue

From the pages of the *Green Rapids Gazette*, June 12, 1868:

> The baptism of Melody McPherson took place at the Community Church Sunday last. Born May 2, she is the daughter of Cord and Rachel McPherson. The McPhersons further celebrated the event by renewing their wedding vows before the altar, with their daughter in attendance.
>
> Godparents to the baby girl were Mr. Jacob McPherson and his wife, the former Lorena Claypool, whose own wedding was the highlight of the social season this past winter.
>
> Friends and acquaintances were entertained at a lavish buffet served at the McPherson ranch, one of our community's most successful horse-breeding establishments.

From the pages of the *Green Rapids Gazette*, June 19, 1868:

The featured attraction at the Green Rapids Theater this Friday and Saturday will be a presentation by the Rochester Opera Company.

Additional information may be obtained by contacting the theater manager, Jacob McPherson, either at his town residence at the Imperial Hotel or at the Circle M ranch.

A concert in early July will be the renowned Mr. McPherson's much awaited local debut as a classical pianist. It is suggested that tickets be reserved well in advance, as this promises to be a notable event. The theater sponsors will attend in a group from New York City, and reservations at both local hotels are at a premium.

* * * * * *

AWARD-WINNING
AUTHOR
TORI PHILLIPS

INTRODUCES...

An illegitimate noblewoman
and a shy earl to a most delicious
marriage of convenience in

THREE DOG
KNIGHT

Available in October 1998
wherever Harlequin Historicals are sold.

Harlequin®
Historical

Look us up on-line at: http://www.romance.net

HHCC

Award-winning author
Gayle Wilson

writes timeless historical novels and
cutting-edge contemporary stories.

Watch for her latest releases:

HONOR'S BRIDE—September 1998
(Harlequin Historical, ISBN 29032-2)

*A Regency tale of a viscount who falls for the courageous wife
of a treacherous fellow officer.*

and

NEVER LET HER GO—October 1998
(Harlequin Intrigue, ISBN 22490-7)

*A thriller about a blinded FBI agent and the woman assigned
to protect him who secretly carries his child.*

Available at your favorite retail outlet.

Mysterious, sexy, sizzling...

THE AUSTRALIANS

Stories of romance Australian-style, guaranteed to
fulfill that sense of adventure!

This November look for

Borrowed—One Bride
by **Trisha David**

Beth Lister is surprised when Kell Hallam kidnaps her on her
wedding day and takes her to his dusty ranch, Coolbuma. Just
who is Kell, and what is his mysterious plan? But Beth is even
more surprised when passion begins to rise between her and
her captor!

*The Wonder from Down Under: where spirited women win
the hearts of Australia's most independent men!*

Available November 1998
where books are sold.

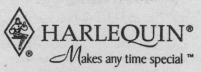

HARLEQUIN®
Makes any time special ™

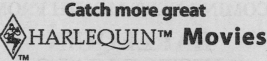 

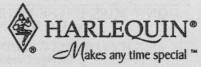

COMING NEXT MONTH FROM

HARLEQUIN HISTORICALS